sometimes love isn't enough...

OUT OF MIND

sometimes love isn't enough...

OUT OF MIND

Jen McLaughlin

Manufactured in the United States of America
E-book ISBN: 978-0-9896684-5-3
Print ISBN: 978-0-9896684-5-3

The author acknowledges the copyrighted or trademarked status and trademark owners of the following wordmarks mentioned in this work of fiction: *Beauty and the Beast*, CVS, *Downton Abbey*, PBS, Target, Porsche, University of Southern California San Diego, Post-it, Aquafina, Volvo, Bruno Mars, Islands, and Harley-Davidson.

Edited by: Kristin at Coat of Polish Edits
Copy edited by: Hollie Westring
Cover Designed by: Sarah Hansen at © OkayCreations.net
Interior Design and Formatting by: E.M. Tippetts Book Designs

OUT OF MIND

Reaching for sunlight...

Finn survived the ambush and came home to me, but in his head, the battle is still raging. He's falling apart and I'm trying my best to pick up the pieces of him, to find the *us* we used to be. I love him as much as I ever did, but love isn't enough to fix this. I thought telling my father about our relationship would be the hardest thing we'd ever have to face. I was wrong.

Lost in shadows...

All I wanted was to be worthy of Carrie. One mission, just one, and I'd be able to give her the future she deserved. Then everything went wrong, leaving me tainted and broken. Carrie wants me to be who I was, but all that's left is what they made of me. I'm no good for her. No good for anyone like this. I have to figure out how to move forward. Alone.

Sometimes love isn't enough...

This one goes out to all the men like Finn who fight, come home, and struggle to fit in with everyday life. Especially my friend Tim, who we all still miss dearly.

CHAPTER ONE

Finn

"Don't let me die...Please don't let me die..."

Explosions boomed in my ears, shooting me upright into a sitting position in bed, gasping for air and crying out into the empty bedroom. Gunshots still echoed in my head, along with the gurgling of Dotter's blood as it poured out of his body until there was nothing left. I looked down at my hands, half expecting to find them bloody. They weren't. But metaphorically? That was a whole other fucking story.

Trembling, I rose to my feet, my broken arm casted and hanging uselessly in a sling. My body was coated in a light sheen of sweat, and even my sheets were dampened and dark. Blinking at the sunlight that crept through the closed curtains, I tried to remind myself where I was. I wasn't fighting for my life. Wasn't watching people die. I was safe.

As safe as I was going to be, anyway.

Pushing the curtains back, I squinted outside. After spending a couple of weeks in a hospital in Germany, followed by another couple of weeks in a hospital in D.C., it was nice to be in a home. But instead of the sandy beaches and hot weather of California, I saw a foot of snow reflecting the sun, blinding me. And we were supposed to get even more tomorrow night. Fucking ridiculous. I studied the position of the sun in the winter sky. Damn, what time was it now? Last thing I remembered, I took a few pills and zonked out. It had been...morning? Maybe? Now, judging from the sunlight streaming through clouds, it was mid-afternoon.

I'd missed a whole day.

Sure. I could act shocked about this, but that happened more often than not lately. I slept away the day, high on painkillers and drunk from whiskey. When I woke up, I swore I wouldn't touch another drink. I'd last an hour or two.

Then I'd do it all over again.

I ran my hand over my shaved head, wincing at how rough it felt. I'd been back in the good old USA for a couple of days now. I still felt like I was trapped in the fucking desert. Instead, I was in the winter wonderland from hell. Carrie's parents' house.

A knock sounded on the door, and I dropped the curtain. I glanced down at myself. I had on a muscle tank and a pair of black basketball shorts. Decent enough, I supposed. "Come in."

The door cracked, and the red hair I'd recognize anywhere appeared before the face I needed so damn much did. "You're up?"

"Yeah." I tugged on my tank and crossed the room. "You can come in."

Carrie entered, shutting the door behind her. She hesitated, looking torn. Her blue eyes were sober and crystal clear, while I was a fucking drunken wreck. I'd been snapping at her lately. Pushing her away. I hated myself for it, yet I couldn't seem to fucking stop.

"Did you sleep good? I thought I heard you cry out."

I fingered the puckered wound on my head. It was still sensitive to the touch and ugly as fuck. Not as ugly as the rest of my scars. Inside *and* out. "I had another nightmare. Same old thing."

She approached me slowly. "Anything I can do to help?"

"Yeah." I met her eyes. "You can come hug me."

She gave me a smile. "Anytime."

Within seconds, she was in my arms. Well, my arm. I glowered down at my broken arm, knowing it was as marked up as my head. You just couldn't see it right now. I closed my arm around her, burying my face in her neck. "Fuck. I missed you."

She tilted her face up to mine. "I missed you, too."

"You should start sneaking in here to see me at night." I dropped a kiss on her forehead. "Then I can at least hold you for a little bit before I fall asleep."

She did sneak into my room every single night, but we never acknowledged her visits. It was our unspoken agreement. Without fail, I would have a nightmare every night. Also without fail, she would come in and comfort me until I fell back asleep. Then, in the morning, we pretended it never happened. I could tell she wanted to talk about it, but she kept silent.

She just gave, without asking for anything in return.

She was too good for me.

"I'll try tonight," she agreed, stretching up on tiptoes to press her mouth to mine.

I tensed and pulled away. I couldn't...she couldn't really want me right now. Not when I looked and felt like this. She stepped back, the disappointment in her eyes way too fucking clear. "I'm going out to refill your prescription. Want to come with me?"

I'd love to, but I couldn't. I wasn't ready for the world to see me yet. "Nah. I'll stay here."

"O-Okay." She watched me, her brow furrowed. "Did you see the sun is shining?"

My heart wrenched. We used to say that, back when I'd been overseas. It had been our code for "I love you." Back when we'd been a secret. Back before her father found out about us. Before he'd threatened me if I ever hurt his baby girl.

I didn't want to hurt her, and yet I was.

I needed to start acting *happy* better. I pasted a big grin on my face. I felt like a fucking clown. "I did. It's so bright."

She nodded, perking up a bit. "Are you sure you don't want to go out with me? It could be fun. Maybe we could go out to dinner? Have a little date."

I started to waver. A date sounded fucking fabulous. It had been so long since I felt normal. Since I felt human. We hadn't had any alone time together, unless you counted stolen moments like this one, and it had been way too long since we acted like a couple at all. I was a fucking mess, and I knew it.

Could I pretend not to be, for her? I could try. "Well..."

I looked over at the nightstand. The mirror over the top of it showed us in perfect profile. She watched me with a hopeful look in her eyes. All red curls, gorgeous skin, and bright blue eyes. She was flawless. And then there was me…Beauty and the Beast.

The wound on my head ran a thin line across my skull, extending down past my eyebrow. My shaven head was patchy at best, due to some lovely hospital clippers that had been used on me. I was told my hair would grow back in eventually, but I was supposed to go out with her like this? I could picture the looks now.

The disgust. The pity.

No. I wasn't ready.

"We could go Christmas shopping, too," she said, her voice excited. "It's only six days away, and I know you didn't get anything for your dad. I still need to shop for mine, too." She grabbed my hand, squeezing it. "We could have fun, like old times."

"I'm sorry, but I can't," I said. "My head…" *is fine.* "Hurts."

"Oh." The smile slipped, but she forced it back into place. She was better at acting happy than I was. "Okay."

"Can you open my pills for me?" I sat down on the edge of the bed. "Maybe get me a drink, too?"

"It's a little early for another pill. You need to wait another hour. And you know you're not supposed to mix booze and painkillers." She looked at me, pressed her lips together, and set my unopened pills on the table. "But I'll grab you some water if you're thirsty."

"Not what I meant, but thanks."

She nodded, grabbed a water bottle, opened it, and handed it over. "You're almost out of pills already. You took too many. I think there should be more."

"I dropped one," I said, averting my eyes. "It rolled away, and I couldn't find it."

"What way did it go?" she asked, dropping to all fours. "I'll find it."

"I don't know. It was dark."

She looked up at me, not saying anything. She didn't believe me. Good. I wouldn't believe me either. I watched her, daring her to argue. To stop treating me as if I might break. She shook her head slightly, stood up, and brushed her hands on her perfect thighs. "Okay, I won't look then."

I frowned and glanced away. "Hey. Have fun shopping."

"Yeah. Thanks." She kissed my bald head, hovering awkwardly. "I love you."

I cringed. She trailed her fingers over my naked scalp. She used to love my hair. Now I didn't have any. "I love you, too."

Once she left, I grabbed the bottle of meds off my nightstand. Another hour, my ass. I'd find a way to open this bottle even if it killed me. After a brief struggle, I managed to pop the lid off on my own. After a while of sitting there in silence, the pill hit me, making the world spin around me. Everything faded away but the blissful silence.

It was the only time I felt like myself anymore.

CHAPTER TWO

Carrie

It had been four months and twenty-three days since I met Finn. He'd told me he was a surfer who didn't have any aspirations above being a Marine, but he'd really been my father's spy. It had been two and a half months since he told me he loved me. I'd told him I loved him, too, and we'd sworn never to lie to each other again. And it had been a month and two days since he got injured, and I thought my world would end. Three days since we came home, and he shut me out of his life. I didn't know how to get back in.

The days kept swirling around my head, over and over again. I guess in a way, I was trying to reassure myself of something. I mean, he was home. And he was getting better. He was trying, anyway. He'd get better. But my world still felt like it was ending. It still wasn't right.

Finn wasn't really Finn anymore.

So instead of going inside my parents' house, I sat in Dad's car for a while, staring up the driveway at the way-too-large-for-normal-humans house I'd grown up in. Part of me wished we'd gone straight to California, instead of back to D.C. like Dad wanted. But Finn's dad was here, and it was winter break, so here we were. Dad let Finn stay at the house, despite his frequent disapproving frowns and his long, lingering looks. But Finn was alive. And he was with me. That's all that mattered, right?

I sighed and slid out of Dad's car, waving at the security dude who got out of his car. He'd wanted to ride with me, but I'd wanted to be alone, so he'd followed me to the store, where I'd wandered around aimlessly. "Finn: Part Two" I liked to call him in my head. Dad had placed a detail on me again, and even though I hated it, I let it slide.

At least he was letting Finn stay at the house.

His room might be on the complete opposite side of the house from my room, sure, but it was something. And it was only temporary. Christmas was coming up, and then we would go home right before New Year's. After that, we'd be fine. And if I kept saying that, maybe it would be true. Finn tried to act normal. He held me close and told me he loved me.

But he wasn't *Finn*.

I opened the front door and blinked. Every single light was on downstairs, and laughter came from the living room. Christmas music played in the formal sitting room, and I could hear my mother on the phone, talking quietly. I was pretty sure I heard my name, so I decided not to go in there. Instead, I'd follow the laughter because I recognized it. It made my whole body tingle and go warm. It was Finn.

Laughing. Actually *laughing*.

I crept into the room, my breath held. My dad, the same man who told me he didn't want Finn and me together, was sitting next to Finn, laughing his butt off at something Finn had apparently just told him. Finn lounged back against the cushions, his casted arm resting against his chest with the help of a sling. He was laughing, too, those blue eyes shining.

So. He'd been drinking again. It's the only time he laughed anymore. He held a mostly empty glass of whiskey in his good hand, and the wound crossing his forehead and creeping into his shaved scalp gave him a ragged appearance. Kinda piratical. All he needed was a hoop earring and some buckskin pants. It was hot. His black tattoos stood out against his paler-than-normal skin, and his dimples were shining full force. He looked happy—normal, even. I knew better.

It was the alcohol talking.

Finn's dad, Larry, was also there, but he wasn't laughing. He was watching Finn with the same concern I felt. The same undying certainty that all was not quite perfect under that flawless smile and never-give-up attitude he kept showing to the world.

"Did that actually happen?" Larry asked, smiling when Finn looked at him. Playing the part, just like me. Was that how I looked? Scared when Finn wasn't looking, and perfectly content when he was? I had a feeling I did. "Or are you making that up?"

I came more into the room, forcing a smile. "What did I miss?"

Dad stood up and held his arms open, a grin still on his lips. "Griffin here was just telling me a story about his buddy from overseas. He was apparently scared of spiders."

"Really?" I hugged Dad. Crossing the room, I bent down, kissed Larry's forehead, and squeezed his hand. Last, but not least, I turned to Finn. "What kind of big, scary fighter is scared of spiders?"

Finn's smile slipped for a fraction of a second. He lifted his glass to his lips, drained it, and smiled up at me as if he didn't spend half the night pacing in his room instead of sleeping. As if he didn't wake up screaming every night.

As if I didn't know all about it.

"That's what we said to him," he said lightly. "But he was. We found that out one night, for sure."

I sat down beside Finn, resting my hand on his knee. He had one leg bent over the other, so it was the perfect snuggling position. He wrapped his good arm around me, his gaze shifting to my dad before he hugged me close. When he held me like this, I almost believed the façade he showed the world. Almost believed we were okay.

"Did you put one on his pillow to mess with him?" Dad asked.

He was being polite, but now that I was here, next to Finn, I could hear the tension in his voice. He didn't approve, but he knew forbidding it wouldn't work, so he was being quiet…for now. I couldn't help but wonder how long that silence would last.

"I did," Finn admitted, a side of his mouth quirking up into a lopsided grin. "When he came into the room, I laid there as if I didn't have a clue what the hell was going on."

Larry shook his head. "I'm sure he was pissed when he saw the beast on his bed."

"He screamed like a little girl." Finn's hand flexed on my shoulder. He gave a long, hard look at the empty glass on the table before turning back to his dad. "That was the second to last day we were there. He didn't sleep the whole night."

Which meant the next day, the guy Finn was talking about had been killed. And Finn had watched it happen. My heart twisted, and I looked up at him. He stared off into the distance, his brow furrowed. He looked lost. I wished I could find him.

Dad cleared his throat. "And that was that."

"Yes, that was that," Finn rasped. He seemed to shake himself, and then he was back on earth again. "He was scared to surf, too. I told him I'd teach him sometime."

"You're an excellent teacher," I said.

"Wait." Dad sat up straighter. "How would you know how good of a surfing teacher he may or may not be?"

I froze. "Uh…"

Finn closed his eyes and sighed. "I taught her."

"You did *what*?" He rose to his feet, his face turning an alarming shade of red. "Griffin Coram, I'll have your skin for—"

"Dad." I glowered at him. "In the scheme of things, do you really think it's that big of a deal? I'm obviously okay."

"*Obviously* okay?" Dad sputtered. "I…he…you…" He cut off. "Argh."

Finn cleared his throat and made as if to rise. "I think that's my cue to grab another whiskey."

"I'll get it." Dad looked at me. "I need the fresh air."

Once my dad left, Finn looked at me and smiled, his blue eyes softening as they usually did when he looked at me. I ran my hand over his head, smiling back at him in return. I used to play with his hair. I missed that. "Oops," I said. "My bad."

"He was bound to find out eventually. Might as well be now," Finn said, reaching out to tug a strand of my hair. "Where'd you go earlier?"

"I picked up your medicine." I reached into my purse and put his bottle of pain pills on the coffee table. I'd be keeping a close watch on how many disappeared. "Remember? I told you before I left."

"I must've forgotten." He ran a hand down his face. "Sorry."

He'd been forgetting a lot of things lately. I wasn't sure if it was from the pills, the booze, or the injury. Maybe a combination of all three. Either way, it kind of freaked me out. "It's okay. Maybe I was wrong and I forgot to tell you."

"Maybe." He shrugged. "Either way, I'm glad you're back now."

Larry stood up. He looked a little bit pale and unsteady. I started to rise, but he shook his head. Finn looked over at him, and Larry gave him a smile. "I'm going to crash early tonight, son. I'm exhausted."

Finn studied him. "You feeling all right, Dad?"

"Yeah, of course. I'm fine," Larry said, shaking his head and chuckling. "Don't you worry about me. You worry about you."

Finn narrowed his eyes. "You look pale. Are you getting sick again?"

"No, not again." Larry headed for the door without looking back. "Good night."

When Finn started to stand, I tugged him back down. "Let him go. He's tired. You can talk to him in the morning."

Finn tensed. "Something's wrong, and he's not telling me. Do you know what it is?"

I was pretty sure Finn's father wasn't doing well. I *thought* it might be something to do with his heart, but I'd never gotten it confirmed. "I don't. I have my suspicions, like you," I said, squeezing his hand. "We'll talk to him together in the morning, okay? Not now."

He nodded and let out a sigh. "You're right. But don't let me forget to talk to him tomorrow. Promise you'll remind me."

I swallowed hard. "I promise." I rested my hand against his cheek, trying to enjoy the moment. "How's the head feeling tonight?"

He met my eyes, relaxing under my touch. "It hurts," he admitted. "A lot."

"Have you had any more pills since I left?"

He shook his head but didn't meet my eyes. "Nope."

"Okay." I hesitated before grabbing his pills. For what had to be the millionth time, I said, "But you've been drinking. You're not supposed to mix—"

"They just say that shit to scare you. I'm fine." His hand shook as he took the bottle from me. He seemed to remember he couldn't open it with one hand, so he held it back out. "Can you help me?"

"Of course." I opened the bottle and poured out a pill, wishing I hadn't asked him how his head felt. I'd had to beg to get a refill for him, since it was a full day too early. "You're not supposed to mix them, and you know it."

"I don't give a damn, and *you* know it." He took a deep breath. With a small grimace, he popped the medicine into his mouth. After he swallowed, he gave me a long, hard look. "I'm fine, Carrie. Don't worry."

I froze, the lid half on. "I didn't say you weren't."

"I watch you all the time. You always look worried, unless you see me watching. Then you laugh and smile." He cupped my cheek and ran his thumb over my lip. "I'm okay. You don't need to worry about me. I'll get through this."

I wished that was true. "I'm not worried about that."

"I know," he said, his tone playful despite the shadows I could see in his eyes. The ones that chased him every night no matter how fast he ran. "I've got you. What more could I possibly need?"

I leaned in and brushed my mouth across his. He tasted like alcohol. "Nothing," I whispered against his lips.

His good hand flexed on my thigh. "Careful. Your dad's coming back any second now."

"He knows about us. Why worry about a kiss?"

"He knows, but he doesn't like it." He leaned back against the couch. "And he definitely doesn't want to see us kissing in his living room." He closed his eyes and pressed his lips together tightly. When he opened his eyes, all signs of tension dissipated. "We won't be here much longer, and then we can go back to normal. We'll be back in California, and I'll be back to annoying you twenty-four-seven."

I smiled, knowing that was what he wanted from me. He loved to make me happy, after all. "I know. I can't wait."

"And, hey, at least I'm home for Christmas. We didn't think I would be." His mouth twisted, and he fingered my sun necklace. "We even celebrated early and everything."

I thought back on the night Finn had created Christmas for me. We'd decorated a tree, shared a romantic dinner, and spent the night in each other's arms. It had been the last time we made love, and the last time I'd seen him *really* smile.

"I know. It was lovely." I kissed him one more time, keeping it short. "Maybe the actual Christmas will be even better. I'll get to show you the present I got for you."

He ran his free hand over his shaved head, touching the shiny, puckered wound. It started at the corner of his eye and then extended to the back of his skull. I knew he was self-conscious about it, but he shouldn't have been. He was gorgeous as always. "I don't think it will top our other one. I can't even use my fucking arm, and we won't be alone.

There won't be any hot holiday sex to finish off the night."

"Oh, I think you could do plenty of damage with just the one arm," I teased, running my hand over his chest. I placed my palm right over the spot where he'd gotten our tattoo. "And if not, well, you can still hold me. That's all I need to be happy. Your arms around me, and us together. Fighting the world as a team."

"You and me against the world, right?" Meeting my eyes hesitantly, he looked down at where my hand rested. His were blazing with heat, desire, and love. He leaned in and rested his forehead against mine, taking a shaky breath. "I love you so fucking much, Carrie."

My heart melted and I blinked back tears. This was the first time he was acting like my Finn, and it was breaking my heart. "I know. I love you, too."

"I don't know what I did to deserve you." His fingers moved to the back of my head, cradling me and holding me closer. "I hope I don't fuck it up."

"You won't." I pulled back and smiled at him, trying to show him there was nothing—*nothing*—he could do to send me running. "We've been over this before. I'm not going anywhere."

He drew in a ragged breath. "I didn't deserve you when I was whole, and I definitely don't deserve you now, looking like Frankenstein's monster."

"*Finn.*" I ran my hand over his head, scowling at him. "Don't you ever say that again. You're perfect. We're perfect." I lightly kissed the spot where his injury started. "And a few scrapes isn't going to ruin that. You're as hot as ever."

He let out a small sound and caught my mouth with his. It was the first time *he* kissed *me* since he came home. Every other time, I'd been the one initiating it, and he'd been pushing me away. He always had a good reason for doing so, but it didn't change the fact that it was true. He was pushing me away, and I couldn't do anything to stop him.

Footsteps approached, and my dad came into the living room. Finn let go of me as if I were diseased and stood shakily. Dad handed him a drink and looked at me. He scanned my face, his brows lowered. Finn took the drink and inclined his head. "Thank you, sir. If you don't mind, I'll take this up to my room. I just took a pill, and I'll be tired soon."

I stood up. "I'll come and—"

"No. I'm fine." Finn offered me a smile, but the real smile I'd gotten earlier was gone. In its place was the one I'd gotten all too used to. "Spend time with your dad. I'll see you in the morning when the sun's shining nice and bright. Maybe we can go out to breakfast."

I watched him go. He snatched up an entire bottle of whiskey off the side table as he passed it, and walked out into the hallway. He was going to drink himself to sleep again. He'd still wake up screaming, though. I knew it and so did he. Or maybe he didn't. Maybe he'd forgotten about his night terrors.

I hadn't.

I took a step after him, planning on ripping it out of his hands, but Dad grabbed my arm. "Let him go. He needs some time alone," Dad said, reaching out and squeezing my hand. "I don't like you two together, and you know that, but I'm telling you this much for your own sake. He needs time and space to accept what happened to him over there, and you need to give it to him. Let him drink. Let him sleep. He'll come out of it."

"But I don't think he needs space." I swallowed hard. "I think he needs me."

Dad flinched. "I think he needs you, too, but not right now. He's not ready yet."

"Why are you telling me this?"

"Because you're my daughter, and I love you." Dad stood. "And because I won't be the one to break you two up. Unfortunately, I think he'll be able to do that just fine without my help."

I stiffened. "We're *not* breaking up."

Dad rested his hand on my shoulder. "Even you have to see the changes already. If you want to make this thing between you work, give him space. He needs it. And pray that he comes out of this resembling the guy he once was."

"How do I know you're not telling me what's worse for him so we break up?"

He hesitated before heading for the doorway. "You don't. You'll have to just trust that I know what's best for you—and him."

He left, and I was alone for all of two seconds before my mom came in. "Did the men abandon you?" Mom asked, her phone still in her hand. She sat beside me, grabbing the remote and switching on the television.

"Did I hear you went shopping without me?"

I forced a smile. "Just to CVS. Nothing too exciting."

"Oh. Well, *Downton Abbey* is on. You know how much I love that show." And it was on the only pre-approved channel in this house: PBS. Educational and political all at once. "Want to watch with me?"

I sighed and settled into the corner of the couch, pulling a throw blanket over my lap. "Sure. Put it on."

As Mom started the show, I glanced over my shoulder. I wanted nothing more than to chase after Finn, take away the whiskey, and hold him until he was better. But something told me Dad was right this time. I probably couldn't fix him with a hug. And maybe it was time to accept one thing about this whole mess.

He needed more help than I could give him.

CHAPTER THREE

Finn

Bombs exploded all around me, punctuated only by the screams of the dying men. I could smell the blood. Taste the fear. Feel the pain. I was sent back there again, living through the attack while everyone else died. But at the same time, I also *knew* I wasn't there anymore. I was in bed, alive and safe—unlike the rest of my squad. It was almost like an alternate universe where I wasn't sure what was real and what wasn't.

Which haunted me now: Nightmare or reality?

I sat upright, my eyes scanning my surroundings. Lightly painted walls and expensive furniture surrounded me instead of blood and bombs. Another nightmare. I'd been stuck in the same hell I was in every night, and no matter how much I drank, nothing made it go away. Nothing saved me. I was starting to think nothing could.

I must have been tossing and turning in my sleep, because my broken arm throbbed like a bitch. My sheets had tangled themselves around my bare feet like a noose, but even so I was still covered with sweat. My door opened and closed. I turned toward it, breathing heavily. It would be Carrie. It was always Carrie. She always calmed me down. Always took care of me.

I loved her for it, but I hated the need for it at the same time.

"Are you all right?" Carrie sank on the bed beside me, her hands reaching for my one good one. "You were having the dream again, weren't you?"

I flopped back down, hating that she was seeing me like this. Scarred. Weak. Broken. Scared. Maybe I should start gagging myself when I went to bed. Or just give up sleeping altogether. "I'm fine," I said, my voice a lot harder than I'd wanted it to be. "Just fucking relax."

She stiffened. If this had been before I'd been fucked up, she would have snapped back at me. Given me as good as I gave her. But she was walking on eggshells around me. Pampering me. I just wanted her to fight with me and be my stubborn Carrie. I wanted that easy camaraderie back so bad that it hurt more than my arm and my head combined.

She nodded, nibbling on her lower lip. "I'm sorry. I—"

"*Don't.*" I rolled out of the bed. "Don't apologize to me again."

"Excuse me?"

"You keep apologizing when I'm the one being a prick. Stop it."

She shook her head. "You're not being a 'prick.'"

"Yeah. I am."

She stood up, too, and curled her hands at her sides. "I know you're stressed and not sleeping well. It's okay to be a little cranky after what you experienced."

"A little bit *cranky*?" I locked the door. "That's the understatement of the damn century."

She ignored me. Just lifted that stubborn chin of hers higher. "I know this is hard for you to deal with, so I'm not going to fight with you, no matter how hard you try to piss me off."

"You never do anymore, Carrie." I crossed the room slowly, never taking my eyes off her. "You're too scared to."

She bit down on her lip. I watched her, studying the curve of that lip. I loved that little pink mouth of hers. And suddenly, I wanted to taste it. No, *needed* to taste it. Wanted to feel normal for one fucking minute of today, before I lost myself in the agony that wouldn't leave me alone. Wanted to go back to how I'd been, instead of what I'd become. "I'm not scared of you, Finn. But tell me, what do you want from me? You want me to fight with you?"

"Sometimes, yes. But not right now—not anymore." I stepped closer. "Right now? I want you. Nothing more. Nothing less."

"*Finn.*" She held her hands out. "You already have me."

"No. I had you." I shook my head. "But I haven't *had* you since I've come back."

Comprehension lit her eyes, and she flushed. "Then you can have me." She closed the distance between us, reaching up to close her palms around the back of my neck. "What are you dreaming about every night? Tell me about it. Talk to me."

Talk? I didn't want to fucking talk. I wanted to *feel*. Forget. Move on. "I c-can't, Carrie." I shook my head, dissipating the bloody images she'd brought to life with her words. "I'll tell you anything you want to know about anything else, but I can't talk about that night. Not to anyone."

"Okay. Okay." She made a soothing sound, as if I were a baby or some shit like that. That needed to end right fucking now. I was a man. A broken man, but a man nonetheless. "You're not ready."

"I never *will* be ready," I managed to say through my suffocating anger. "It's not something I'm willing to relive through conversation. I already see it every night, and that's enough for me."

She shook her head. "But if you talk to someone, it helps."

"Yeah, well, you're not a therapist."

A flash in her eyes answered me before she even opened her mouth. A hint of the real Carrie shined through. About damn time. "No, but I *am* going to school for it."

"Occupational."

She pressed her lips together. "Still—"

"Nope. Not happening."

She narrowed her eyes on me. "You don't have to talk to me if you don't want to, but you need to talk to someone. It will help you recover."

Recover, my ass. Therapists made you talk because it made them money. End of story. It wouldn't help me. Wouldn't fix me. They'd just tell me to pop some pills and call me healed. Bullshit. I would do it my way, in my own time. "I'm already recovering."

She pursed her lips. "I'm not talking about the visible injuries, Finn."

"Yeah, well, they are the only ones that matter, as far as I'm concerned." I hauled her closer. "Can you ever want me again, even with how scarred I am now?"

She shook her head, and for a second my worst nightmare came to life. "Finn, I never stopped wanting you, and I never will." She rested her hands on my chest, and I almost collapsed from the relief surging through me. "So how can I possibly answer if I'd ever want you again?"

I tried to believe that. Tried to be optimistic like I'd been before I went overseas and almost got blown to pieces like the rest of my buddies. But she had the benefit of not seeing inside my head. She didn't know just how far gone I was—so she was still blissfully optimistic. Her world still had rainbows and butterflies and all that shit.

But me? I saw it all, and part of me thought it might be better for her if I walked away. But we'd promised to stay with each other. Promised no more running or lies.

Her eyes lowered, and her stare lingered over my abs before dipping even lower. Good. She could see what I fucking wanted right now—*her*. I wanted to remind her why she was with me, since she probably couldn't see it anymore. Not when she looked at my wounds.

All she saw was what I used to be.

She hesitated. "Finn, I don't know if you're ready yet…"

"Why wouldn't I be ready?" I stepped closer, and she tilted her face up toward mine. Her pupils flared, and she bit down on her lower lip again. "I've been ready since I met you."

Her mouth twitched into a reluctant smile. "You know what I mean. With people recovering from trauma, sex can be a trigger. It can make things worse. I don't want to make you suffer—"

"The only way I'll suffer," I cupped her face with my good hand, my thumb under her jawline, "is if you say no. So don't say no."

Part of me needed to know she still wanted me, scars and all. She might be right, and this might not be good for my head, but fuck it. I needed it. I needed *her*.

Carrie

I knew this wasn't a good idea. But when he looked down at me like that, all blue eyes and soft words, I couldn't stop myself from giving him what he wanted—even if it wasn't what he *needed*. The two didn't always go hand in hand, did they?

Reaching up on tiptoe, I curled my hands around his neck and kissed him, keeping it light and easy. I didn't want to scare him off or be too pushy. I didn't need to worry, I guess. He backed me across the room, his breath coming fast, his hand flexing on my chin. I knew he was frustrated with feeling helpless and broken, and I wished I could help him.

Wished he would let me help him.

I spun him so his back was toward the bed and pushed him gently onto it. Good thing he'd locked the door. As long as we were quiet, no one should know what we were up to. I straddled him, skimmed my hands up under his shirt, and sighed with satisfaction even as it bugged me that he was wearing a shirt. He never used to sleep with a shirt on. Was he hiding his wounds from himself, too? It seemed that way.

I pulled back and studied him. His eyes were shut, and his cheeks flushed. He looked so freaking hot like this. Turned on and ready for me. All mine. "Are you sure you're ready?"

He smoothed my hair off my face. "Of course I'm sure."

"Okay." I reached for the bedside light, but he snatched my hand before I could turn it on. "What? What is it?"

"No lights," he rasped, his fingers tightening on mine. "I like it like this."

"Finn…" I swallowed hard. "You don't need to hide from me."

"I'm not. I don't want your dad to know." He let go of my hand and hauled me closer. "That's all."

I wanted to believe him, but I didn't. He hadn't let me see him yet. Hadn't even taken his shirt off in front of me. But I couldn't push it. Couldn't push him. "Okay."

I kissed him, holding myself back again. I wasn't sure how to be with him when he was being like this. Should I be bold? Or should I let him take the lead? I was out of my league here, and I knew it. He broke off the kiss and cursed under his breath before saying, "If you don't want this from me anymore, then you can leave. I understand."

"I want this." I tried to kiss him again, but he didn't let me. "Finn, what's wrong?"

"You're acting as if you can't stand the thought of kissing me," he rasped, his hand flexing on my hip. "I get it. I'm fucked up now and—"

I slammed my mouth down on his, shutting him up before he insulted himself again. It was killing me to act as if he was going to break at any point, and I was done listening to him put himself down. Freaking *done*. He was gorgeous, injuries and all.

His mouth opened under mine, so I slid my tongue inside, seeking his. As soon as I found it, heat shot through my body, making me tremble. I deepened the kiss, needing more of him. Needing to kiss him, touch him, love him. It had been too long since I'd gotten to kiss him like this. Feel him like this.

His uninjured hand skimmed up my side before running down my arm. I shivered and ran my hands down his pecs, to the waist of his boxers. He arched his hips a little bit, pressing his erection against my core. God, that felt good. *So* good. For the first time since he'd come home, I wasn't thinking of him as Finn, injured Marine.

He was my Finn, and I needed him as badly as he needed me.

"Fuck," he moaned, arching into me again. "Lose the clothes."

"Yours first." I slid down his body, pressing my open mouth against his neck.

He gripped my hair tight, holding me in place. "Help me get these off."

I closed my hands over his boxers and nipped at his abs through the shirt. He hissed and tightened his grip on my hair. I wished I could see him right now. See him watching me with those blazing blue eyes I loved so much. But for now, quiet and rushed would have to do. I lowered his boxers over his hips, and he helped me get them off by lifting his hips slightly. I tossed them off the bed and climbed between his legs. "Condom?"

"Drawer," he said, his voice strangled. "Left side, top."

I didn't bother to ask him when and how they'd gotten there. I climbed over him and retrieved one, but didn't put it on him yet. I lifted his shirt and licked his abs, grinning when he groaned. I loved driving him insane. Loved making him squirm with need. Loved *him* so much it hurt. I skimmed my hands up his thighs while flicking my tongue over the head of his cock. My cheeks heated as I did so, knowing I was totally disobeying pretty much every rule my parents had laid down when they allowed Finn to stay here to recover…

And not even caring a little bit about it.

He gripped my hair, begging for more without making a sound. I closed my mouth around him, swirling my tongue over the smooth skin of his erection. He squirmed, moving restlessly against the white sheets. "*Carrie.*"

I sucked him in deeper, taking as much of him into my mouth as I could, and yet still wanting more. I'd never get sick of this. Never get sick of him. I cupped his balls, squeezing gently as I increased the suction, going up and down with perfect timing.

He let out a ragged moan, but bit it back abruptly. It brought me back to a time when he'd teased me about being too loud in bed. He'd proceeded to prove his point by making me scream his name repeatedly, and I'd done so quite happily. It had been back when we'd thought we were going to D.C. together. Before he deployed.

My heart squeezed tight at the memory. Of his laughter ringing in my ears on that day. He'd been so light. So free. I didn't think he'd ever be that way again.

"*Carrie*. I need you so damn much." He threaded his hand in my hair and tugged me up his body. "Kiss me. Love me."

My heart twisted at the need in his voice. I couldn't help it. "Always."

I kissed him, making sure to not press my weight on his broken arm, while putting all the emotions I couldn't put into words into that kiss. He didn't want to talk about anything, and that was fine for now. But he needed to know I was *here*. Needed to know I wasn't leaving. His lips hesitated under mine, almost as if he was receiving my message loud and clear, and then he groaned and held me against his body as tight as he could with a casted arm between us.

Then he let go and picked up the condom, ripping it open with his teeth before holding it out to me. "Put this on me."

I took it and rolled it down his cock with trembling hands. Once the condom was firmly in place, I tried to kiss him again, but he pressed his fingers against my mouth. "Get naked first. Then I'll make you come so many times you'll lose count. It's been too long."

He was always alpha in bed—and out of it—but this was different. And it was hot. I slid off the bed and quickly stripped out of my pajama pants and tank top. Next, I shimmied out of my underwear. I stood there for a second, knowing I was silhouetted in the moonlight for him. And he seemed to appreciate the view, judging from the way his voice rasped when he said, "Get back here now."

I climbed onto the bed, my heart racing as I crawled between his legs and kissed him again, my bare butt in the air. It felt decadent to be so casual about what we were doing—and where we were doing it. He curled his hand around the back of my head and hauled me closer, kissing me passionately. My stomach twisted into a tight coil, demanding more.

Demanding what I knew he could give me. It had been so long. *Too* long. And I needed more. I let out a moan of my own when he dipped his hand between my thighs, finding my clit easily. He rubbed two fingers against me in a circular motion, applying the perfect pressure to send me over the edge.

He broke off the kiss and bit down on my shoulder, drawing a ragged gasp from my lips. "*Finn.*"

"You like that?" he asked, his voice rough and low. "You want more?"

"God, yes." I dug my nails into his sides, making sure that I didn't bump against his injury as I squirmed. "*More.*"

He rubbed my clit rougher, making me bite back a scream. God, I was so close. I could feel the pressure building higher and higher, and soon I would break. He knew it, too. I could tell by the way he was playing with me. Torturing me.

It was oh-so-delicious and incredibly frustrating.

I didn't know whether to beg for mercy, or kick his butt for doing this to me.

"Did you touch yourself while I was gone?" He increased the pressure. "Did you rub your fingers against yourself and pretend it was me? Did you come with my name on your lips?"

I groaned and moved my hips restlessly. I was almost there. Almost to heaven. Part of his words didn't even register with me. I was that far gone. "I...I can't talk like that."

"Answer me." He thrust a finger inside me, and I whimpered and buried my face in his neck. I had to be quiet. Had to make sure no one knew what we were doing. "Did you fuck yourself when I was gone?"

Of course I had, but it had never felt like this. Only he made me feel this good. But I couldn't tell *him* that. "J-Just keep touching me. Don't..." I moved against his fingers, straining to get even closer. "You...dare...stop."

And then he did. He stopped touching me. Just hovered there, almost brushing against me, but remaining still. Yeah. I was going to beg for mercy. Then, after I was done, I'd kill him. "Tell. Me."

"*Finn.*" I grabbed his hand and pressed it back where I wanted it. No, where I *needed* it. He couldn't stop now. Not when I was so close. "Please."

24

"Tell me the truth, and then I will."

"Y-Yes. I did it, okay?" I moaned when he rubbed me again, but too lightly. Not enough. Not nearly enough. I knew I was being too loud, but even knowing it didn't make me stop. "Finn, please."

"You touched yourself and imagined it was me?" He nibbled on my neck and thrust a finger inside me again. Thank freaking God. "Was it my lips or my fingers when you did it?"

I whimpered, low and desperate. "Your lips. Always your lips."

His fingers stilled. "Then I can't disappoint you now." His hand was gone, and I wanted to shout, scream, and cry. He slapped the side of my ass. "Climb on top."

"I am on…" Comprehension lit up within me, as well as desire. So much desire. "You don't mean for me to…"

"I do." He tugged my leg. "Hurry the fuck up. I need to taste you. To make you come on my mouth."

I trembled just from the words. And the image…oh my God, the image that gave me. I wanted it *now*. I positioned myself so I straddled him, a knee on either side of his head—and clear of his injured arm—and then lowered myself to his face. It was so dirty and raw and right. So freaking right.

God, yes.

His tongue touched my clit, and I closed my hands over the top of the headboard so tight it hurt my palms, and dropped my head against the light blue wall. God, this must look so hot. Him under me, with me basically sitting on his face. We'd never done it this way. It was different and amazing. And oh my God…

His good hand cupped my butt, his fingers digging in enough to hurt just enough, and his mouth moved over my clit with the perfect amount of pressure. I stopped thinking, stopped picturing this, and just lost myself in his touch. The tightness in my belly grew harsher, focusing on his mouth moving over me.

His tongue, his teeth, his hands…

Everything within me gathered real close before exploding in fragments of pleasure and need. I collapsed with my forehead against the wall, and he kept his tongue pressed against my sensitive clit as I came back down from the high he'd given me. By the time I could gather my thoughts, he moved his tongue, which was featherlight and almost nonexistent on me.

I came again, explosive and hard. Much harder than the first time.

I tore free of his grip when he tried to keep going down on me, and he let me. I slid down his body, kissing him hard. He tasted more like me than him, but I didn't care. I needed him. Needed this. I positioned his cock at my entry and lowered myself on him, swallowing his groan with my mouth.

His hand gripped my hip while his broken arm rested on his chest, and he urged me to move faster. I didn't have any complaints about that. I pumped my hips fast and hard, my breathing growing more and more fevered with each thrust. His fingers dug into my thigh, and a tortured groan came from him as he tensed beneath me.

I closed my eyes and moved even faster. I was *so* close to coming again. I could feel it. Taste it. Sense it. I pressed my mouth to his and lost myself in the pleasure, the kiss, and him. The orgasm took me by surprise, even though I'd known I was close. But it felt different this time. More whole. As if it was more intense than ever before, and maybe it was.

He froze beneath me, his back curved and his fingers tight on me, and then he collapsed onto the mattress, his breathing unsteady and hard. I melted against his chest, my head on his good shoulder and my hand curled under his neck. "Wow."

His hand flexed on me. "Yeah," he rasped.

Something in his voice told me he wasn't all right. I lifted my head and checked his broken arm. I hadn't been lying on it or anything. I tried to search the darkness to see his face, but I could only make out vague shapes. I couldn't see him. "Are you all right? I didn't hurt you, did I?"

He laughed, but it wasn't his laugh. It was strained. "I'm fine. I'm just tired, that's all."

"Oh." I scooted off him. "You'd tell me if you weren't all right, right? We promised, no more lies."

"Honestly? I don't think you'd want to know whether I was lying right now." He stood up, removed the condom, and came back to the bed. "You don't need to know everything that's in my head. I just need time to adjust."

That's exactly what my father had said. That he needed time.

"Okay. Then I'll give it to you. Just know I'm here to talk, or whatever."

After a second of hesitation, he lay back down and wrapped his arm around me before kissing my forehead. "I know you are. If I need to talk, I'll let you know."

"That's all I can ask for, minus one thing."

He stiffened. "What?"

"Don't lie to me again." I propped myself on my elbows. "Whatever happens, whatever you go through, just don't lie to me. I can handle a lot, but not that."

He nodded slowly, his shadowed face intent on mine. "Okay. No lies. But don't ask me things I'm not ready for. The stuff that happened over there…"

His voice cracked, but he cleared his throat to hide it. It broke my heart that he was so vulnerable, yet unwilling to show it. "I won't push," I promised. "Not yet."

"I can't talk about it." His jaw flexed. "I won't."

"Okay." I scooted up and kissed him. "Want me to stay until you fall asleep?"

He hesitated. "Would it make me less of a man if I said yes? If I admitted I needed you more than I need medicine? You're the reason I keep going. You're why I'm still here, instead of in that fucking nightmare I can't escape."

My heart… Yep. It totally melted.

"Nope, not at all." I sat up and pulled the covers over us before settling back down on the pillow. It was weird, in a way, how you went from sitting on a guy's face to snuggling under the covers and holding each other for support. "It would make you the man I love more than anything."

His fingers flexed on my hip, and he nodded. "Are you too tired?"

I was freaking exhausted. I'd been sitting up with him almost every night. But if he knew that, he'd send me away. His sleep was more important than mine, so I lied. Ironic, considering I'd just lectured him about not lying to *me*.

This was different. He needed me here.

"Nope. Wide-awake. I had coffee earlier." That much was true.

He smiled. I didn't see it, but I could feel it. "I wish I could manage without sleep like you. I used to be able to…before…"

He broke off. He wasn't going to finish that thought.

I rested my hand over his heart. "You'll get there again."

"I know." He yawned, loud and long. "It'll happen soon."

I smiled and ignored the tears in my eyes. "Get some rest. I'm here with you, and I'm not going anywhere."

"And neither am I," he whispered sleepily.

CHAPTER FOUR

Finn

The next afternoon, I stood at the window, watching the snow fall to the snow-covered lawn, and let myself breathe it in. I'd dozed off on the sofa for a little while after eating my lunch, and I'd woken up sweating and screaming. Not knowing exactly where I was or even if I'd live. Like fucking usual.

Good thing no one had been here to see or hear it. It was bad enough *I* knew about my weakness—I didn't need Senator Wallington knowing too. He'd already warned me he wouldn't stand by and watch me hurt his daughter when he'd visited me in the hospital in Germany. His words may have been cryptic, but they were crystal clear.

I know you love my girl, Griffin. And I know she loves you, too. I get why you fell for her. Who wouldn't? It doesn't mean I'm happy about it, though. Or that I'll accept it. Get well, son. For both of our sakes.

That last part? Yeah, it meant "get better, or get the hell out of her life." I knew it. He knew it. And I wasn't getting better. Not yet. Maybe not ever. My good hand tightened on the coffee mug I held. I wanted something stronger. Something to take the pain away. But I resisted, for Carrie.

I'd gone through hell and back to keep her at my side.

I wouldn't…no, I *couldn't* lose her.

A car pulled up, and I narrowed my eyes. It wasn't Carrie or her parents. They were out getting a Christmas tree. They'd waited till the last minute since Carrie hadn't been home to go with them until a few days ago. I'd stayed behind because walking around in the freezing cold with an aching arm while the senator frowned at me wasn't the best thing for me. Carrie had tried to stay behind but I'd insisted she go.

She needed to spend time with them before we went home. Needed to feel normal as badly as I did. I knew it, so I made her leave by telling her I wanted to nap.

I had. Then I'd had a nightmare. Go fucking figure.

The red Porsche parked at the front, but I couldn't see who got out of it. I made my way over to the front door just in time for the butler to open it. "They're not at home, Mr. Stapleton."

"I know. Carrie texted me and told me, but I thought I'd stop by and wait." He laughed. "She told me she wouldn't be much longer because they're freezing outside."

"Ah, well, come in. You can wait in the family living room, if you'd like."

I stood in the shadows, waiting to see who the fuck this was. Carrie had been texting him, but I didn't know a single thing about him. "Thank you, George."

He knew the butler's name?

"Can I get you a cocktail?" George asked.

Another laugh. "I'd love a whiskey, if you don't mind."

I stepped closer. There was a shuffling sound, and then a tall blond guy stepped through the door. He was handsome, had bright green eyes, and was wearing an impeccable blue sweater and a pair of khakis. He looked...fucking perfect, damn it.

He was everything I wasn't right now. Who the hell *was* he?

He pulled off his scarf and kept talking to George, but I didn't hear a word. I was too busy trying not to be jealous of a guy I didn't even know. He laughed and turned my way...and the smile faded. He looked me up and down, concern clear in his eyes. I *knew* I looked like hell. I *knew* I was a wreck. But seeing him looking at me as if he felt sorry for me?

Fuck no. Not happening.

"Hi," he said, hesitating. He crossed the room and held out his hand, offering me his non-dominant hand since he knew I couldn't use my broken arm. How thoughtful of him. "I'm Riley. You must be Griffin, right?"

Son of a bitch, he was nice, too.

I knew right away, within seconds of eye contact, that while this guy was rich, he was *not* another Cory. This guy was kind and seemed to be a guy that even I could like, under different circumstances. In fact, even I had to admit he was the perfect guy for Carrie…

If it wasn't for *me* being in the way.

"It's Finn," I managed to say without my voice cracking. I set my mostly empty coffee mug down on the side table and shook his hand, not dropping his stare. He was sizing me up, and I had a feeling he'd find me lacking. So I stared right the fuck back. I wasn't one to back down, even when I was clearly the one who lost this battle. My mind was not whole, and neither was my body. "And you are…?"

"Riley Stapleton." He was a little shorter than me, but not by much, and he was strong. His grip didn't relax on mine at all, even though I didn't let go of him as quickly as I should have. "I'm a friend of Carrie's, and our dads are political affiliates."

I nodded and released him. He watched me with bright green eyes. His flawless skin and impeccably styled hair made me run a hand over my own roughly shaved head, ending up on my long, jagged cut. "I've never heard of you."

He smiled easily. "It's not too surprising. I didn't really become friends with Carrie till the holiday party. And after that, she left and stayed with you. We've only been talking via text and phone." He nodded toward my arm, his eyes warm and compassionate. "I hear you're doing better?"

"Oh yeah. Much." I looked him up and down, trying to dislike him on principle, but failing. He genuinely seemed to care. Un-fucking-believable. "So you were there when the call came in about me?"

"I was."

I flinched. "How bad was it?"

"It was pretty bad," Riley admitted, laughing lightly before motioning me into the living room. "Please. Let's sit. I don't want to tire you. Carrie would be angry with me."

Tire me? What was I, a fucking baby? "I'm fine."

"Still. Let's sit."

Damn it, I should have been the one to invite him to sit, since I kinda sorta lived here. I should have been polite and mannerly, and invited him inside. Instead, I'd questioned him in the foyer like a dickhead. I led him into the opulent room, hovering by the couch awkwardly while Riley seated himself. I sat beside him, letting my broken arm rest against my chest, and gripped my knee with my hand.

George came in with two glasses of whiskey and set them in front of us. He left the bottle behind and I knew it was because of me. One drink wouldn't hurt, would it? I eyed it, knowing I wanted it way too badly and unable to stop myself from picking it up. I drained it in one gulp, turning to Riley with more confidence. I wasn't used to this feeling. It fucking sucked.

I felt inferior and incompetent in the face of such perfection.

"So." I looked at him again. He'd been watching me drink. When I met his eyes, he quickly looked away and picked up his own whiskey. "You're a friend of Carrie's, huh?"

"I am." Riley's hand tightened on his crystal glass. "You don't need to worry about me, man. I'm not after her or anything."

I blinked at him. "I never said you were."

"I just wanted to make that clear. I mean, she's a great girl, and you're a lucky guy." Riley looked down at his drink and shrugged. "But anyone with eyes can see she loves you, and I've never come between a guy and a girl before. I won't be starting now."

"You don't get why she loves me though, right?" I poured more whiskey with a trembling hand. "You don't understand why we work."

Riley let out an uneasy laugh. "I get it perfectly fine." Riley reclined against the couch and watched me. I half expected to see criticism in his eyes. Or judgment. There wasn't, damn it. "You seem like a good guy. Why would I question that?"

"I'm not one of you." I motioned down his body. "I'm different."

"Different is good sometimes." Riley took a small sip. I forced myself not to gulp down the contents of my whole glass. "I'm not like her father any more than she is. Don't assume I am just because I run in the same circles."

I set the bottle down and raised the glass to my lips. As I drank, I thought on his words. He was right. I was judging him, and that wasn't fair of me. "I'm sorry."

Riley started. "Excuse me?"

"You're right. I shouldn't make assumptions." I lifted my glass to him and tried to brush my prejudice and insecurities aside. "If you're a friend of Carrie's, you're a friend of mine."

He seemed surprised at my about-face. "Uh, good." He shifted his weight. "How's the arm doing?"

I looked down at the sling. "Still broken."

"That's unfortunate," Riley said dryly, amusement in his eyes. "Maybe tomorrow it won't be?"

"Maybe." I smiled. I couldn't help it. "What do you do when you're not here?"

Riley took another sip. "I'm still in college. Upstate California, but I'll be finished with my bachelor's degree soon. Then next year I'll be moving to Southern California for my master's and doctorate."

So he'd be by Carrie and me soon. Fucking fabulous. "Let me guess, somewhere really close to the University of California in San Diego?"

"Yeah." Riley flushed and looked out the window, so I took the opportunity to study him. I tried to picture him as this villain who was out to steal my girl, but I couldn't. I really wanted to, but it wasn't there. "That's the plan anyway."

I nodded even though he wasn't looking at me. "I plan on starting at Carrie's school soon, too."

Riley turned back to me. "Oh yeah? What major?"

"Uh…" I racked my memory for what I'd decided to do, but the word wouldn't come. I knew it, but my fucking mind wouldn't work. Another side effect of being almost blown to pieces, I guess. I couldn't remember a damn thing. "I'm still deciding. Things got a little confused when I came home like this."

Riley nodded. "I can see why. I wish you all the best of luck, man."

"What are you going for?"

"Law, of course." Riley twisted his lips. "My father wouldn't have it any other way."

I was about to ask him what he would do if it weren't for his father, but the front door opened. "Is that Riley's car I see out front?" Senator Wallington asked. "Where are you, boy?"

George cleared his throat. "He's in the living room, sir."

"They're back," Riley said unnecessarily. My brain might be scattered, but it wasn't completely useless. Riley rose to his feet and smoothed his shirt. "You need a refill?"

I looked down at my glass. I hadn't even noticed I'd finished it again. How many had I had? My head was spinning a little bit already. Shit. "No, thank you. I'm fine."

My voice slurred on *fine*. Riley was polite enough to pretend he didn't notice. "All right."

"Riley? Sorry to keep you waiting. We had to search for the perfect tree and—" Senator Wallington stopped in the doorway, his eyes going from me to Riley. I didn't have to be sober to know who he preferred. "Oh. I see Griffin was keeping you company." He eyed the whiskey on the table, and then pointedly looked at my empty glass. "Hopefully you two got along all right."

I flinched. Riley laughed and dragged his hand through his perfect hair. I missed my fucking hair. "How could we not? He was wonderful. Welcomed me into the home with open arms."

"Indeed." Senator Wallington eyed me dubiously. He wasn't flat-out rude, never that. But I knew he didn't like me with Carrie. He tolerated me. Nothing more. "I'm glad to hear it."

I looked past him. "Where's Carrie?"

"She's coming." The senator gave me a tight-lipped smile. "She stopped to talk to your father."

Right. My father. I should have been spending time with him instead of drinking in the living room. I had questions to ask him. "Oh."

Senator Wallington turned to Riley. "Come and see the tree. It's humongous."

"Sure thing." After a quick nod, Riley turned to me. "You coming, Finn?"

I shook my head. I didn't need to go out there with a man who hated my guts to stare at a tree that would be inside the house soon enough. Especially when my head was spinning like a fucking carousel. I'd rather wait for Carrie to come inside. "Nah. Go on without me."

Senator Wallington eyed me suspiciously, but grinned at Riley. "Come on, then."

Riley went outside with him, not looking back again. Unable to resist, I stood at the window and watched him and the senator as they stood next to the car with the tree on the roof. It was fucking *huge*. Would probably fill up my entire apartment.

But in this house? It would be just right.

As I watched, the senator threw his arm around Riley's shoulders and said something that made Riley laugh. He'd never accept me like that. Broken or not, he never would have been so friendly to me. It was time I accepted it. I was second choice.

Hell, probably his last choice.

Riley gestured to the tree while saying something that had the senator grinning. Carrie and her mother came up. While her mother beelined for Riley and the senator, Carrie started for the door. Her father called her over, and she turned to him and walked to the car.

As she talked, she turned to Riley, smiled, and smacked his arm while also laughing at something he said. She didn't hit me anymore. Was probably too scared to hurt me or some shit like that. As a matter of fact, she didn't smile with me anymore. Not like that. I hadn't seen her smile like that for way too long. Not even with me.

But without me?

She looked happy. A hell of a lot happier than she'd been.

I grabbed the bottle of whiskey off the table and stalked out of the living room, out into the foyer, and headed for the servant's entrance into the kitchen. I needed to clear my head. Maybe some fresh air would help me think clearly, since I couldn't seem to do that anymore. Hell, if I was smart, I'd see the one thing that was staring me right in the fucking face, even if I was too selfish to admit it.

She was better off without me.

And she was better off *with* Riley.

CHAPTER FIVE

Carrie

I took my teal cashmere cowl off and peeked into the living room. Empty. Riley came up behind me and helped me remove my coat, and I smiled at him in thanks as I strained to see if Finn was lurking somewhere. He was nowhere to be found, even though he'd been with Riley only minutes before.

Part of me wondered how that had gone. Finn had a tendency not to like guys who were my friends, so it made me think maybe Finn tried to scare Riley off. Or maybe he'd been as taken in by him at the first meeting as I'd been. Something about Riley screamed for you to like him instantly. Outside, he'd been cracking jokes to me about how much my father kept pushing him toward me, despite my very real boyfriend inside the house.

On top of that, he'd told me he'd met—and loved—Finn.

That made me like him even more. He obviously had good taste. "Where were you two hanging out?" I asked him.

"In the living room." Riley hung my coat on the coat stand and motioned me forward. "I'm sure he's still there. Let's go find him."

We walked into the living room, but it was clear he wasn't there anymore. An empty glass sat on the table, but nothing else. "He's not here." I picked it up and sniffed it. Whiskey. So, he'd been drinking. "But he obviously was at one point."

"Yeah. With me." Riley watched me closely. Too closely. "That's my glass, though. Not his."

Hope surged through me. "Oh. He wasn't drinking?"

"He was. He must have cleaned up after himself when he left." Riley shrugged. "He must've put the bottle away, too."

I swallowed hard. He'd probably taken it with him to finish it off. But Riley didn't need to know that. I'd hoped that after last night, he might not feel the need to drink himself into oblivion. I'd hoped... It didn't matter what I'd hoped.

It hadn't happened.

I gave Riley my back while I composed myself. Once I was ready, I turned to him with a bright smile. "I can get you a refill, if you'd like."

"Yes, please." He hesitated, reached for my hand, but dropped it by his side without me having to reject him. Good, because I didn't want to. "Are you okay, Carrie?"

"I'm great," I said, forcing a cheerful note to my voice. "I mean, it's hard to see him like this." I motioned toward the empty glass. "But he's working his way through it. We're working our way through it."

"I didn't ask how *he* was." He stepped closer, watching me from under his lashes. "I asked how you are."

I swallowed past the lump in my throat. "I told you. I'm fine."

"Carrie..." He looked over my shoulder and smiled brightly, changing his tone of voice. "Ah, there you are. We were about to send out a search party for you."

Finn stood in the doorway, watching Riley and me with narrowed eyes. When I smiled at him, he smiled back, but I could see the look in his eyes didn't match. Not at all. If anything, he looked sad. He set down his empty glass, and put the bottle on the table. It was almost empty. "I went looking for my dad, but I couldn't find him."

Riley picked up his cup and headed across the room, talking about having another drink. I trailed behind him, my eyes on Finn. He seemed as if he was being friendly enough. He hadn't called him Miley or anything else that was close to his name, but not quite right. "I was just talking to him when I came home. He went out to the store."

"Oh." He ran his hand over his head. He used to tug on his curls when he was nervous. Is that what he was trying to do? "I would have gone with him if I'd known. He shouldn't be going out alone."

But he hadn't wanted to go shopping with me? I wasn't sure what that meant. "Sorry, I didn't think you'd want to."

He smiled at me. "It's fine. Now I get to spend time with you… and Riley." He popped the lid off the whiskey and poured Riley a good amount. "Can't let you drink alone, now can I?"

Riley grinned. "Course not. Short Stuff over here isn't old enough, so I've only got you."

"Yeah, she's not quite old enough yet," Finn murmured as he poured himself another glass. He watched me as he poured, almost as if he was daring me to say something. To start a fight with him. And, man, I wanted to. "We've had a few discussions about that, though, haven't we, Carrie?"

I curled my hands into balls and bit down on my tongue. Glancing at his glass pointedly, I said, "We have. Too much alcohol is never a good thing."

He laughed. "She thinks I drink too much when I'm stressed out." He turned to Riley and held his glass out for a toast. "Lately, that's been all the time, hasn't it?"

"Finn…" I started, but he threw his arm over my shoulder and hugged me close. I stole a quick look at Riley. He was watching Finn with concern in his gaze. My cheeks heated. "You doing okay?"

"Fabulous now that you're back." He kissed my forehead, his lips lingering. Despite my uneasiness about his current state of mind, my heart flared to life as the gesture. It was so much like something the old Finn would do. "I missed you."

"Did you nap?"

He fingers tightened on his glass. "Yep."

I wanted to ask him if he'd had the nightmare again, but I wouldn't in front of Riley. "Great. So I see you met Riley?"

"I did." Finn led me to the couch, making sure I sat between him and the arm of the couch. Riley sat on Finn's other side. "We were talking about the night you two became friends."

I stole a quick glance at Riley. "Oh yeah?"

"Yep." Riley sipped his drink, looking slightly uncomfortable if his furrowed brow was any indication. "How long are you two staying here?"

"We go back on the thirtieth."

"Is that what we decided?" Finn blinked. "I thought we were leaving on the twenty-seventh."

I shook my head and rested my hand on his thigh. "No, because you have an MRI that morning." I softened my voice. "Remember? I put it on a Post-it."

"No. I don't remember." Finn took a long drink, his leg going hard under my hand. I could practically feel the frustration rolling off him. "How long are you in town, Riley?"

"Through the afternoon of the first. Then it's the red-eye flight back to California that night."

I nodded. "We were going to stay through then, too, but I thought it would be best if we got Finn back to Cali so we could start setting up his physical therapy appointments, and all the other stuff that goes with his injuries." I lifted a hand before letting it fall to my lap. "There's a lot to organize before classes start."

Finn cursed under his breath and stood. "You make me sound like I'm an old man who can't take care of myself. I'm injured, not useless. I can organize it all."

"I know. I didn't mean—"

"I know you didn't mean anything by it, Carrie. It's just that I'm realizing I'm not your boyfriend anymore. I'm a fucking burden." He gripped his head and gave me his back. "You know what? Forget I said that. I think I'm going to excuse myself before I say something else I'll regret."

I lurched to my feet. "Don't go. I'm sorry."

"I told you to stop fucking apologizing to me," he snapped.

"But—"

My dad came up behind Finn. "Is every—?"

Finn whirled on my dad, fist raised, his breathing coming fast. He looked a second away from clocking my dad in the jaw. Dad jumped back, his eyes wide and his hands up in surrender. I ran to Finn's side, and Riley bolted around the couch to Dad. "*Finn.*"

"Shit." Finn covered his face with his good hand. "I'm sorry. You snuck up on me." He shook his head, but didn't drop his hand. "I'm sorry. I'm sorry."

"Shh. It's okay, Finn." I locked eyes with Dad. "It's okay. He's all right."

Dad broke gazes with me, his face pale but otherwise seeming unaffected. "Yes. I'm fine, Griffin."

Jen McLaughlin

Finn turned to me and finally showed his face. He looked ravaged. Terrified. *Broken*. It's the first time he'd dropped the act around me, and it hurt so freaking much. I opened my arms, and he dove into them, bending down and hugging me with his good one. "Fuck, Carrie. I'm sorry. I love you. I'm *sorry*."

"Shh." I hugged him as tight as I could, meeting Riley's gaze over Finn's shoulder. "I'm here with you."

They needed to go. Needed to let Finn recover without an audience. He seemed to get my message. "Mr. Wallington?" Riley said a bit haltingly. "Let's go check on your tree and see if the household staff needs any help. It's a fine tree, if I may say so myself."

Dad looked less than willing, but good manners won out. "Sure thing. Let's go." He started for the door but froze. "Carrie, if you need help, I'll be right out there."

I nodded but didn't answer. I was too busy holding Finn and trying to calm him down. Once we were alone, I kissed the top of his head. "I'm here, and you're okay."

"I'm not okay. I'm *not*." He clung to me so tightly I could barely breathe. His face was pressed into my chest, but I could still feel him shivering in my arms. "Shit, I can't do this to you anymore. I can't be this guy."

My heart stuttered. "You didn't do anything to me, Finn. I'm fine." I ran my hands over his bald head, skipping over his puckered wound. I didn't know if they still hurt. "You're fine. We'll get through this."

He shook his head but didn't release me. "You don't deserve this."

"Hey. Stop that." I pulled back and forced him to look at me. Cupping his cheeks, I narrowed my eyes on him. "*You* don't deserve this. You went there because you were trying to make life better for us. For me. If anything, this is all my fault. If we hadn't met, and you hadn't loved me, you never would have taken this job." My voice cracked. "Anything you're going through right now, it's on *me*. Not you."

He shook his head frantically. "This isn't your fault. It's mine. I lived. They died." He stared off into the distance. "They all died in front of me. I saw it happen. They all just *died*. Why did I live? Why me?"

I swallowed back a sob. He looked so lost. "Because I need you."

"I need you too." He seemed to snap back into reality. He turned to me and his face softened a fraction. "So damn much, but it's not fair.

None of this is fair."

Was it not fair that he needed me, or was he saying it wasn't fair he was still alive? I wasn't sure, and I wasn't sure I really wanted to find out. "I know it's not."

"I can't do this to you," he repeated. "I won't do it. I won't ruin you. I won't take you down with me."

His words filled me with fear. It was as if he was telling me he was leaving. We'd promised to love each other forever. He couldn't leave. I gripped him even tighter. "Stop talking like that. You're scaring me."

"You should be fucking scared of me." He laughed harshly. "*Look* at me."

"I *am* looking at you." I leaned in and kissed him gently, even though my fingers ached to slap him until he stopped talking nonsense. "I'm always looking at you. You're gorgeous, brave, kind, and loving. You're Finn, and I love you just the way you are. Forever, no matter what."

He drew in a ragged breath. "Yeah, but I think you see the old me. Not the 'me' I am now. The *me* I'll always be from now on. The guys died. Every. Single. One."

"But you lived." I shook him a little. "You're here, with me. There's a reason for that, don't you think?"

"I know, but I'm not here," he whispered. "Not really. You'd be better off if I just—"

"Don't you even think about finishing that thought," I hissed. "I'm telling you right now, I won't accept it."

He averted his eyes. "But it's true. You're just too stubborn to admit it."

I pushed him a little bit, anger taking over and making me forget I might hurt him. What had he been about to say? Was he going to say I would be better off if he'd just leave me...or if he'd died? Either way, he was wrong. *So* freaking wrong. "I will kick your ass so fucking hard you won't be able to sit straight for a week. Do you *hear* me?"

That seemed to bring him back to life. His lips even twitched as he turned back to me. "Is that so? A whole week?"

"Yeah. That's so." I curled my hands into fists so hard my nails dug into my palms. "I can't live without you. I can't do anything if you leave me. Don't think it. Don't dream it. Don't even *say* it. I'll never forgive you if you do. Not in a million years. Got it?"

His Adam's apple bobbed as he swallowed. "I hate doing this to you. Hate being fucking broken. This isn't who you fell in love with."

"We're all broken in different ways. You feel shattered now, but it'll get better." I ran my fingers over his jawline. It was so strong. So resilient. Just like him. He didn't realize how strong he still was. "Love is about staying with each other, in sickness and in health. I'm not leaving because you've been injured. And you can't push me away. I won't *let* you do that to us."

His resolve cracked. I could see it, as if it was a physical thing. "Carrie…"

"No. Don't *Carrie* me."

I kissed him, trying to convey the depth of my devotion and love in that simple kiss. He clung to me, making a broken sound in the back of his throat. His hand trembled as he cupped the back of my head, deepening the kiss.

Something crashed behind us and he jumped to his feet, shoving me behind him. Riley stood at the door, his eyes locked on us. "It's just me," he said softly. "I'm going to head out now. The snow is getting pretty heavy."

Finn relaxed marginally. "I'm sorry about earlier. I…well, I'm…"

"Dude." Riley held up a hand. "No explanations needed. Seriously."

Finn gave him a long look and nodded. "Thanks, man."

"Are you sure you can make it home okay?" I glanced out the window. The snow was coming down really heavily now. I felt bad that he'd come all this way to visit us and I'd basically said hi and that was it. "You just got here."

"I'll be fine." Riley smiled. "I might be in California now, but I'm still used to the D.C. winters. I'm not that much of a surfer boy."

No, I only had one surfer boy in my life.

Finn gave him a small smile. "It was nice meeting you. Hopefully the next time we see each other, I'm a little more put together."

"I think you're exactly the way a man should be after going through what you went through." Riley offered his hand. "Take it easy."

Finn shook it. "You too."

"I will." Riley turned to me and hesitated. "Carrie? Want to walk me out?"

I looked at Finn. "I should probably—"

"You should walk him out." Finn let go of me and stepped back, running his hand over his head. "Don't worry. I'll be right here when you get back."

I didn't want to leave him, but I couldn't refuse. That would be rude. "All right."

Riley started for the door, and I fell in to step with him. As we turned the corner, I peeked over my shoulder. Finn stood exactly where I'd left him. All alone.

"He's having a hard time," Riley said under his breath. "Be patient. I had a buddy come back from Iraq like this. He was drinking. Having panic attacks. It lasted for a long time. If he'd had someone who loved him the way you love Finn, then maybe…" Riley shook himself. "Keep being loving and kind, like you're doing. Don't let your dad tell you Finn needs space. He doesn't. He needs you."

I blinked back tears. "Finn thinks I'm better off without him, though. He told me so."

"Right now, he thinks it's true. Men like him push away their loved ones. They think they're failures and not good enough to be loved." Riley opened the front door and grabbed his coat. I followed him outside, hugging myself. "He will keep pushing you away. Just keep pulling him closer."

I nodded and swallowed hard. "I'm trying."

When we reached the front of his car, Riley brushed a finger across my cheek. It came back wet. I hadn't even realized I'd been crying. "Keep trying. And if you need to vent, give me a call. I'm an excellent listener."

I nodded and forced a smile. "Thank you. You're a good friend."

"I know," he teased. "You'd be a fool to not take me up on that offer. I'm a catch."

"Yeah, you are." I laughed. "I should hook you up with someone from my dorm."

"I don't know about that. I'm not ready for love yet."

"You still love your ex?"

He hesitated and avoided my eyes. "Yeah. Something like that."

"Well, when you're ready."

"It's a plan." He opened his car door and started to get in. "Bye, Carrie."

"Wait." I stepped closer. "How long did it take your friend to get better?"

"He didn't. He shot himself in the head a month and two days after he came back home. I found him that way." Riley met my eyes. "Take care of him, Carrie. And watch him closely."

I nodded and walked backward as I watched Riley get into the car, eager to get back to Finn. God, just the thought of him doing something like that…

I couldn't even think it.

CHAPTER SIX

Finn

Ring, ring, ring.

No matter how many times I called, the result hadn't changed. Dad's voicemail picked up, announcing joyfully that he couldn't come to the phone right now. I sighed and hung up without leaving a message. I'd already left him one. The snow kept coming down heavier and heavier, and it would only get worse after sunset.

Hell, even Riley was leaving.

I walked to the window and peeked through it, watching them like a voyeur. Riley had pulled his car up when they'd been carrying the tree inside, so I could see them perfectly from where I stood. When Riley reached out and touched her face, I wanted to scream at him to back the fuck off my girl, but I didn't. I just watched.

They looked good together.

Pushing away from the window, I straightened my spine and grabbed my pills off the table, staring down at the small orange bottle. It was time for another dose, judging from the pain ripping through me.

"You need help with that?" Carrie's mom asked hesitantly.

I jumped, my heart racing. Would I ever stop panicking when someone walked up behind me? Or would I forever be the scared, pansy-ass, shell of a man I'd once been? "Yeah. I can't open it, ma'am."

She approached slowly, as if uncertain of her welcome. "I'll open it for you."

"Thank you," I said, holding it out to her. "I appreciate that."

Senator Wallington followed her into the room, his blue eyes locked on mine. As his wife opened my pain meds, he grabbed an unopened bottle of Aquafina off the bar. My half-eaten turkey sandwich was still there, too. "You'll need this opened, too, I presume?"

I licked my parched lips. I'd rather have a stiff drink, but the water would look better in front of them. God knew I already looked bad enough. "Yes, please, sir."

He twisted the lid off and handed it to me. "You doing all right? Mixing alcohol and pills is generally discouraged."

"I'm fine." In a half an hour or so, I'd be feeling even better. I set the water down. Next, I took the pill from Carrie's mom and popped it in my mouth, watching him the whole time. "Sorry about earlier."

"It's all right." He sat down and crossed an ankle over a knee. "What time is your father expected back? It's getting nasty out there."

"I'm not sure. I called him a few times, but he's not answering." I shifted on my feet, blinking when the room spun. Weird. I didn't remember it doing that before. "I might have to go out and look for him. Maybe Carrie knows where he went."

"Where who went?" Carrie asked, her voice tight. "Sit down, Finn. You look dizzy."

I wasn't dizzy. I was fucking high. But I sat down anyway. She came to my side and curled her hand with mine, holding on tight. She seemed freaked out by something. "My dad. It's getting bad out there, and he isn't answering his phone."

"We can go look for him if you want," she said quickly. "He went to Target."

I nodded. "Let's go. I'm worried he'll—"

"You're not going anywhere," Senator Wallington said, his eyes on Carrie. For a second, I'd thought he was talking to me. "We'll send out security in an all-terrain vehicle. You're not going out in this mess in your Volvo."

"I'll go," I said.

"No, you won't. If you go, *she'll* go." Senator Wallington arched a brow at me. "Do you really want her out in this?"

I looked out the window, squinting. It looked blurry. "I guess not…"

"That's what I thought." Senator Wallington smoothed his suit jacket. "I'll send Cortez and another man."

"Hugh, are you sure we should make them go out in this?" Carrie's mom asked, her voice worried. "It's getting pretty dark out there, and the roads are bound to be treacherous."

"All the more reason that we need to find Larry," Carrie said, her voice insistent. "I can do it. I'll be—"

"*No*," Senator Wallington snarled. "Absolutely not."

"Hugh. We need to—"

"Someone needs to go," Carrie insisted.

"Enough of this!" I shouted, heading for the door. I stumbled on my second step. "*You* can argue about who should go. *I'm* going before it's too late to get out of here."

Carrie rushed after me. "You can't drive. You're…you're…" She paused, and I could see her arguing with herself how best to get me to listen. She should just say it. *You're drunk. Say it, Carrie, say it.* "Your arm is in a sling, so you won't be able to control the vehicle if it slips."

She didn't say it.

"I don't care, Carrie. He's my dad." I yanked the door open. "I'm not losing him, too."

"Not losing who?" Dad asked, blinking at me. He looked past me, no doubt seeing Carrie, Senator Wallington, and Mrs. Wallington all hovering in the doorway. "What did I miss?"

"You," I snapped, curling my hand around the knob so tight it hurt. "What did you need that was so important you had to drive in the snow?"

"My medicine," Dad said calmly. He held up a prescription bag and shook it under my nose. "I knew the weather was going to get worse, so I figured it was now or never. I chose now."

"I don't know what medicine was worth risking your life over." I snatched the bag and struggled to pull out the orange pill bottle. I scanned the pill name before looking at Dad with a hollow pain in my chest. I recognized the name of the meds, damn it. "Why are you taking this? What aren't you telling me?"

"My heart is acting up." Dad took his medication back and dropped it into the bag. "It's not a huge surprise. Your grandfather had issues, too."

"Yeah. I remember." I swallowed hard. It was all coming together now. "And he died of a heart attack. Did you have a heart attack? Is that why you didn't come to California when the senator did?"

Dad flushed. "Yes."

Anger rushed through me, red-hot and burning everything in its path. It collided with the ice-cold fear also coursing through my veins, creating a monstrous storm within me. "And you didn't tell me because…?"

"Can I at least come inside before you ask me a million questions?" He huddled into his coat, his bright red cheeks looking chafed. "I'm freezing."

I hadn't even realized I still stood in the doorway with the door wide open, blocking his entry. I backed out of it and looked over my shoulder. Carrie's parents were gone, but Carrie still stood there. She looked unsure of her welcome. I met her eyes. "Did you know about this?"

"I didn't *know*, but I suspected." She wrapped her arms around herself. "I didn't tell you because I didn't have confirmation. We were going to talk to him today, remember?"

I nodded once. "Yeah. I remember. You didn't remind me, though, like you promised you would."

"I'm sorry. I—"

"Can we talk in my room, son?" Dad came inside and closed the door, looking at me with disappointment clear in his blue eyes. "I'm exhausted."

"Of course." I forgot all about being pissed he didn't tell me about his illness. He looked even paler than he'd been, and I couldn't shake the feeling that he was acting as if he was feeling much better than he actually was. You know, like *me*. "Let's go. Did you eat dinner?"

"Of course I did." Dad rolled his eyes and shuffled toward the stairs. He looked weaker than ever. Same gray hair. Same blue eyes. But so much fucking older. "I have a bad heart, not a bad stomach."

I forced a laugh. "That's true. You were never one to skip a meal."

"And I never will," he said, laughing along with me.

As soon as he turned around, the smile on my face disappeared. I stopped at Carrie's side and leaned down until my mouth was a whisper away from her ear. "We'll talk later."

She caught my hand. "Take it easy on him. He's worried about you."

"And *I'm* worried about him." I watched him climb the stairs, one slow step at a time. The pain pills finally kicked in, giving Dad a weird shimmery haze around him. Almost like an aura—or what I guessed an aura looked like. Fuck if I actually knew. "I just want to know all the details. Then I'll let him sleep."

"Okay." She rose up on tiptoe and kissed me. "I'll see you soon."

"I'll be waiting."

"The sun is finally shining," she said softly.

I tensed. "Yeah, it is," I managed to say through my swollen throat.

Not because it made me happy, but because it made *her* happy. Those words used to mean so much to me when she said that, but now it brought back memories of men dying. Of Dotter's blood squirting all over my face and in my mouth. It meant something completely different to her—and it sucked that was the case now.

Fuck, I wished…

I wished we could go back.

We made it into his room, and I switched the light on. I hadn't been in his room since we got here. I'd been so absorbed in what I'd been dealing with that I totally missed all the signs. That's the kind of man I'd become. A whole shitload of orange pill bottles sat by his bed. I walked up to them and ran my fingers over the lineup. "You should have told me."

"What good would it have done? When it's our time to die, it's our time. There's nothing you or anyone can do to stop it."

I threw the covers back off his bed. "Lay down."

"I will." He scratched his head. His half-bald head. When had that happened? He's always seemed so strong. Ageless. Now, as I thought it over, I realized he was over fifty. Too young to die, but old enough to be way too fucking close to it. "There's nothing you can do to stop time from moving on. Nothing you can do to change the past."

I let out a harsh laugh. "Yeah. No kidding. I learned that up close and personal. One might even say I had a front row seat."

"I know, and I'm sorry you did." He ran his hands over his hair. "I wish I could change that. Wish I could take it all away."

"Yeah, well, you can't change what already happened."

I opened his dresser and pulled out a pair of pajamas. They were blue and had stripes on them. They'd been his present from me last year for Christmas. That seemed as if it was a lifetime ago, not only one year. It had been before I met Carrie. Before I learned what love really was.

51

Before I'd watched my whole unit die and then lived to tell about it.

A hell of a lot could happen in a year.

"No, but we can change how it affects us." Dad pulled his sweater over his head, and I handed him the pajama top. "You're pushing her away."

"I know. I can't help it." I picked up the pants and held them out as Dad shrugged into his shirt. "I keep saying I'll stop. Keep waking up with the best intentions. But then I fuck up and I still push her away."

"You have to stop hurting her. Have you talked to her about it?"

I hesitated. "We haven't really talked much at all."

"Because you're pushing her away."

"Yes." I crumpled his pants in my hand. "Sometimes I think she would be better off without me."

He shook his head. "She wouldn't be. She'd live. She'd laugh. She'd smile. But she wouldn't be better."

Dad's hands were shaking too badly for him to button the shirt himself, so I tossed his pants to the side and went to help him button his shirt…right until I realized I could barely manage to button my own damn shirt. So I just stood there, helplessly watching my father struggle to dress himself.

How the fuck had I missed this? How could I be so self-centered?

"You're not self-centered. You're recovering. There's a difference." Dad frowned at me. Those pain pills must've messed with my head. I hadn't even meant to talk out loud. "But the kind of love that you two have doesn't come around often. To waste it on pride and self-pity would be a crime."

I swallowed hard. Damn it, he was right. I was being an idiot, but I already knew that. I just couldn't *stop*. Too bad they didn't make a pill for that. "I hate that she's stuck with this. Stuck with me."

"She's not stuck with you; she chose you." Dad caught my hand and squeezed it tight. "You can't lose her, too. Don't let that happen, because I guarantee you'll regret it if you do."

I met his eyes. "Are you saying I'm losing you?"

"I'm saying I'm old and sick." Dad lifted a shoulder. "It's not rocket science, son. Everyone dies. I'm not sad that my turn is coming. You shouldn't be either."

"I can't lose you, Dad."

"I'll try my best to stay, but it's not up to me." Dad pointed up toward the ceiling. "It's up to Him."

At first I thought he meant Senator Wallington, whose bedroom suite was upstairs on the third floor, but then I realized he meant God. The same God I wasn't even sure I believed in anymore. Why would the "merciful" God kill all my squad members, but let me live? Why would He take my mother away?

And why was He trying to take my father, too?

Later that night, I sat in my dark bedroom, staring out the window. The moon was full, and it made me think of the last time I'd seen it that way. I'd been with Carrie on my bike. We'd whipped through the streets of San Diego, and she'd clung to me the whole time. We'd been so wild and free and in love.

My dad kept insisting I stop pushing her away, but maybe I should be pushing her away even harder. Maybe I should break it off with her. Set her free. Wouldn't that be better than this? I eyed my pill bottle. It hadn't been long enough for me to take another one yet, but the urge was there. I tried to ignore it.

The door opened, and I lurched to my feet unsteadily. She slid inside the door, shut it, and then stood somewhere close to it. I couldn't see her because it was too dark. "Finn? Are you in here?"

For a second, and only a second, I debated not answering. She would go away, and I could drink myself into oblivion, and top it off with another pain pill or two. But then I remembered I loved her, and she loved me, even if I was an ass. "I'm here."

I heard her come closer. "Can I turn on the light?"

"I prefer the dark. It soothes me."

"Okay." Her weight dipped down on the bed beside me. "How's your dad?"

"He's dying." My voice cracked on the last word. I couldn't fucking help it. I needed him here. God didn't need him. *I* did. "It's not fair."

Her arms wrapped around me from behind, entwining in front of my heart, and I clung to her joined hands with my good hand. It felt good. Right. Human. "I'm so sorry. But he's still here. He could live another twenty years and surprise us all."

"Yeah. Maybe. He is stubborn like that." I laughed. It felt foreign in my throat. "Must be where I got it from."

She was silent for a second, almost as if she couldn't believe I made a half-assed joke, and then she laughed. It washed over me, soothing my soul. "Yeah. Must be."

"That was the wrong answer," I teased. My fingers twitched on hers. "You were supposed to say I'm not stubborn at all."

"I would, but we promised not to lie to each other." She kissed my shoulder. "So the truth it is, love."

Love. She hadn't called me that since Germany.

I closed my eyes, pretending I hadn't just found out my dad was sick. On top of that, I pretended I wasn't fucked up. Pretended we were in California, not D.C. Then I opened my eyes and woke the fuck up. "I appreciate that about you. You always tell me the truth."

She shifted behind me. "I try to, anyway."

"Do you still love me, Carrie?" I tightened my hand on hers when she tried to pull away. "And before you answer that, let me be clear. I'm not talking about the man I was before I left. I'm talking about the man I am now. *Me*. Do you love *me*?"

"Of course I do." She wiggled free. I let her this time. "This will pass, Finn. I know you're upset because it's been a battle every second of every day, but it'll get better."

"It might not." I stared out the window. "I might be like the moon now. It will come and go in phases, but I don't think the pain, the sheer helplessness and anger I feel at the world right now, will ever fully go away."

"Why are you angry?" she asked, her voice whisper light.

"Because He took everyone else, but He let me live." I shook my head and forced a laugh. "No matter how many times I look at it, and no matter how many different ways, that will never make sense to me."

Her hand found mine and held on tight. "Do you wish you'd died?"

"I don't think you want honesty on that question," I said, my throat tight. "Not tonight, anyway. Ask me another time."

She made a weird sound, but stayed silent on the issue. "I'm glad you lived. It might make me selfish and horrible, but I'm glad."

"You don't think it would be easier on everyone if I'd just died?"

I asked, my voice oddly distant in my own head. "I think He made a mistake. I think I was supposed to die, too. That's why I feel the way I do. That's why I can't let myself be happy. I'm supposed to be dead, like them. Hell, I feel like I'm dying already."

She cried out. "Don't say that. It's not true."

"I have to be fucking honest, right?" I rubbed my head, my gaze on my casted arm. "This is me right now. This is the real me. No pretending I'm okay. No lies."

She crawled into my lap and cradled my face. "I know, but I'm here. And I'm not letting you waste away. I refuse to let you wither away into nothing because you feel like you should be dead. If you were supposed to be dead, you'd be dead. You're here, and you're mine."

"I'm a drunk and I can't even relax or sleep." I bit down on my tongue hard. "Why do you want me to stay?"

"Why would I want you to leave?" She kissed me, perfect and sweet and so very *her*. She pulled back, but I could still taste her on my lips. "I love you, and I'm not leaving you. I'm here to stay, and so are you."

I dropped my forehead to hers. I *wanted* to believe it. Hell, deep down I *did* believe it. Once upon a time, I'd been sure we would get our happy ending. I'd known, deep down to my soul, that we were meant to be together forever. That I was the best man for her, because no one would make her happier than I could, because our love was just that fucking strong. I'd been certain of it.

I couldn't say the same thing anymore.

CHAPTER SEVEN

Carrie

There was a shift in him tonight. I could feel it. Sense it. He was still trying to convince me he wasn't good enough for me, just like when we'd first gotten together, but now it was more of a hindsight type of thing. He wasn't pushing me away, but he was being painfully honest with me.

Maybe he was actually starting to heal.

It was way too early for recovery. I knew that. I'd done my research. Even now, I had an open book on PTSD and all its lasting effects on my nightstand. It was part of my bedtime routine. I also had countless books on being the support system for someone with PTSD, and how best to handle certain types of episodes. That's what he'd had today.

An *episode*.

He worried that he might not go back to normal. I wasn't sure he would either, but I knew one thing: he might never get back to normal, but he would get better. And if he didn't ever return to normal, well, then, he would have to achieve a new standard of normal. We'd have to adjust our expectations.

His hand skimmed down my sides and settled on the curve of my hip. "Ginger..."

God, I'd missed him calling me that. He used to do it all the time. Now, it was always Carrie. *Carrie* this and *Carrie* that. Never Ginger. "Yeah?"

"I'm going to stop telling you to leave me." He caught my hand. "I'm going to stop pushing you away, but know this: I still think you could do better. This isn't a heroic action of mine; it's a selfish one. I don't want to lose you, because I need you. But you *should* walk away from me."

My heart twisted painfully. The fact that he believed this, with all his heart, broke mine. "You're wrong. You're the most unselfish man I've ever met." I wiggled my hand free. "And I think you're blind to yourself."

"I think it's the other way around," he said sheepishly. He ran a hand over his head, probably looking for those curls again. With a grimace, he dropped his hand to his lap. "I'm going to try to get better for you."

"Don't do it for me." I undid the last button of his shirt. "Do it for you."

"No." He ran his hand up over my body, tipping my head back. "For *us.*"

I swallowed hard and unclasped his sling, my knuckles scraping against the hard cast. Desire unfurled in my belly at the way he watched me. I couldn't see it, but I could feel it. "Let's get you out of this shirt."

"Only if you get out of yours, too," he said, his tone light.

Hope, small and distant, flared in me. I'd been right. He was different tonight. Maybe his talk with his father had helped. Whatever it was, I was happy for the change. "That could be arranged."

I took the sling off and laid it on the side. He flinched. "I think it's time for another pill."

"Has it been four hours yet?"

He hesitated. "Yeah, a little over, I think."

I gently slid his shirt off his shoulders. His hard muscles taunted me. I wished I could run my tongue over each one, but he wasn't ready for that. "And when was your last drink?"

"With Riley."

"Okay. I'm going to turn the light on so I don't spill them."

Silence. "All right. But stay on my lap."

"Gladly. It's my favorite place to be."

He chuckled lightly. "The feeling is mutual."

I stretched my arm and turned on the light by his bed. It was very dim. Perfect for what I needed. I grabbed the bottle and undid the cap. When I turned back to Finn, he was watching me with a soft look in his eye. One that I hadn't seen in a long time. I swallowed and poured one big pill into my palm. "Do you need a drink to wash it down?"

"I *need* you." He took it and tossed it into his mouth. "But, yeah, I could go for some water. My bottle is next to the lamp."

I closed the meds and set them back where they'd been. Picking up the water, I undid that cap, too. "We need to get you a glass in here."

"I'm fine."

He tipped his head back and chugged the water. As he did so, I let my gaze skim over his body. He had injuries, sure, but he looked beautiful to me. Even more so than before, if anything. His ink still stretched over his muscles, and his muscles were still ridiculously hard and huge.

The heart under those muscles was still the same, too.

My stomach tightened and I forced my gaze away. I didn't want him feeling pressured to do anything with me. Heck, last night had been pushing it. Although, it had seemed to maybe help a little bit… But the books said it didn't.

"You can turn out the light now," he said. I looked back at him, and he looked so vulnerable it hurt. "I know it's not a pretty picture."

"Finn, you look delicious." I skimmed my fingers over his shoulders. "When I look at you, it takes all my control not to attack you. You don't see what I see." I touched the cut on his shoulder. "I see bravery. Love. A good man."

I lowered my hand over the tattoo he'd gotten for us. It said: *the sun is finally shining*. Our code word for *I love you*. Guess we didn't need a code anymore, though.

Everyone knew about us.

"I'm only good because of you," he whispered. "You're the only good part about me."

"That's a lie." I placed my hand over his heart. "Your goodness is in here. It was there long before you met me. It was there when we met, and it's what made me want to kiss you that first time. It's what makes me want to kiss you now."

He made a small sound and squeezed my thigh. "Then fucking kiss me already, Ginger."

There he went using that nickname again.

He kissed me, his hand skimming up my body, and over my breasts, before settling on my lower back. He pulled me closer as his lips crashed over mine, stealing away all my thoughts. All my doubts. All he left behind was this. *Us.*

His tongue slipped between my lips, and I whimpered into his mouth. He swallowed my cries and his own moan melded with mine. I pressed down against his erection, my entire body begging for more, and I knew I was lost.

I always had been when it came to Finn.

Finn

I could feel her hesitation. Her doubt. She was worried she might break me even worse than I already was, but it didn't matter. I needed her more than I needed my sanity.

I needed her to need me.

And I knew the exact second she stopped fighting me internally. She melted against me and gripped my good shoulder, her nails digging in. I deepened the kiss and cupped a breast, toying with her nipple with the perfect amount of pressure. When I tugged hard, she cried out into my mouth, grinding down against my cock.

When she pushed down, I arched up, stealing her breath in the process. Good. I still had it in me. I might only have one good arm, but I'd still make her come so hard she wouldn't be able to look at me without blushing for a week, damn it.

Her nails dug into my shoulder, her other hand dipping past my broken arm and between us to massage my cock. "Finn. God."

"Undo my pants," I commanded, my own voice a little bit broken. "Then take yours off, too, but hurry up. I need you."

A desperate need to be buried inside of her consumed me. While she took her pants off, her hands trembled over every button and zipper. It consumed her, too. I could see it. Even though the light was on and I was looking like I now looked, she still wanted me.

This was what love was.

She dropped to her knees between my thighs and undid my button. I gritted my teeth and helped her remove my jeans. Next went my boxers, and then she grabbed a condom out of the drawer by my bed. Instead of putting it on me, she lowered her mouth to my cock and licked it.

Holy fucking shit.

"Carrie, not tonight. I need…I need…" I grabbed the condom and ripped the foil open with the help of my teeth. "I need to fuck you. Hard. Hot. Now."

"*Yes.*"

Her cheeks flushed, she rolled the condom on my cock. She straddled my hips, her pussy right where I needed her, and lowered herself onto me with a soft sigh. With my good hand, I gripped her ass and drove into her fully. She let out a strangled scream, biting down hard on her lip. I paused. "Are you okay?"

"No." She shook her head, still biting her lower lip, and smacked my uninjured arm. "You stopped. Don't. Stop."

Game fucking on. I moved beneath her, and she rode me hard. I could tell she was close, and I was close, too. So fucking close. "Touch yourself. I can't do it, so you have to do it for me. You have to be my hands. Play with yourself like I do."

She skimmed her hands over her belly. There was no hesitation. My Ginger was getting bolder. I loved it. "Where do you want to touch?"

I used my good hand to roll her nipple between my fingers. I wasn't gentle or sweet at all, and she loved it. "Massage your clit while I fuck you."

She let out a moan, lowering her hand inch by torturous inch. When she started moving her fingers in a circle, masturbating in front of me, my stomach tightened and twisted. I almost came right there. I needed her that bad. "Oh my God. *Yes.*"

I squeezed her breast and pumped my hips up hard. She moved over me faster. Her fingers picked up speed, too, and then she was arching her back and tensing. Her pussy squeezed down on me, and I let myself go. I didn't close my eyes this time. I just watched her as she came; her lids squeezed shut and her pink lips parted.

She was fucking gorgeous.

I came so hard it almost hurt, and I clung to her as well as I could with one hand. She collapsed against my good shoulder and I let myself fall back against the mattress. I rubbed her back gently, trying to catch my breath. She seemed perfectly content to stay there on me, snuggled up as if we hadn't just fucked each other rather than sweet lovemaking.

We'd both needed it.

She traced an invisible pattern on my shoulder. Or maybe she traced my tattoo. I couldn't tell. "When I sleep next to you, do you have the nightmares?"

"No." My hand stilled on her back. "But you usually only come in after I've already had at least one."

"Want me to stay the whole night?"

Fuck yeah, I did. "Your dad won't like it."

"If he isn't happy with it, we can go get a hotel room." She lifted up on her elbows, resting on my chest. It was then that I realized she hadn't even taken off her shirt. I'd have to make sure she got naked for me next time. "Your peace of mind is more important to me than my father's rules."

The painkillers kicked in, thank fucking God, making my mind all fuzzy and loose again. "Then stay. I miss sleeping with you in my arms. Maybe you'll chase away the nightmares."

She nodded against my chest. "Get on your pillow. You look like you're about to pass out."

I scooted up backward to my spot, rolling halfway over on my side. I didn't even bother to remove the condom. She rolled me onto my side more fully, removing it for me. Even though I wanted to protest, I couldn't say a word. My eyes closed, and I started drifting off into my drugged la-la land.

Maybe with her here at my side, I'd actually sleep. Maybe she was my pretty little dreamcatcher, fighting to keep the demons at bay.

She turned off the light, pulled on some clothes, from the sound of it, and then slid into bed beside me. As she tucked me in, my last conscious thought was how very like my father I was right now. I'd tried to help him undress for bed so he could rest, and now Carrie was doing it for me. He and I were kinda the same.

We were both slowly dying from the inside out.

CHAPTER EIGHT

Carrie

I got ripped from my sleep when Finn's door flew open, banging against the wall. Finn cursed and sprung up as well as he could, picked up a knife I hadn't even known he had from beneath the bed, and faced the door, breathing heavily. I scooted back against the headboard and blinked against the hallway light. Finn was completely naked, holding a knife, and mumbling under his breath.

He looked...terrifying.

"Who's there?" he snarled, positioning himself between me and the *threat* at the door. "Speak now before I kill you."

"It's me." A man cleared his throat. And, God, I recognized that voice. "Senator Wallington. Sorry to barge in unannounced, Griffin, but you have to—"

"*Stop.*" Finn looked over his shoulder at me, his face highlighted by the moonlight. I could see that the look in his eyes was somewhere between anger, fear, and desperation all mashed into one. He still held on to the knife. "Can you please give me a second to get dressed? I'm... I'm not decent."

I couldn't see my father, but I could picture him taking in Finn's nakedness. And he'd realize *why* Finn might be naked in three, two, one...

"Who is in there with you?" Dad asked calmly. I heard him come closer. "You're not alone." It wasn't a question.

"Stop right there." Finn stepped forward, blocking the light switch. "You're not turning that light on, sir."

"The hell I'm not," Dad growled under his breath. "If you're messing around behind my daughter's back, I assure you that my wrath is worse than what you experienced over there. You will never sleep again without picturing *my*—"

Finn let out a strangled sound. "I'm not cheating on Carrie, sir."

"Then who…?" He broke off. "Carrie. That had *better* not be you behind him."

I closed my eyes in embarrassment. This was hell. Right here. Right now. I opened my mouth to talk, but Finn beat me to it.

"Which is it you prefer, sir? For me to be cheating on her, or for her to be here instead of someone else?" Finn asked, his voice strained. He set down the knife on the nightstand. "What makes you think someone is here at all? Maybe I just sleep naked."

"I can see it all over you," Dad said, his voice tinged with disgust. "*Who* is back there?"

A light shone, and I cringed away from it. Damn those flashlight apps on the iPhone. Finn tried to jump in front of me, but it was too late. He'd seen me in Finn's bed. *Gr-eeeeat.* "Hi, Dad," I said softly, waving a hand. "Fancy seeing you here."

Dad shut off the light, completely ignoring me. "I was quite clear about my rules, Griffin."

"Yes, sir." I saw Finn's shoulders droop. "I'm sorry."

"I came to him, Dad. Not the other way around." I tugged the covers higher, even though I had a shirt on. I felt exposed. "Stop yelling at him and yell at me."

"Or better yet, tell me why you're in my room at—" Finn picked up and lit up his phone, "—one in the morning."

"I…you…" Dad trailed off, making a frustrated sound. "It's your father. Get dressed and come quickly."

"My dad? But what—oh God." Finn tossed his phone to the side, and I lunged out of the bed. "Oh God."

Before he could turn the light on, I already had his plaid pajama pants out of the drawer and was holding them out for him. The room flooded with light, and I thanked God I'd gotten dressed before I'd fallen asleep because my dad was standing right there watching us with disapproval clear in his eyes.

"Is he okay?" I asked, helping Finn into his pants. He was trembling. "Is Larry...is he...?"

"Dead," Finn said, his voice hollow. He met my eyes, looking broken and terrified. "She's asking if he's dead."

My dad's face finally cracked. "No, but he had another heart attack. The ambulance is on its way, but with the snow this heavy, it might take a while."

"Shit," Finn said, his voice broken. He closed his eyes, his jaw flexing. "Please, no. Not him, too. Not my dad."

I swallowed and placed a hand on his biceps. "Shh. Let's go to him and—"

Finn shook me off and pushed past Dad, bolting toward Larry's room. He was only wearing his pajama pants, so I grabbed a sweatshirt out of the drawer and followed him. Dad stepped in my path before I could leave the room. "Carrie."

I glowered at him. "Now isn't the time to lecture me for disobeying you. Finn needs me."

"I know. And I'm angry. Make no mistake." Dad hesitated but grabbed my hand. "It's bad, Carrie. He's dying. He won't make it this time. I can see it."

My heart slammed to a halt and sped up, all within the span of two seconds. My chest heaved, the tears that wanted to escape choking me, but I refused to let them free. "B-But he can't die. Finn...h-he...*no.*"

I slipped past him, running after Finn. If my dad was right, and Larry was dying...God, this would kill Finn. He was already going through so much. Could he possibly recover from this, too? He was still an unstable mess after all he'd been through overseas. If he had to bury his father on top of that, he would never be the same.

He'd never be able to heal.

I stopped in the doorway of Larry's room. Finn knelt at his side, holding Larry's hand with his uninjured one. "Dad, I'm here. You'll be okay. Help's coming."

I hovered in the doorway for a second. Finn kept talking to Larry, but Larry looked...oh God, he looked dead. His skin had an ashen gray color to it, and there were no signs of life left within him. Finn squeezed

Larry's hand and called out to him, but there was no reply.

He was dead. Larry was dead.

I blinked away the tears blurring my vision, not even bothering to try to hold them back. I hugged Finn's sweatshirt to my chest and stepped forward, my grief choking me. He must've heard me. He turned around and his gaze fell on me. He looked scared, but not sad. It confused me until I realized…

Oh my God. He didn't know.

"Is the ambulance here yet?" Finn asked, his voice rushed. "He said my name when I got here, but then he passed out."

I pressed my lips together tight. I couldn't break down. Couldn't cry. "They're not here yet." I went around to the other side of the bed and touched Larry's hand. It was already getting cold and a little bit stiff. So freaking fast. "Finn…"

He shot me a look. "Don't talk to me like that. He'll be fine." Finn dropped his head to the mattress. "He *has* to be fine. We were just talking. Just…" Finn lifted his head and glowered at me. "Stop looking at me as if he's dead. He's not. He's okay. Got it?"

I nodded, not sure what to do or say. "O-Okay."

Finn placed a hand on Larry's forehead. "He's cold. Can you get him some extra blankets?"

"Uh, y-yes. Sure." I left the room and opened the linen closet down the hallway. As I pulled out some comforters, Mom and Dad came around the corner, talking quietly. When they saw me, they stopped in their tracks. "He's still alive, right?"

I closed the door and juggled the blankets. "I don't think so. But Finn…he doesn't know. I think he knows, but he can't know. He can't accept it yet."

Dad rushed past me, his face pale, and Mom hugged me. "Oh dear. This is going to hit all of us hard, but Griffin, well, he's going to have a difficult time."

I released a huge sob, clinging to my mom and letting the comforters hit the floor at our feet. "I'm so scared. He can't handle this right now. It's going to kill him."

"I know." Mom hugged me tight. "He'll need you with him."

I nodded, let go of Mom, wiped my hands across my cheeks, and then picked up the blankets. I felt like shit, and knew it was only going to get worse, but Finn needed me at his side. I had to pull myself together. At some point, he would realize Larry was gone, and he'd need someone at his side when that happened. He'd need me.

"This is going to kill him," I repeated.

Maybe I was in shock or something.

"I know." Mom grabbed my hand and didn't let go. "But he has *you* to help him."

"I don't think I'm going to be enough this time," I said, my voice hollow and distant in my own head. "I'm not enough."

Finn

I clung to Dad's hand, praying with my eyes closed. I didn't fucking pray anymore. God had stopped listening to me a long time ago. He'd taken my mom. Taken my unit. And now He was trying to take my father, too. Well, fuck that.

I wouldn't let Him.

"You can't have him," I whispered, my face pressed to my father's cold hand. Where the hell were those blankets, anyway? "I still need him. He's not done here yet."

A footstep sounded in the doorway, and I didn't bother to lift my head. I couldn't look at her right now, those sad blue eyes of hers shining with pity. I didn't need her pity. Dad wasn't dying tonight. She could save her empathy for someone else.

Anyone else.

"Did you get the blankets?" I asked.

"She's getting them," Senator Wallington said. Oh. It wasn't Carrie behind me this time. "I'm just coming to check in on Larry. To s-see how he's doing."

I struggled to my feet and stood between him and the senator, looking at him defensively. "He's not dead."

"I didn't say he was." He held his hands up. "He's my friend, Griffin. I just want to see him, like you. To make sure he's okay."

I hesitated, letting him pass through. For some reason, I didn't want anyone looking at him too closely. Didn't want them to tell me he was…

I stopped that thought right fucking there.

Carrie's dad sat on the opposite side of the bed and reached for Dad's fingers with his trembling hand. "Larry." He closed his eyes and swallowed hard. "I'm so sorry."

"*No.*" Rage swept through me, strangling me with the strength and depths it struck in me. I snatched Dad's hand back and gave the senator what I hoped was an eat-shit-and-die look. "You don't get to say a word about being sorry for him. He's *fine.*"

He stood up and covered his face. "Look, son, I know—"

"I'm not your son!" I held Dad's hand to my chest. "You don't even like me, and don't approve of me and Carrie at all. Let's not mince words tonight."

He dropped his hands. "I don't *dis*like you, Griffin."

"But you don't like me, either."

He didn't say anything to that.

I squeezed my dad's hand. Was it just me, or was it even colder? "Where is the ambulance? And where's Carrie with the blankets?"

"I'm here," she said from behind me. She came to my side and gently laid blankets over Dad. "You doing okay?"

I swallowed hard at the look of concern in her eyes when she glanced my way. She was looking at me as if she was scared I'd fall apart. I wouldn't. "I just want the ambulance to get here already. Then I'll be fine."

Senator Wallington cleared his throat. "Griffin, your father isn't cold. He's—"

"Dad, don't." Carrie kneeled beside me and rested a hand on my upper back. "Just don't. Let me handle this."

"I don't need to be *handled.*" I looked at Carrie, swallowing hard when I met her eyes. There wasn't pity, but there was sadness. So much fucking sadness. As if she knew he was gone, accepted it, and was worried for *me.* "He's not dead, Ginger. He can't be dead. I…he…*no.*"

The senator stepped forward again. "I know this is hard, Griffin, but—" Sirens sounded outside the window, and he cut himself off. "They're here now."

"About damn time," I said, my voice even. I knew what he was trying to say, but I didn't believe him. I'd know it if my father was dead, damn it. I'd seen dead. *This* wasn't it. "Can you let them in? I don't want to leave him alone in case he wakes up."

"I'll do it," Carrie's mom said. I hadn't even realized she was here. "You stay with them, Hugh. Just in case."

Just in case *what*?

Senator Wallington nodded. Carrie rested a small hand on my arm. "It's going to be okay, Finn."

I nodded, but didn't say anything. I could sense more than see the long, shared look between Carrie and her dad. I ignored it. "I know."

She laid her hand over mine and I clung to her, needing her strength now more than ever. But I didn't let go of Dad. It seemed like it took ages for the paramedics to come inside, but when they did, I finally released Dad's hand, but not Carrie's, and moved out of their way. They came to the side of the bed and checked his pulse.

Carrie's dad leaned down and whispered something to the man. After he finished, they both looked at me. The paramedic bent over Dad, his fingers doing something I couldn't see. Senator Wallington approached me, his eyes filled with sadness and acceptance. I wasn't accepting a damn thing he told me. "Griffin, I know it's hard, but he's gone. There's nothing we can do to save him now."

"You're wrong." I shook my head, my vision blurring. My heart thudded in my ears, and I backed up, dropping Carrie's hand. I looked at the paramedic, who looked fucking terrified of me. "He's alive, right? *Tell me he's alive.*"

The man looked at Senator Wallington before studying me. "His heart gave out. If it's any consolation, he went fast. There wasn't time to—"

"*No!*" I fell to my dad's bedside and shook him. "Dad. You have to wake up. Wake up right now, and show them you're not gone." I shook him harder. "Wake. *Up.*"

Carrie let out a sob behind me and squeezed my shoulder. "Finn, he—"

"No. Don't." I shrugged her off and shook Dad again. His lips were already turning that bluish, dead-like color that all corpses got. "But he was just here. He was just talking to me…*no.*"

Senator Wallington covered his mouth, his eyes watering.

Carrie nodded. "I know, but he's gone."

"No." I swallowed past my aching throat. I ran my fingers over his cold forehead. He looked like he was sleeping. Not like he was gone forever. "I need you. Dad, *please.*"

Nothing. He'd left me, too.

Everyone kept fucking dying.

I stood up, roared, and punched the wall. My fist sank into it, sending pain flying up my good hand, but it didn't numb the pain in my heart. The absolute, agonizingly real pain that choked me. So I punched the wall again. And again. And again. I lost count after the fourth time. When that stopped feeling satisfying, I started breaking shit.

Anything.

Carrie cried out my name, and tried to rush to my side, but her father held her back. He tossed her to a paramedic, who grabbed her arms and held her back, then stood in front of her protectively. Tears streamed down her face, and she was shouting words, but I didn't hear anything. All I heard was my own heartbeat thundering at breakneck speeds. And these words kept repeating in my head: I lived. He died. They all died.

It wasn't fucking *fair*.

By the time I was focused on the world around me again, I had no idea why the hell everyone was crying, or why Carrie was holding her face and sobbing her heart out. I collapsed against the wall, my breath coming out in ragged gasps. I stared at my feet, because why the fuck not? They were the only things standing still right now.

Everything else was spinning.

Someone came close to me, and I snapped my head up. It was Carrie's dad. He looked scared of me. I was kind of scared of myself, too. "Griffin, you need to calm down. Don't make them sedate you."

I stiffened when he came closer, blinking rapidly. The room was in shambles, vases and glasses were broken, and Carrie was sobbing. The paramedic was still holding her back, and everyone was looking at me like I was crazy. Even Carrie looked scared.

What had I done?

I tore my gaze from Carrie's wet face, looking down at my hand in surprise. It was dripping with blood, all over the pristine white carpet, and the skin was ripped back from the knuckles. It looked as if a storm had gone off in the room, and that storm had been me.

I'd done this.

"C-Carrie?" I looked up at her, swiping my forearm across my cheeks. It came back wet. I'd been crying? I didn't fucking cry. "He's gone?"

She shoved the paramedic off her and stood, her legs barely supporting her. She took an unsteady step toward me, and then another. Her father watched, looking as if he was going to step in the way. She shot him a look, brushed past him, and walked up to me. "Y-Yes, he's gone."

I choked on a sob, and she threw herself at me, hugging me tight. I clung to her with one arm, letting myself cry. I hadn't cried since my mom died, and now here I was again. *Alone.* "I'm alive, and he's dead. They're all dead."

I buried my face in her neck and squeezed my eyes shut. I didn't want to see the senator watching me, looking horrified and sad. Didn't want to watch as the paramedics zipped my father in a black bag and hauled his lifeless body away. And I didn't want to accept the fact that I was the only one who kept living, while everyone else around me died.

Who was next? Carrie? I was a toxic bomb, killing everyone who cared about me.

She hugged me tighter. "It's not your fault. None of this is your fault."

But she was dead wrong. It should have been *me.*

CHAPTER NINE

Carrie

A little while later, I pulled the blankets over Finn's shoulders, kissed his forehead, and turned out the light. He hadn't really said anything after he'd gone insane and started breaking things. He kept just staring off into the distance, talking when spoken to, but in a way that told me he wasn't really there. He might have been holding my hand, but he might as well have been across the country—or the world, for that matter.

He was gone.

Right now, he was buried in grief, and there was nothing I could do to help him. Sure, I could love him and be here for him, but I couldn't bring his dad back. He'd already been struggling with the deaths he'd seen, and now he had one more to add to the pile. The worst one since his mother died.

I was scared he was going to drift away from me. Heck, he'd already started to. Absentmindedly, I touched the tender spot on my cheekbone. When he'd started bashing the wall, I'd tried to stop him. Tried to calm him down. Stupid, really. When a huge guy is going insane and breaking things, you shouldn't jump in the way.

If he knew something he'd broken and/or thrown had hurt me by accident, he'd never forgive himself. That's why he'd never find out. It hadn't been on purpose, after all. He didn't need to know.

I stood up, ready to find my bed. It was already five in the morning, but I could maybe sneak in two hours before the household rose and started preparing for the funeral. I almost cried out when he grasped my hand. He'd finished almost a whole bottle of whiskey and taken two pain pills. For once, I hadn't even harped at him for mixing the two. But I thought he'd been out.

"Carrie?" His voice slurred. "Where are you going?"

I sat back down. "Nowhere. I'm right here."

"Don't leave me," he whispered. "I can't lose you, too."

I squeezed his hand. "I'm not going anywhere, love."

He drifted off to sleep again, and I rested my head on the mattress. Dad came up behind me, his shadow falling over the two of us. "Are you going to bed now?"

I shook my head, but didn't bother to lift it. "He needs me tonight."

"Carrie..." He came closer. "I care about him. I really do, but if he continues in this self-destructive behavior, this has to end. He's dangerous right now. He could hurt you."

I sat up straight and glowered at him. "His dad just died. Think about that before you go judging him. When he flipped out, he wasn't himself." I looked back at him. His brow was wrinkled, but his breathing was even and deep. He appeared to be asleep. I hoped he was. He didn't need to hear this. "He wouldn't...he doesn't *do* this stuff. He's not himself right now."

Dad nodded. "That's exactly what I'm worried about."

"I'm not leaving him. I love him."

"I know, and I know he loves you. I never disputed that." Dad headed for the door. "You can spend the night. I happen to agree with you on one point—he needs you right now. But leave the door open."

He walked out into the hallway, leaving us alone. His words kept ringing in my head. I pressed my fingers to my cheekbone. Dad hadn't seen me get injured, thank God. His reaction would have been just as bad as Finn's if he ever found out about it.

"He's wrong." Finn's eyes opened again. He pulled the covers back with his bandaged hand. "I would never hurt you. I'd sooner kill myself."

I couldn't tear my eyes off his injured hand. The paramedics had taken care of it after they removed Larry's body. They'd also asked us if we wanted to press charges against Finn for the damage done to our home. Dad and I both said no immediately. Mom had agreed with us after a small moment of hesitation.

He had a broken arm and a busted hand. How was he supposed to take care of himself now? Easy. He wouldn't. I would have to be his hands.

"I know," I whispered, climbing in beside him. "Don't listen to him."

His unbroken arm wrapped around me, holding me close. He kissed the top of my head, letting out a shaky sigh after. "I love you, Ginger. You know that, right?"

I blinked back tears and nodded, not answering him.

"I'm sorry I lost it like that. Something just…I don't know. I didn't think I'd lose him, too. Not yet." His voice cracked, and he let out a strangled groan. "I didn't know I'd be so alone. Didn't know I could hurt more than I already was."

I lifted my head and cupped his cheek. "You're not alone, Finn. You have me and my parents."

"I know." He paused, the words slurring together. "But it's just not the same. Nothing's the same anymore. And I'm sorry for that, too."

"Things don't have to be the same to be good," I whispered. I ran my thumb over his lower lip, like he used to do to me. "People change. As long as we change together, we'll be fine."

"I don't think you have any idea how much I need you, Ginger." He rested his bandaged hand on my hip. "I love you so damn much. You have no idea how much."

"I do, because that's how much I love you." I kissed the spot above his heart before resting my hand over it. "Now get some rest. It's almost morning."

He nodded sleepily, and within seconds he was breathing evenly again. Tears fell from my eyes, and I didn't wipe them away. If anything, it would draw notice to them and possibly wake him up, and he didn't need to know how upset I was. I needed to be the stronger one right now.

For him. For us. For me.

These next couple of weeks would suck for all of us, but once we got through them, the healing process could start. Finn would bury his father, and over time he would stop drinking so much. His arm would heal, and then he would stop taking meds. Maybe he would be able to laugh again. Smile again. We could go home to Cali, and he'd be able to surf, ride his bike, and start school. Everything would be fine.

Everything *had* to be fine.

A few hours later, I woke up when someone knocked on the door lightly. I rolled over and squinted toward the noise, trying to remember where I was and why someone was knocking. Then I remembered it all. Oh, boy, did I remember it all.

Mom looked at Finn and the way he was holding me, her lips pressed together. "It's time to wake up. We have to start the funeral arrangements."

"All right," I whispered. "I'll be right there. I think he should sleep a bit more, because—"

"I'm up." Finn's bicep flexed under me. "I'll be down."

Mom nodded, giving me one last look before she left the room. I lifted my head and studied Finn's face. His eyes were bloodshot with dark circles under them, and he looked as if he hadn't slept at all. His blue eyes met mine, and he tried to give me a small smile. "My arm's asleep, I think."

"Oh." I scooted back and sat on the side of the bed, facing him, hugging my knees. "Hey."

"Hey yourself." He lifted his arm and rotated it, flinching. "Ow. What the hell happened to my hand?"

I looked at him, not certain what to say. "You don't remember?"

"I remember losing my shit, but I'm a little sketchy on all the details." He reached out to brush my hair off my face before glaring down at his bandaged fingers. "Oh, fuck. I broke stuff, didn't I? Punched the wall and all that?"

I swallowed hard. "Yeah. It's okay, though."

"In what world is that behavior okay, Carrie?" He sat up and rested his arm on his knees, in almost the same position as me. His slinged arm was the only difference. "Hitting things and throwing fits are never okay. I'm not a child."

"Your dad just died." I flinched when he paled at the words, reaching out to squeeze his foot. "I think we all understand why you lost control like you did. No one holds it against you."

He met my eyes, but glanced away just as quickly. "I do. I hold it against me."

"Finn…"

He got out of bed. "Don't make excuses for my behavior. You deserve better, and you know it." He turned back to me, his bandaged hand at his side. "What if I had hurt you? What if I…?" He broke off, his jaw flexing. "God, what if I lose it and hurt you, Carrie? I'd never forgive myself."

I fought the undeniable urge to press a hand to my cheek, hiding the mark he'd made last night. I knew he hadn't meant to. He'd been out of his mind. Inconsolable.

But I wasn't making excuses for him.

I shook my head. "It will never happen, so you don't need to worry about it. You'd never hurt me like that."

"I promise to try to do better. I know yesterday was—" he sighed, "a fail of epic proportions. Today will suck too, and the next day. But I'll do better."

I gave him a small smile. "You're doing just fine."

"No, I'm not." He sat down on the edge of the bed, glowering down at his bandaged hand. "Can you take the bandage off? I need to have at least one hand."

"Are you sure—?" When he gave me a look that clearly said *take it the fuck off*, I came around the side of the bed and knelt at his feet. "If it hurts too much, I can put it back on. I watched them do it yesterday."

His Adam's apple bobbed. "I can't believe he's gone. Just like that. No matter how much I see death, no matter how many times I lose someone, I will never get over how fucking fast it happens. One second they're there, and the next…just gone."

I undid the silver clasp that held the Ace bandage on before slowly unwrapping it. "I won't pretend to know what you're feeling right now, because I can't possibly understand it until I'm there, but I know it sucks, and anything you need? I'll give it to you."

He met my eyes. "I know. You're too good to me."

"You keep saying that."

He shrugged with one shoulder. "Because it's true, and I promised not to lie to you anymore."

I shook my head and bit down on my lower lip, focusing on the task at hand. From what I could see of his knuckles, things weren't looking promising for him. He thought he'd be able to use his hand, obviously, but it looked mangled, bruised, and thoroughly unusable.

After I finished the task at hand, I settled back on my haunches. He flexed his fingers, paling and flinching. "Fuck, that hurts."

"I know." Automatically, I reached for his pain pills. At some point, the bottle had fallen to the floor and rolled partially under the bed. There were only three left, so I'd have to get more this afternoon. That meant he'd taken more than he was supposed to. There should still be six. "I'll open this and—"

"*No.*" He rolled his shoulder, flexing his hand again. "I'm done taking those things. They're fucking with my head. Flush them."

I looked down at the bottle in my hand. "What if the pain gets worse later?"

"It's going to get worse. There's no way it won't." He looked back at me, his eyes solemn and way too somber. "But if they're here, I'll find a reason to take them, and then I'll turn into a raging fuck-head again. I'm done with those, and I'm done with drinking. I'm just done with it all."

I blinked rapidly, trying to fight back the tears of relief I felt. For a while there, I'd been worried he might become addicted to the escape the pills and booze gave him. I worried he might fall apart, and there would be nothing I could do to save him. But he was saving himself. *Thank God.*

"Okay. I'll get rid of them."

"Thank you." He held out his hurt hand, and I latched on to his wrist so he could pull me up to my feet without too much pain. "For everything."

I reached up on tiptoe and kissed him. I'd expected him to be a mess this morning, but if anything, he seemed stronger than before. More determined to be the man he wanted to be. I wasn't sure what to make of it. "You ready?"

"Yeah. My dad wouldn't have wanted me to fall apart. I promised him—" His voice broke, and he stopped talking. He ran his hand over his head, watching me. "I promised him I'd pull myself together and stop being an ass. I'm starting now. It's what he would have wanted."

I rested my hand over his heart. "He was very proud of you. You know that, right?"

"I know he *was* proud of me." He closed his eyes. "But he wasn't proud of the man I'd become since I came back home."

The thin wound that ran down his forehead looked more pronounced this morning. I reached out and traced my hand over it. "I think you're wrong. He knew you were in there, and he knew what you were going through—what you went through to get back here. He didn't judge you at all."

He caught my hand, trapping my fingers against his jagged gash. "He didn't, but I did." He gave me an inscrutable look and released his hold on my hand. I didn't miss the pain that crossed his eyes at the movement. "Let's brush our teeth, then we'll go down. There's a lot to get done today. I have to contact the church, get a coffin, write a eulogy…"

I nodded. "One step at a time, together. Okay? First step? Teeth."

"Okay." He kissed the top of my head. "Let's go."

I followed him out of his room. For a second, just a second, I wanted to grab him, shove him back inside the bedroom, and lock the door. Inside here, he was just my Finn. It was the only place where we felt and acted normal. As soon as we got out there, with my parents and the rest of the world, there was no telling what would happen.

And selfishly…I wanted to keep him *just like this*.

CHAPTER TEN

Finn

"That one." I pointed to the wooden casket at the end of the row, my throat tight and my arm throbbing like hell. Everything hurt, but I refused to ask Carrie to get my prescription refilled. I deserved the pain. Every. Fucking. Second. It fueled me. Made me put one foot in front of the other. Distracted me from the *real* pain that was killing me.

The pain of losing my father.

Carrie tightened her fingers on mine. "It's beautiful. He would have loved it."

"Thanks."

I closed my eyes for a second. It was ridiculous that people spent so much damn time picking out a casket based on what the dead person lying in it would have liked. They wouldn't ever see it—so why the hell did it matter if it was the right color? Or if it had top-of-the-line pillows? They wouldn't feel a fucking thing.

They were blissfully, blessedly unaware of all these proceedings. If Father Thomas was to be believed, Dad was in a much better place now. He was with Mom in heaven, smiling down on me. I'd rather they got their asses back down here with me. That way I wouldn't be the only one left.

Senator Wallington pulled the man aside and spoke to him in a low tone. He'd come along with us, and kept adding things—then insisting to pay since he'd "adjusted" the order. I knew what he was doing. He was taking care of the bills for me, but trying to do so in a way that I wouldn't take offense.

I gritted my teeth and looked down at Carrie, forcing a smile. If it was the last thing I did, I wouldn't let her know how fucked up I was right now. Oh, who was I kidding? She knew. She'd seen me last night. I still couldn't believe I'd let myself break like that, and in the process broken so many things in that damn bedroom. I could have hurt someone—hell, I could have hurt Carrie.

I would fucking walk away before I ever, *ever* let myself hurt her.

End of story.

I looked into her eyes, trying to latch on to the serenity that I usually felt. She looked different today. She'd put on makeup, even blush. Was she trying to look less exhausted for my behalf? If so, she was failing. I knew how tired she was because she'd been taking care of me. Well, no more.

Tonight, I'd make sure she went to bed at a decent time.

"All right. We're all settled." Senator Wallington came over. "I added a few things to the order, so I paid for the coffin myself. I hope you don't mind."

Enough. "Sir, I can't let you keep doing that. I have money, and I can—"

He held a hand up. "You caught me. I promised him I'd take care of the bills when his time came. I won't break that promise, no matter how much you hate it. Besides, last time I checked, you were too injured to work. You'll need to save money, since you don't know how long you'll be unemployed."

I flushed. I hadn't even considered the fact that I couldn't do my job anymore. Or was that not what he meant? Was he suggesting I was fired from being Carrie's bodyguard not because of my injury, but because of our relationship? No one would guard her better than me, damn it.

My own life depended on her survival.

"Dad, he can still guard me." Carrie frowned at him. "An injury won't stop him from babysitting me for you."

"Oh, and how would he stop a kidnapper with a broken arm and a mangled hand?" Her dad cocked his head. "Will he kick them? Shout for help?"

Carrie glared at him. "He'll heal."

"Yeah, but until then, he can't work as a guard." He looked over his shoulder while straightening his tie. "Besides, contracts were broken and lies were told. I'm still not sure what I'm doing about that yet, but now isn't the time or place to discuss this. All I was saying was that I was paying, and I wouldn't take no for an answer. That's it."

I inclined my head, not dropping his stare. "Yes, sir."

I practically spit out that last word. Fuck, I needed a drink. I understood what he wasn't saying: I wasn't getting my job back. I'd lied to him. Fallen for his daughter. Lied some more. And then gone crazy. It wasn't exactly a shocker that I'd lost my job.

"We'll talk later," the senator repeated.

"No need. I understand completely."

Carrie might not realize it, but I'd known all along how this would end when he found out about us. I'd be fired and looking for a new job. It's why I'd left on that assignment in the first place. Why I'd tried to better myself, only to end up broken and damaged.

Carrie shook her head. "This isn't over, Dad."

"This has absolutely nothing to do with you, and like I said—" He motioned security over. Cortez and Morris walked over our way, their expressions solemn. "It's not the time or the place."

After Cortez nodded at me, he turned to Senator Wallington. "What can I do for you, sir?"

"You're going to leave with me," he paused, "and Morris?"

Morris stepped forward. "Yes, sir?"

"You stay with them."

Carrie stiffened. "We don't need a guard."

"It's fine," I said, catching the senator's eyes. He didn't trust me around his daughter anymore. That much was clear. And honestly? I didn't blame him. "I can't protect you, Carrie. He's right."

He was *so* fucking right.

"I don't want anyone watching me besides Finn," Carrie protested. She shot Morris a smile. "No offense, but I've already got my—"

"*No.*" Senator Wallington balled his fists, his face turning an alarming shade of red. "I've put up with a lot from you, Carrie, but this is not up for debate. Morris stays."

I squeezed Carrie's hand. She was about to start a fight, right here in the fucking casket store, for the love of God. "It's fine, Carrie. He's right."

She whirled on me, eyes narrowed. "No, he's not. You wouldn't let anything happen to me."

"I'm not quite myself." I smiled, even though I wanted to fucking scream. "You can't deny that."

She hesitated. "But still…"

"It's just for now. Things will go back to normal after I heal. Isn't that right, sir?"

Senator Wallington met my eyes. "Right."

"See?" I let go of her hand. "Where are you going, sir?"

"I'm going to stop at my office on the way home. I'll be home in time for dinner." He hesitated. "Riley might be stopping by. He heard about your father, and wants to give his condolences."

"Excellent."

"That might not be the best idea," Carrie said, looking at me. "You might need some down time."

"Then he can keep you company." I smiled again. It fucking hurt to smile when everything was breaking inside me. I wasn't worried about her and Riley. I trusted her, and that meant I had to trust him, too. "My head is killing me, so I do need to rest. It'll be good to know you have a friend nearby while I'm sleeping."

She bit her lower lip. "All right, if that's what you want."

I didn't. What I wanted was a fucking drink, but I couldn't have that, could I?

So I nodded. "It's what I want."

The next day was Dad's funeral. It was cold, dark, depressing, and fucking hard to get through. There were tons of people there. People I'd known over the years. People Dad knew. And then friends of the senator. We'd actually had to turn some people away, as we couldn't all fit inside.

It should make me feel happy to know so many people cared about him, but instead I felt empty. I sat in a room surrounded by people who cared about my dad, but there were only two people in this room who actually gave a damn about *me*—and one of them was in the coffin at the front of the room.

People came to say goodbye to my dad, but every once in a while, I heard someone laugh as they caught up on the "good old times." I wasn't fucking laughing. I hadn't laughed since the night before my dad died.

Hell, I didn't know if I'd ever laugh again.

After I delivered my eulogy, which I'd managed to get through without breaking down, I stared at the open casket as Father Thomas droned on and on about redemption, heaven, and hell. I couldn't take my eyes off Dad, knowing it was the last time I'd ever get to see his face again. I think part of me was hoping this was all a dream or some shit like that. Like he'd pop up and be all, "Ha! I tricked you, didn't I?"

But he didn't move. He was really *gone*.

I clung to Carrie's hand, my dry eyes stinging. She sniffed beside me, tears running down her cheeks, and I almost envied her. I couldn't let myself go again. Couldn't release the grief. Look what had happened last time. So I sat there, staring straight ahead, and pretended I was anywhere but here. Surfing. Riding my bike. Laughing with Carrie on my lap.

Some undetermined amount of time later, Carrie shook my knee. "Finn? You ready?"

I blinked, looking around in surprise. The room was empty. Only Carrie and I remained. We sat in the middle of the front row, and everyone else waited outside. I could see them through the window. Waiting for the next step—the gravesite. "N-No. I'll never be ready."

"Take your time." She didn't let go of me. If anything, she held on tighter. "They can wait for you."

"Fuck." I swallowed hard. "I have to say goodbye now, don't I?"

She nodded slowly. All traces of her tears were gone, and she looked at me with clear eyes. "Yes. You have to say goodbye."

I looked over at the casket. After he was in the ground…what then? I just went about my life acting as if I was normal when I wasn't? "This sucks."

"Yeah, it does." She kissed my temple. "Do you want to say goodbye alone?"

I thought about it before nodding. "Wait for me outside?"

"Always." She let go of me and started for the door. She wore a black dress and a black pair of heels. Her long red hair fell down her back freely, and she looked gorgeous. "And Finn?"

I stood up and straightened my black suit jacket. "Yeah?"

"You're not alone. You have me."

My heart clenched tight. She was right, and I knew it, but I still felt alone. I was the only family member left. My grandparents were long gone. And now my parents, too. But I didn't say any of that. "I love you."

She smiled sadly, her red lips parting to show her perfect white teeth. She had a lot of makeup on again today. "I love you, too."

After she left, I turned to my father. The undertaker nodded at me and retreated to the back of the room to give me privacy. He joined the group of pallbearers, talking quietly. They all gave me their backs. I was alone. It was time to accept it.

I walked up to the casket slowly, each step taking longer than the next. By the time I reached the side and knelt beside it, my feet felt as if they weighed a thousand pounds each and my palms were sweating. I reached out and held his hand with my only semi-functioning hand. It didn't feel like his skin, and yet it did. "I'm going to miss you, Dad."

He didn't reply, obviously, but I swore his fingers tightened on mine.

"I'm going to go to school. I'll make you proud. I know I made a big mess of things. I know I screwed everything up." I looked up at the window. Carrie stood there, next to her parents. Riley was with her. I tore my eyes away. "But I did some things right lately. I know what I have to do, and I'm going to do it."

I looked at my dad again. He was pale and lifeless, but he was still *here*. And soon…he wouldn't be. "I wish you hadn't left me. Everyone is dying. Everyone but me. I just don't get it. It's not fair."

I swallowed past my throbbing throat. Visions of Dad teaching me how to drive hit me. "Remember when you used to blare the radio and crank the windows down when you were teaching me how to drive? That way when I mastered driving with the music blaring, nothing would faze me after that." I let out a small laugh. "And you used to sing Tom Petty at the top of your lungs, your face glowing every time I mastered a new skill, and I told you I was going to pretend like I didn't know you if you didn't quiet down." I cleared my throat. "I never would have done that to you. I loved you then for being so silly and free, and I love you even more now. Just thought you should know that."

I dropped my head onto the side of the casket, swallowing hard. "And I keep remembering how you looked the day I went away to boot camp. You looked so proud of me that day—the proudest I've ever seen you look. Your eyes were all bright and shiny with tears, and you smiled throughout the whole damn ceremony." I lifted my head, my eyes stinging. "You haven't looked at me once like that since we got back to D.C. I'm sorry I let you down. So sorry—"

I broke off. Knowing he'd died while being disappointed in me killed me. He might not have told me as much, but I'd seen it in his eyes that last night we had together. Heard it in his voice. He'd wanted me to do better, and I hadn't had the chance to do so. His last memory of me would be me as a pill-popping drunk.

I curled my hurt hand into a fist, grimacing through the pain. I deserved it. "I love you, Dad. And I'll never stop loving you. Never stop missing you. I'm sorry I fucked it all up, but I'll fix it. I promise."

Was it just me, or had someone touched me on the back? I looked, but I was still alone. I gave my dad one last look, stood up, cleared my throat, and nodded at the men in the back of the room. "I'm done. He's all yours."

I walked out the door, my eyes scanning the crowd until I found her. As I walked toward Carrie, I heard whispers of "the heir" dating "the help," and I knew they were talking about Carrie and me. Someone snickered and replied about how it was fun "to date below rank sometimes," but that it "wouldn't last past the grieving."

Fuck them. Fuck them all.

Riley bent down to Carrie, talking to her quietly, and she shook her head. I approached slowly, not wanting to interrupt the two people in this room who everyone would agree was a perfect match. She must have sensed me coming, because she broke off midsentence and rushed to my side.

"You okay?"

No. "Yeah."

She claimed my hand again. It hurt like hell, but I didn't care.

I needed her too badly to let go yet.

CHAPTER ELEVEN

Carrie

I walked into the empty family room, a glass of water in my hand, and sat down on the edge of the couch. The whole day had been nonstop mingling, comforting, crying, and then more crying. Finn had gone upstairs to lie down for a few minutes, and I'd escaped the crush of people still hanging around our house.

I wish I could have lain down, too, but my mom would've had a heart attack if I escaped mid-party. Bad manners and all that jazz. I finished off my water, set it down, and laid back against the couch. Silence. Silence was good. The door opened behind me and I leapt to my feet, forcing a smile to my face. When I saw it was Riley and my dad, I let the smile slide away and sank down on the cushions. "Oh, it's you guys."

"You sound disappointed." Riley sat beside me, amusement in his eyes. "Were you hoping for someone else? Maybe someone with tattoos?"

I shook my head. "He's resting. He just went upstairs."

"That's good," Riley said.

Dad opened the liquor cabinet. "Riley, would you like a—?" He squinted. "Oh, wait. My scotch is missing. Maybe Griffin took it up with him."

"No. He's not drinking anymore." I looked down at my lap. "He stopped after Larry died."

"Uh…" Dad closed the cabinet, a bottle of whiskey and two glasses in his hands. "I thought I saw him drinking last night. Are you sure?"

I swallowed hard. He'd sworn he wasn't drinking anymore, so that didn't sound right. "I'm positive he isn't drinking. He's not even taking pills anymore. I flushed them all."

Dad and Riley exchanged a long glance. "Okay," Dad said.

"I, for one, haven't seen him drinking today," Riley said, offering me a smile. "Maybe you were mistaken after all, Mr. Wallington."

"Yes. Maybe." He poured two glasses of whiskey, putting the bottle back into the cabinet. After handing the glass to Riley, he headed for the door. "I'll leave you two alone. If I don't go back to help with the guests, your mother will kill me."

I looked at Riley and rolled my eyes. It was clear he'd brought Riley in here just for this purpose—to leave us alone together. Once the door closed behind him, Riley shoved his glass at me. "Drink it. You need it more than I do."

"Oh, thank God," I said, downing the nasty beverage in one gulp. I didn't know why anyone would drink this crap willingly. I swiped my forearm across my lips and handed the empty glass back to Riley. "Is this ever going to end?"

"Is what ever going to end?"

I stared out the window. Snow was falling again, and the sun was setting, casting the sky in hues of pink and orange. It looked so peaceful. Too bad it was anything but peaceful in here tonight. "The pain. The nonstop crap being piled on Finn. First he gets injured, and then his father dies. How much can one man take?"

"Finn's strong." Riley got up and made his way over to the cabinet. He refilled his cup, drank it, and poured some more. "He'll recover, and he has you to help him."

"Yeah, but what if I'm not enough?"

Riley gripped the side of the cabinet with both hands, his knuckles going white. Pushing off it, he came back to my side, sat down, and offered me his cup again. "How could you not be?"

I took the drink, swallowing it quickly. I didn't even flinch that time. "Easily. I'm not his father, and I can't give him back his father."

"You don't need to be his dad. You just need to be you." He shrugged before crossing one ankle over his knee. "That's all he needs."

"Yeah…"

90

I stared off into the distance, watching the snow falling. It would be Christmas in a couple of days—two, I think? I'd lost track of the days. But it didn't matter, I was only thinking of the days because there wasn't really much more to say. I *knew* I wasn't enough. If I were enough, he'd be sitting next to me, instead of Riley. If I were enough, he wouldn't be sitting in his bedroom alone, instead of being with me. Ever since my father basically fired him yesterday, he'd been quiet. We'd slept together again, with the door open, but he'd barely said anything besides "good night" to me. It scared me.

Riley reached out and touched my cheekbone. "What happened there?"

"It's nothing." I flinched away and covered the bruise with my hand. All my crying must have removed the heavy makeup I'd put on to hide it. I couldn't let Finn or my dad see it, so I'd have to reapply. "Nothing at all."

Riley's brows slammed down. "Did someone *hit* you?"

"N-No, of course not." I stood up shakily, walked to the mirror, and studied the mark. I'd need to sneak up to my room for some concealer. "It was an accident. I'll go get my—"

"*Carrie*," Riley said. He caught my gaze in the mirror. He looked ready to kill someone. "Was it Finn?"

"No. Yes. Kind of." I closed my eyes. I didn't want to look at Riley right now. Not when he looked so freaking angry. "When his dad died, he went a little crazy. Punching things and throwing crap around. Breaking stuff. My dad tried to pull me back, but I moved too fast. Finn kept hitting things, and stuff was going all over the place, and something went flying…and bounced off my cheek. He didn't mean to do it, and he doesn't even know it happened. That's how far gone he was. My dad was there. He saw the whole thing." A white lie. My father had seen it, sure, but he didn't know I'd been hurt. I spun around and gripped the mantel behind me. "You can't say anything to Finn, though. If he knew he hurt me…I don't know what he'd do."

"But he *did* hurt you."

"Not on purpose." I crossed the room and grabbed Riley's hands. "Please don't tell him. Finn can't ever find out about it. It would kill him."

Riley shook his head. "But—"

"I can't ever find out about *what*?" Finn asked from the doorway, his voice low and broken. "What did I miss in the five minutes I was upstairs?"

Riley tensed and dropped my hands, and I stumbled back. I realized, at the last second, what it looked like. It looked as if we'd been caught red-handed in an intimate moment, and we'd been talking about keeping secrets. "It's nothing, Finn."

Finn met my eyes, his gaze neither accusing nor untrusting. "Then tell me what it is if it's no big deal."

"Look, man." Riley cleared his throat. "It's not what you think. I would never—"

"I know. I assure you, I trust Carrie implicitly." Finn looked at Riley, staring him down. "But you should leave us so we can talk in privacy. Now."

It was the first time I'd seen him actually act like my arrogant Finn in way too long, and it sent a shaft of pain to my chest to know it was because he'd overheard me. Why hadn't my father closed the freaking door? "You can go, Riley. We'll be fine."

Riley looked at the spot on my cheek where I knew it was discolored, shifting on his feet uneasily. "Yeah. Sure. I'll go find my parents."

"Close the door on your way out," Finn said. He watched Riley pass, doing the manly head nod they all seemed to do, and then turned his attention back on me. As soon as the door closed behind Riley, Finn crossed the room and stopped directly in front of me. "What's going on, Ginger? What are you hiding from me?"

"I…it's nothing."

"If it's nothing, then you wouldn't be acting like this." He reached out and caught my chin, lifting my face up to his. His gaze latched on to mine. "Tell me the truth. We promised, no more lying."

I crumpled my dress in my hands. "Did you drink last night?"

"What?" He blinked at me. "No. Why?"

"Dad said he saw you drinking."

He shook his head. "I promised not to touch it anymore, and I didn't." He looked at the empty glass on the table. Slowly, he turned back to me. "Were *you* drinking?"

I flinched. "Riley got me a drink…well, two. Two drinks."

"It's okay. Just because I can't handle it right now doesn't mean you have to be scared to have one." He lifted a shoulder. "I still don't like it, but hell, I'm not in charge of you anymore. I got fired."

"No, you didn't. Not technically. He just said—"

"He fired me." Finn flexed his jaw. "Plain and simple. I knew it was going to happen, so it's not a surprise."

"You'll be fine once your arm heals. If nothing else, he probably meant you couldn't do it for a while," I said in a rush.

"Carrie." Finn met my eyes again, his own looking a little bit hard. "He didn't fire me because of my injury. He fired me because I fell in love with you. I knew it was going to happen, and I did it anyway."

I flushed. "But—"

"It's *okay*." He pressed his fingers to my mouth. "I made plans for this, remember? I can call Captain Richards and see if the offer for college is still open and—"

"Wait. You want to stay *in*, after what happened to you?"

He frowned at me. "Well, maybe. If I'm not discharged. That's always been the plan. What else am I supposed to do with myself?"

"Go to college. Be normal. *Live*."

"This is me being normal." He stepped back, letting go of me. Then his brow crinkled, and he grabbed me again, turning my face toward the light. He paled, and his fingers faltered on my chin. "Where did this mark come from?"

"It's nothing," I said quickly, my voice quivering. I tried to think fast. "It's a silly bruise that I can't even remember—"

"Don't fucking lie to me," he said, his voice hard. "Did Riley hit you? Is that what you were talking about earlier? Is that what you couldn't tell me?"

"N-No." I closed my eyes and shook my head as best as I could with him holding me like that. By the time I opened my eyes, he looked like he was ready to explode. "Of course not. Please. It's nothing."

"Then who did it?" He ran his fingers over the discoloration, his voice tinged with concern. "I know it wasn't your dad, and the only other person you were with besides him was…was…" His gaze snapped back to mine, comprehension turning the blue stormy and violent. "*Me*. Holy shit."

I shook my head frantically. "Finn, you didn't do this. Not really." I tried to grab his hand, but he jerked away and backed off, his eyes wide. "It wasn't you. When you went crazy that night, something flew back and scraped against me. It was nothing."

He growled, his chest rising and falling rapidly. "It's everything! I fucking *hurt* you."

"It was an accident!" I cried out, holding my hands in front of me and taking another step toward him. He backed away again. "Don't you see? This wasn't you. It was just a freak occurrence—"

"Stop. Making. Excuses." He ran a hand down his face. The empty hollowness I saw in his eyes killed me. "I hurt you, Carrie. The one person I swore I would never hurt. The one person I swore I would never, ever let down. The one person left on this world I need—and I hurt you? How the fuck is that *okay*?"

"Because you didn't mean to do it, damn it," I shouted, stomping my foot. "Why do you insist on always making yourself out to be the bad guy who ruins everything? This was an accident. Simply an accident."

"Fuck that." He stalked to the bar and yanked it open. "Me hurting you is never, ever acceptable. You've been tiptoeing around me, acting like you're scared to set me off—and now I see why. You should have been scared, damn it."

He was right. I'd totally been walking on eggshells around him, and look where it had gotten us. Here. "You know what? You're right. I've been scared about doing anything to set you off or make you upset, but maybe you need that now." I slapped his uninjured arm, and, man, it felt good. "Stop being an asshole. Stop hurting me. And stop acting like *this*."

He flinched, but I knew it was from my words, not my blow. "I can't. I keep hurting you, and it's not fair."

"Then don't do it again," I snarled, wanting to hit him again, but holding myself back. "Simple solution, really. No need for dramatics and heartbreak. You know where you can start? Close that stupid cabinet, and back away from the alcohol. You *promised* me you wouldn't drink anymore. Why don't you follow through on that? It's a good start."

He froze with his hand on the knob. "I hurt you, Carrie. What makes you think I'm worthy of keeping promises? What makes you think you can trust me at all?" Then he looked at me and he looked…different. It reminded me of something, but I couldn't put my finger on it. "What makes you think I give a damn about what promises I've made you if I can hurt you like that? You can't fucking trust me. Not anymore."

I curled my hands into fists. He was ruining everything, all because of a stupid mark he hadn't even meant to put there. God. "Stop this right now, or maybe *I'll* decide *I'm* done with you. Is that what you fucking want?"

He hesitated. Actually hesitated. "And if I do?"

"You don't," I said quickly, not giving up on him. I couldn't. "I know you, Finn. This isn't you." I wrapped my arms around myself. "Stop being like this."

He yanked the cabinet open. "Ah, but you're wrong. This *is* me now, Carrie, and it isn't changing. The problem is, neither are you. Which is why..." He hesitated, his knuckles white on the handle. "Th-This isn't working anymore."

I gasped, unable to believe what he was saying. What he was *doing*.

And then, oh God, then I realized what I was thinking of when he'd reminded me of something earlier. The way he was looking at me right now, all cold calculation and separated, it reminded me of when we'd first met...

Before he loved me.

Finn

She gasped behind me, and the pain she felt right now sliced through me. I'd swear it did. *You have to stop hurting her if you love her.* That's what Dad had said before he died. It was time I did what he'd asked. I'd been selfishly keeping Carrie at my side, treating her like shit the whole time.

It was time to admit that I wasn't getting better anytime soon. I was hurting her constantly, and I couldn't do it anymore. I'd been ignoring it up until now, but seeing that bruise on her face? Well, I couldn't fucking ignore that. I always swore I'd leave her before I'd hurt her. It was time to follow through on that promise.

"Finn, don't do this to me. You didn't even know it happened," she whispered, her voice broken and shaken.

I closed my eyes, pain ripping through me. "Is that supposed to make it better? That I was so fucked up I didn't even realize the person I love more than life itself was hurting?"

"It's not like that," she said, her voice growing stronger with each word. "You were upset. Anyone would have—"

I slammed my hand down on the bar. From the corner of my eye, I saw her jump. Good. Maybe if I scared her more, she'd finally give up on me. I'd already given up on myself. "Anyone would *not* have done what I did. I'm not fucking normal, Carrie. I'm a mess, and all I can think about at any given time of day is drinking, pain pills, or *dying*. That's all I care about anymore."

"You care about me. Don't pretend like you don't. You can say it all you want, but I'll see it for what it is. Another fucking lie." She glared at me. "I can't help you if you refuse to help yourself."

Good. She was mad. When she cursed, I knew she was pissed.

"You're right. You can't, so stop trying to." I set down a glass and filled it with whiskey. I didn't even want the drink, but I had to make a point. Had to show her that right now, I wasn't capable of being saved. She needed to physically see it to believe it. Lifting it up, I toasted her. "That's why I'm letting you go."

She watched me as I downed the whole fucking drink in one swig, her cheeks flushing. Then her gaze snapped back to mine, flashing fire. "You don't get to *decide* what's best for me. You don't get to *let me go*. I get a say, damn it. And fuck you for thinking I don't. I'm not walking away because you think you're too scary for me. You're not. You're just being an asshole."

"I know I am, damn it." I laughed harshly, letting all my frustration and anger out on her. Because even though I knew this was the right thing to do, it was killing me. This conversation hurt more than the IED or the broken arm, or even my father dying. It. Fucking. Hurt. "Jesus, Carrie, do you see me right now? Do you even fucking see me?"

"*Yes!* I've never *stopped* seeing you. Never stopped loving you. I've been here, with you, this whole time!" She stalked across the room and shoved my shoulder. "And what do I get for it? This! You giving up on yourself. On us."

I twisted my lips into a poor imitation of a smile. "Yeah, well, that's me. I'm an asshole. It's how I was before you, and now I'm back to my old ways. Get used to it."

She came closer, her eyes shining with tears and anger. So much anger. She looked like she was going to hit me again, and I wanted her to, because I deserved it so damn much. But she stopped short. "You're upset and not thinking clearly. You need to put away the drink and go to bed. In the morning—"

"I'll feel exactly the same." I met her eyes, squaring my shoulders. It was time to really hurt her, and I didn't want to. But if I could hurt her this one last time, she would be better off. Free of the emotional wreck I was. It was time to help her be happy again, because I never would be. "I can't love you like this, and you can't love me like this." I paused, gathering up the nerve to say, "I don't love you anymore, Carrie."

She gasped and covered her mouth. I immediately wanted to take the words back. "Wh-What? Don't say that if you don't mean it. Don't you dare say it again."

Of course I didn't *mean* it, but I'd say it anyway. I had to, for her. "I. Don't. Love. You. Anymore. We're done."

Tears poured out of her eyes, and she shoved me backward. I stumbled this time, welcoming the pain it sent shooting up my arm. "You're only saying that because you refuse to help yourself. You're giving up. Lying to me again. We swore—"

"I swore a lot of things." I forced a cocky grin. It hurt. "I lied to you, plain and simple. It's what I do. But I'm not lying now. This isn't about giving up. It's about letting go. We're over. The love is gone."

"Finn…" she whispered, broken and hurt. "I don't believe you."

I poured another drink, hating myself for every single drop that went into it. Hating myself because I'd let it get to this. Let it go this far, when I should have never let her fall in love with me in the first place. We were fucking doomed from the start, and I'd known it. I'd just chosen to ignore it. Now, I was even more fucked up than before.

She deserved better, damn it.

"Yeah, well, believe it." I saluted her with the glass. "It's over, Ginger. I've been faking feelings for you this whole week. I'm too tired to fake it anymore just so you don't get hurt. I'm done protecting you."

She lifted her chin stubbornly. "I can't save you if you're giving up."

"I don't want you to fucking save me!" I shouted. "I want you to leave me the hell alone!"

She backed up, her lower lip trembling. "Fuck you, asshole."

"And she finally sees the truth," I drawled, my heart ripping in two. "It's about damn time you accepted it."

Tears poured down those smooth cheeks of hers, and her blue eyes were coated in moisture, making them brighter than usual. It went against every single instinct inside of me not to walk up to her and hug her. To not take it all back. She might not know it now, but I was doing her a favor. I had to remember that, even if it was too late to save her from the pain. I couldn't regret loving her. Knowing her. So, no matter how selfish it might be, I didn't regret the time we had together. I'd never love someone the way I loved her.

She'd always be the one for me. I just couldn't be hers.

"Even so, I'm not giving up on you—but you need to fight, too. You're going to realize this is wrong. You're going to regret this, and I'll forgive you. But you can't say things like that to me and expect me to forgive *that*." She reached for my hand. If she touched me, I'd be a goner. I'd lose my resolve to save her. "I love you, and I'll always love you, but this isn't okay."

"Don't say that," I rasped, backing away from her. I ran my hand over my shaved head, wishing I could tug on my hair. Wishing I wasn't me. "You need to forget this ever happened. Move on. This was all a huge mistake between us. Stop trying to be a rebel, and stop trying to piss off Daddy Dearest all the time. Marry a guy like Riley."

I choked on the words. This wasn't right. She was supposed to marry *me*.

Fuck, I needed to get away from her.

"I'm not marrying anyone but you," she said, her voice completely calm. "When you wake up in the morning, come find me. Say you're sorry, and maybe we can forget this happened. *That's* how much I love you."

Without warning, she lunged across the distance between us, closing it with one giant step. Her arms snaked around my neck and she kissed me. She tasted like tears, whiskey, and Carrie. God, she felt so fucking good. So fucking right. How was I supposed to give this up? Give her up? I'd never get to taste her again, and that hurt, too.

I broke off the kiss, a ragged moan escaping me. Tears burned my vision, but I turned away from her before she could see. "It's over. Just give up already. I don't want to be with you anymore. It's…it's your fault this happened to me. I blame *you*."

She gasped and backed off, covering her mouth. I hated myself right then, for striking where I knew she'd be weakest. I knew, deep down, she blamed herself for this. And I'd used that to hurt her. To make her back the hell off.

I deserved to die right now.

The door opened. Senator Wallington walked in, took one look at me, skimmed over to Carrie, and rushed inside. "What's going on here?"

I poured myself another drink. "Your dreams have come true. I've finally accepted I'll never be good enough for your baby girl, and I broke up with her."

Carrie shook her head but didn't say anything.

She just stared at me, looking broken.

I faced her father, letting all my rage at this situation come to the surface. Letting them see how much of a fuck-up I was, finally. "Since she's having difficulty accepting this, why don't you tell her how wrong I am for her? Did you ever tell her about that time I almost got fired for bringing a girl back here with me? We got caught naked in the—"

Carrie cried out and spun on her heel, giving me her back and hiding her gorgeous face from me. I wanted to demand she turn around so I could see her. After all, I wouldn't be seeing her again. I needed to see her—to memorize everything about her.

"Griffin, you're drinking. You're not thinking this through." The senator cleared his throat. "Maybe you should put that aside and go to bed—"

"Sleep won't change a damn thing. I'm done trying to make myself better for this family. Done trying to be good enough for her, when that will never happen." I chugged the drink before I slammed the glass on the bar. "Be happy. You got what you wanted. You predicted it, even. Warned me in the hospital that I'd become too dark for her. Well, you're right. So I'm leaving."

"Then go," Carrie said, her voice so soft I almost missed it. "You don't love me anymore?"

I looked at her, wanting nothing more than to take it all back, but she was finally accepting it. I couldn't give in to temptation now. "I can't love you anymore, not like this."

Carrie flinched, but didn't say a word. Senator Wallington wrapped an arm around her shoulders. Glaring at me, he said, "Then you need to leave."

I laughed, even though I wanted to shout at the top of my fucking lungs. "I've got nothing left here, so I'll gladly leave."

"You had me," Carrie said, her voice steady despite the tears streaming down her cheeks. She lifted her chin and stared me down. "But that wasn't enough, was it? It was never enough, because this was always my fault. You blame me."

I met her eyes, my heart shattering into pieces. I wanted to deny it. Wanted to tell her how much she meant to me, but I just stared back at her, not saying a word. Carrie stared right back at me, not flinching. She waited for a second, obviously giving me one last chance to take it all back. I wanted to do it so damn badly. But instead I inclined my head, agreeing with her without speaking, because quite frankly? I couldn't even if I tried right now.

The tears I was holding back were choking the life out of me.

She swallowed hard, nodded, and walked out of the room. The last vision I had of her was her leaving the room, her head held high, as she walked away from me.

And she didn't even look back.

CHAPTER TWELVE

Carrie

I dashed up the stairs full speed ahead, slowing down once I rounded the corner. I walked down the hallway toward my room in a daze. I couldn't believe what had just happened, and yet in some ways, I'd known it was coming. The whole flight to Germany, I'd been going over and over in my head how I'd done this to him. Our relationship had ruined him. Had ruined his life. How could he ever love me after that?

Easy. He didn't. He'd told me as much.

I'd ruined our chances at a happy ending. He blamed me for his injuries. So did I. Over the last month, I'd seen him pushing me away constantly, and I'd made excuses for it. I'd seen him deteriorating in front of my eyes every single day, and I'd let him. He hadn't been shutting me out because he was healing. He'd been shutting me out because he didn't want me around. He'd realized he didn't love me anymore.

I couldn't fix that.

I'd been out of my league with him, and he'd been going slowly out of his mind—with no one to help him stay afloat. We'd been a ticking time bomb, and it had only been a matter of time till it all exploded. I covered my mouth and choked on a sob, picking up the pace before someone saw me. My mom opened her door at the same time I ran past it. All it took was one look at me, and she was following me into my room.

She closed the door behind her and opened her arms for me. "What happened?"

I shook my head, my hands fisted together in front of me. "He...he doesn't love me anymore, and it's all my fault."

"What?" Her face fell. "Oh no. I'm so sorry, baby."

"How...why...oh my God, he doesn't *love* me."

And then I burst into tears. I threw myself into her arms, finally letting myself cry. Really, *really* cry. I'd never cried like this before, and I didn't think I ever would again. There would never be another love like Finn's in my life, and I knew it. Knew this was it, the best love of my life. Gone forever.

"Shh." Mom rubbed her hand down my hair, over and over again, soothing me without words. But really, what was there to say? Nothing would ease this aching emptiness inside of me. Nothing ever could. "Shh, baby."

I couldn't believe it. It was over. He was gone.

Our first fight. Our first kiss. The way he'd laughed at the movie we'd watched that first night we spent together. Him on our "Christmas night," so stoic and scared, but determined to better himself for *me*. It was all gone. All a memory.

I shouldn't have let him go overseas. That had been my first mistake. My second had been blindly believing in love. I wouldn't be making that mistake again.

Love obviously didn't conquer all.

By the time I finished sobbing all over Mom, she was soaked and I was exhausted. I pulled away from her and avoided her eyes, feeling like a child all over again. "Thanks, Mom. I'm okay now."

Only I wasn't. Not at all.

"Our first heartbreak is always the toughest." She tucked my hair behind my ear and gave me a small smile. "It'll get better."

I swallowed hard, looking away. I didn't want to talk about it. It hurt too much. "I think I'm going to stay up here for the rest of the night, if you don't mind? I'm not fit company."

"That's fine, dear. People are clearing out now." She stood up. "I'll get you some cookies and milk. That always makes you feel better."

That might have worked for scraped knees and bad dreams, but nothing would fix this. I smiled anyway. "Yeah. That sounds lovely."

"Okay. I'll be right back. Why don't you get more comfortable?"

I nodded, not saying anything. As soon as the door closed behind her, I ripped the stupid black dress off and threw it across the room. Next went my bra, my panties, my tights. *Everything* had to go. Everything that reminded me of this day.

I hated him a little bit right now. I loved him. But, God, I hated him too.

I stood naked in front of the mirror and looked at myself. I looked a little bit crazy right now, with black mascara running down my cheeks and my hair a hectic, frizzy mess. All I wore was the tattoo I'd gotten for Finn—which he'd never gotten to see—and the necklace he gave me.

I closed my fingers around the clasp, ready to take it off…

But I couldn't.

He might not love me anymore, but God, I loved him so much. I ran my fingers over the sun pendant before pulling pajamas out of my closet. I barely had them on when the knock sounded on the door. I sat down on the bed and started twisting my hair into a ponytail. "Come in."

The door cracked open, but instead of my mother, Riley poked his head in. I wanted to tell him to fuck off, channeling Finn one last time, but it wasn't his fault Finn kept saying Riley was better for me. It wasn't his fault Finn didn't love me anymore.

"Hey," I said, my voice coming out hoarse and kind of frog-like. "You leaving?"

He came inside, leaving the door wide open, carrying a tray of cookies and milk. "Yeah, I'm about to head out, but your mom asked me to bring these up real quick." He set them on my nightstand, his green eyes studying me. "You okay?"

I laughed. It sounded foreign to my ears. "Do I *look* okay?"

"It's Finn, isn't it? You got in a fight because of the bruise. Maybe I could talk to him?" Riley shoved his hands into his pockets. "See if he needs a guy's perspective on things? It might help."

I looked down at my lap, wringing my hands into knots. "He doesn't love me anymore, and he blames me for his injuries. For his dad…for all of it…"

Riley's eyes went wide. "What? Bullshit. He loves you."

"No, he doesn't." I bit down hard on my lower lip. "He told me he doesn't love me. We're done. I wanted to be with him the rest of my life, and now it's over. Just like that. Gone. Dead."

"Shit." Riley hesitated for a second. He sat on the bed beside me and pulled me into his arms, but not too close. "I'm sorry. Are you sure he meant it? Maybe he just thinks he isn't good enough for you anymore, and is pushing you away. It's standard PTSD behavior."

I shook my head, blinking back tears. I refused to cry again. Finn had made me cry too much as it was. I knew why he was being this way, and I even understood it. But it didn't mean I had to roll over and accept it without feeling mad, hurt, and betrayed. This sucked. "He looked me in the eye and said it to my face. It's over."

Riley smoothed my frizzy hair back. "I know how you feel right now, but it'll get better. Over time, it'll hurt less."

I fought the urge to throat punch him for that platitude. It wouldn't get better, and it wouldn't fade. It would always hurt, like a festering, open wound that never healed. Did anyone realize how much I needed Finn? This wasn't puppy love, and it wasn't infatuation. It was soul-searching, heartbreaking, undying *love*.

"Yeah, I don't think it will. But thanks anyway, Riley."

I pulled back and looked into his eyes. He gazed at me with so much compassion that for a second, only a second, I wished I could have fallen in love with him instead. He was so nice. So perfect. I could totally see why Finn wanted me to be with Riley.

Too bad he didn't get to pimp me out like a rental doll.

Riley patted my head. "Give it time. You'll go back to school, hang out with friends, and it'll all fade away to a painful memory."

I nodded, not having it in me to argue anymore, and swiped my hands across my damp cheeks. "I'm sorry you had to witness all this drama."

"It's fine. We're friends, and friends help each other out." He pointed at the plate. "They also share their cookies with each other, and those look delicious. So…?"

Despite the blinding pain I was in, I laughed. I actually laughed. "Fine."

Reaching out, I grabbed a cookie for the both of us. We ate in silence. What would Finn do now? Where would he go? Would I ever see him again? Did he really not love me? How could something so strong and real die so fast?

I guess I'd never find out.

Riley took his last bite and dusted off his hands. "Well, I guess I'll get going. Remember, this too shall pass."

Another useless platitude. My fingers twitched with the urge to maim him. "Yeah. Sure." I finished my cookie, my eyes on the door. "I can't believe I'm going back to Cali alone. That he's not going to be there…"

"Hey, I'll see you in California, don't forget. You won't be all alone. I'm not that far away. We could get together over the weekends and drink the pain away."

"Yeah." I nodded without really listening. My mind was on Finn. "That'll be fun."

He walked past me, dropping a brotherly kiss on the top of my head. "Rest up. It'll look better in the morning."

I highly doubted that.

Finn

This was the end. There was no coming back from this.

She could never love me again after what I'd done. What I'd said. I'd had a similar thought before, when she'd found out who I really was in California. Back then, I'd still been naïve enough to think we could be together. That had been before I morphed into a monster who hurt everyone I loved.

It had been before I became…*me.*

"You need to cool it," Senator Wallington snapped. "I'm going to give you the benefit of the doubt and assume this is the alcohol talking, but you're done treating my daughter this way. And I'm cutting you off too."

Senator Wallington snatched the whiskey up and held it against his chest, making sure I didn't get another glass, I could only assume. He didn't need to worry. I didn't want any more. She was gone, so there was no one left to horrify. I didn't need to make her hate me anymore. She already did. "Don't worry. I'll be gone soon."

"Carrie loves you, and you're being an idiot." The senator shook his head. "I don't know what's gotten into you, but you need to snap out of it before it's too late."

I laughed. "*Now* you're championing us?"

"No, I'm championing her. She loves you, and you broke her heart just now." He cocked his head, his gaze scanning over mine. "How's that feel?"

"Like fucking hell," I rasped, curling my hand into a fist. "But she'll realize I did her a favor once she moves on. I hurt her. You see that mark on her face? It's from me. I did that."

Senator Wallington stiffened. "Excuse me?"

"The night my dad died. Something I did hit her." I tightened my fist. "I hurt her."

His eyes narrowed on me. "In that case, maybe you're right. Maybe you need more help than we can give you. Go find—"

"Save your words of wisdom for someone else. I don't need them anymore." I laughed harshly. "And, hey, she can marry Riley now. Have trust fund babies who don't have a daddy with tattoos behind them. That should make you happy."

The senator shifted on his feet. "You know that's not true. If I wasn't okay with you being here, you wouldn't be here, damn it. What would your father say about how you're acting right now?"

"*Don't.*" I took a step toward him, fury raging through me. It felt better than the agony. "You don't get to say that to me. He knew I was messed up, and he told me to stop hurting her. Now I am, because we're done. She'll move on, and I'll…I'll…" *I'd go crawl into a hole somewhere and forget the world existed.* "I'll be fine, too."

The senator scowled at me. "Go to bed. Talk to her in the morning when you're sober. And if you don't want to fix this, get the hell out of my house before dawn. She doesn't need to see you again."

I stormed past him. Every step I took felt harder than the last, because I knew if I was going to follow through on my promise to stop hurting her, I needed to leave before I caved. Senator Wallington was right. I needed to leave tonight.

I went outside, ready to run away right then and there, but I had too much shit upstairs in my room. I'd have to get at least some of it if I wanted to make a clean break. I sank down to the ground and covered my face with my hand, unable to believe that my life had come to this. How had this happened?

How had I lost her too? I had nothing left.

No reason to go on living.

I'd turned into a drugged-out, alcoholic, raging lunatic—and I'd hurt Carrie in more ways than one. I'd never wished I was dead more than in this moment.

Some unknown amount of time later, I stood up and went back inside. I passed Riley on the stairs, only just managing to hide my surprise at seeing him coming down from the direction of Carrie's room. Irrational, misplaced jealousy hit me in the gut. I nodded at him. "Hey."

"Did you mean it?" Riley asked, his voice hard. "Do you actually not love her anymore?"

I stopped mid-step, my hand tight on the banister. So. Carrie had already told him about the breakup. That hadn't taken long. Again with the jealousy. I wanted to take a swing at him. Kick his ass until he couldn't stand up. I didn't. "I really don't see how it's any of your business. We broke up. That's all that matters."

"Ah, but you see, it's not." Riley crossed his arms. "I had a friend with PTSD once, you know."

I shrugged. "Your point?"

"He killed himself after pushing all of his loved ones away." Riley laid a hand on my shoulder, and I swallowed hard. Shrugging free, I gave him a look that clearly told him to keep his hand to himself. "Don't be him. Don't do anything stupid. If you love her, don't let her go. And don't think you can let her go and then sweep back into her life when you're all better. Someone else will snatch her up, and it'll be too late. She'll have a long line of guys waiting for her to get over you."

I cocked a brow at him, but damn it, he was right. Just the thought of her being with someone else tasted bad in my mouth. "Will you be the first in that line?"

Riley twisted his lips. "If I thought I stood a chance in hell? Yeah. But she loves you, and you're an idiot to throw it all away."

Again. He was right. But so was I. This was the right thing to do. I was sure of it. I kept dragging her down, drowning her slowly. It was time to sink alone. "Then I guess you'll win in the end, because I'm not changing my mind. I'm no good for her like this." I caught his gaze. "But if you manage to get her to fall for you, you damn well better take good care of her, or you'll answer to me."

With that, I climbed the rest of the way up the stairs. When I opened my bedroom door, I stopped in the frame, one foot in and one foot out. She was there. In my room. The first thing I noticed was that she'd changed into pajamas. The second? That she wasn't crying anymore. She didn't look pissed, though. She just looked empty.

She looked up when I came into the room, her ravaged face sending a fist of pain through my chest. The black makeup that had streamed down her cheeks like a child's first finger painting had been washed off at some point. Christ, I couldn't do this anymore. Couldn't keep fucking hurting her. I closed the door behind me and collapsed against it.

"Carrie…"

She stood up unsteadily. "Don't worry, I'll leave you alone in a second. I just wanted to ask you something without my father standing there watching." She met my eyes one last time. "Are you just pushing me away for my own good? Or did you really mean it when you said you didn't love me anymore because of what I'd done to you?"

No. No, no, no, no, no.

I opened my mouth, ready to beg for forgiveness, but then I saw it. The bruise I'd given her. "Y-Yes. I meant it." I swallowed hard. "Too much has changed between us. I went over there to make myself better for you, to save us, but instead it ruined everything. I'm sorry for that. I'm sorry it has to be this way, but I can't love you like I used to, and you shouldn't love me either."

She bit down hard on her lower lip and nodded, still not crying. "I think it's my fault, too. I totally get it if you can't love me because of what I did to you." She bit down again, even harder. "But we promised each other no more lies. If you do this, if you say this, you can't show up later and take it all back."

I shook my head, even though I wanted to hug her. Kiss her. Love her. "I'm not lying."

"Okay." She tilted that stubborn chin of hers up again, looking more like her father than ever before. "If it wasn't for me, for *us*, you would have never been offered that job. You would have never been hurt, and you'd still be the you that you so clearly want to be. I'm sorry for that. So, so sorry."

My heart wrenched. She couldn't take the blame. It wasn't on her shoulders, damn it. She wasn't the broken one here. "It's not your fault. None of this is your fault. It's all me. Forget what I said earlier. I didn't—"

"Don't go backing down now," she snapped. Then she regained that calm she'd been showing me, and looked at me with a cool smile. "One more thing. I love you, and I'll always love you, but I don't want to ever see you again if this is the end. Don't come looking for me. Don't come check on me. It's done."

I counted to three in my head. I wouldn't tell her the truth. I wouldn't fall to my knees and beg her to forgive me. And I definitely wouldn't tell her it had all been an act. That I hadn't really broken any promises to her.

That I loved her with all of my fucking heart and always would.

I closed my eyes. "Carrie…"

"Don't." She headed for the door. "Just d-don't."

She was making this so damn hard, when all I was trying to do was save her. She needed to leave before I snapped. But when she grabbed the knob, finally ready to leave me alone, I laid my hand over hers. Stopped her. Her skin was so soft. So perfect. So *mine*. How was I supposed to live without her by my side? How was any of this right?

"You won't see me again," I promised, meeting her gaze before looking at the bruise again. It kept reminding me I was doing the right thing. "Someday you'll love someone who actually deserves your love, and I'll be happy you found him."

"Yeah. Okay." She looked away first, tears finally escaping her eyes. "Whatever."

I moved away from the door, and for the second time that night…

I watched her walk away.

CHAPTER THIRTEEN

Carrie

Month one

Without opening my eyes, I shut off my blaring alarm. I slowly rolled over and blinked at the window. The sun was shining bright and cheery, completely opposite of the weather in D.C. It had been so weird coming home without…without *him*. I refused to even think his name—it hurt too much. I fingered my necklace, still staring outside at the bright blue sky. Funny that it was so pretty and cheery outside, when my life felt so dark I didn't want to move. I rolled over, pulled the covers over my head, and went back to sleep.

Finn

I chugged back another shot, squinting through the dim bar across all the bodies, shouting, and laughter. A girl with red hair turned my way, smiling coyly when she spotted me watching her. It only made me think of Carrie, which made me want to drink more, damn it. I motioned the bartender over, pointing at my empty shot glass. Where was she right now? Was she happy? Sad? Did she miss me as much as I missed her? I didn't know, but fuck, I wish I did.

CHAPTER FOURTEEN

Carrie

Month two

I sat up in bed, smoothing my messy hair out of my eyes. I was five minutes late to class, so I needed to move fast. Throwing the covers over the side of the bed, my feet hit the bare floor within seconds. After I tossed my scattered homework into my bag, I hobbled over to my closet, eyeing the shirt I'd left curled up in a ball on my pillow. Finn's shirt. It had taken me three weeks to find it mixed in with my stuff; I'd been that much of a mess. Now I slept with it every night. It calmed me, even while it made me cry. I couldn't let it go.

Couldn't let him go.

Finn

I sank onto the bench, a bottle of beer in my hand, glowering at the ocean. I had thought it would bring me peace, being back out here in California. Being near her. But she didn't even know I was here, and I hadn't gone near her. I looked down at my ripped jeans and trailed my hand over my scar. The cast was off my arm now, but it still hurt like a fucking bitch. Everything hurt. I had no meaning to my life. Nothing to live for.

No one who cared.

CHAPTER FIFTEEN

Carrie

Month three

I entered my dorm room, smiling as I shut the door behind me. I'd been out to dinner with Marie and her latest love interest, Sean. For the first time in months, I thought maybe I was starting to feel alive a little bit again. I walked up to the window, staring out into the night. I played with my necklace as I stared at the full moon, wondering where he was right now. If he was okay. If he was happy. I glanced down to where he used to always stand while watching over me...and my heart stopped. I swore, I freaking *swore*, I saw him out there, looking up at me. Pressing my forehead against the glass, I squinted into the darkness, desperately seeking him.

He wasn't there. I'd imagined the whole thing.

Swallowing past the tears that welled up in my throat, I rested a hand against the glass window. "I miss you, Finn."

The door opened behind me. I swiped the tears away and left the window.

Finn

I looked up at her, my heart racing so fucking hard I swore she could hear it. I saw her scanning the shadows, looking for me. Had she seen me, or had I imagined that? I tightened my fist around the bottle of whiskey I always seemed to carry around with me, wanting so badly to step into the light and shout her name at the top of my lungs. To beg her to forgive me. To love me again. Then I saw the empty bottle in my hand…and I hated myself.

"I miss you so much, Ginger," I whispered, dropping the bottle to the grass at my feet. "So fucking much."

I stumbled forward. I shouldn't be alive. Shouldn't be here anymore. Maybe I should go to the beach, take all my pills, and end it. End the suffering, pain, and agony. No. That wasn't painful enough. I deserved worse.

I deserved to fucking suffer.

Slowly, I made my way to the store, my heart in my throat the whole time. As I stood in the camping aisle, staring at the rope that could end my life, I tried to think of how best to do it. Where best to do it. I didn't have a house, and hanging myself from a tree seemed too poetic. I just stood there calmly contemplating the best place to die, and I didn't even care.

I'd hit rock bottom.

CHAPTER SIXTEEN

Carrie

Month four

I blinked up at the blinding light, covering my eyes with my hand. Peeking through my fingers, I just managed to catch sight of the bright blonde hair hanging down over my head. I'd been blissfully sleeping moments before, but now the light was freaking killing me. "God, Marie. What the hell?"

"Get up." She yanked the covers off me, leaving them tangled around my feet. "We're going out."

I pulled the covers back up over my sweats and loose T-shirt. "What? No. I'm not going out. It's…" I looked at the clock. "Uh…eight o'clock at night."

Wow. I'd have sworn it was at least midnight.

"Yeah. Just noticing the pathetic depths to which you've fallen, huh?" She ripped the covers off again. This time I let her. "It's a Friday night in spring, the weather is perfect, and we're going to a party whether or not you like it. Enough moping around over him."

"I'm not moping," I protested, sitting up and rubbing my eyes. "I'm just tired."

"You've been moping ever since you came back from D.C., and you know it. You woke up and he was gone. It was over. It was tragic and sad.

He broke your heart." She put her hands on her hips. "I've allowed you four months to get over it, but enough is enough already. You need to come back to the land of the living. Finn's gone, but you're not."

I swallowed hard at the mention of his name, my fingers automatically closing around the sun pendant. Had it really been four months? It felt like only days ago that I'd woken up to find his room empty. No goodbye. No hugs. Nothing. Just empty, like me.

I nodded. "I know that."

"Then get the hell up." Marie headed for the drawers, rummaging through them and slamming them shut in progression. "Ugh. You need one of my dresses. All of yours aren't right."

"Right for what?" I asked, shoving my hair out of my eyes. "I really don't want to go to a party. I'm tired. And there's—"

"'No other Finns out there.' Yeah. I got that loud and clear the other twenty times you told me." She rolled her eyes and pulled out one of her black dresses. I hated black dresses now. They reminded me of *him*. "How's this?"

"No."

She rolled her eyes and pulled out a dark green one. "This?"

"Marie..." I met her eyes. "Don't make me go. I-I'm not ready."

"You'll never be ready." She sat down beside me and hugged me so tight I couldn't breathe. I didn't mind one little bit. "But all you've done is sleep, hang out with me, study, and study some more. The only person you get dressed nicely for anymore is Riley, and even that's a chore for you. Do you really want your life to be like this forever? To be stuck in mourning like this?" She squeezed my shoulder. "You broke up with him, he didn't *die*."

It felt like he had. I hadn't heard a word from him since he'd packed up and left my parents' house in the middle of the night. Lately, I kept thinking I'd seen him here and there. Outside of my classes. At the gym. At the cafeteria after dinner. But then I'd look again, and he wouldn't be there. His ghost kept haunting me, even though he was still alive.

Hernandez was my guard now, and by unspoken agreement we didn't discuss Finn at all. I didn't ask, and he didn't tell. Heck, I didn't even know if they still talked. It was better that way...or so I kept telling myself.

Maybe Marie was right.

Maybe I needed to stop being so darn sad all the time. It had been four months, and he'd obviously moved on with his life. Maybe I should try to do the same, no matter how dull and boring it might be now. "Where's the party?"

"At Sean's fraternity." Marie's eyes lit up at the mention of Sean. All I knew about the dude was that he was loud when they made out, and he had a hell of a smile that Marie couldn't shut up about. "You in?"

I sighed. "Yeah, I guess so. I'll have to let Hernandez know."

I'd told her who I really was two months ago, when I'd finally stopped moping around long enough to actually form a coherent sentence. We'd gotten even closer since she knew the real me. It was so refreshingly fun to not have to hide my identity from someone like Marie.

"Oh." Marie's smile faded. "Does he *have* to come? He ruins the fun with that frown and serious disposition of his. And those judgey eyes."

"He'll stay back," I said, grabbing my phone. "And he won't stare at you. Why do you hate him so much?"

"He's Finn's friend. That makes him the enemy in my book," Marie said. She stood, the dress still in her hands, looking less than convinced. "I wonder if Riley could come down to meet us? What do you think?"

I pulled up Hernandez's number and jotted off a quick text. *Going to party.* "I doubt it. He'd need more notice than twenty minutes."

"Well, about that…" Marie fidgeted, her gaze skittering away. "I kind of sort of invited him down yesterday. Thought it might be time for you to open your eyes and see the boy's in love with you."

I tightened my grip on the phone. It vibrated, but I didn't look at it. "No, he's not. We're friends. That's it. Why does everyone keep shoving us together like we're suddenly going to fall in love or something?"

Marie snorted. "*You* might want to be friends, but *he* wants more."

"No, he doesn't." My stomach twisted at the thought. "He really doesn't."

"Yeah. Sure he doesn't." Marie pulled out a clean—maybe?—towel and chucked it at me. I caught it reflexively. "He'll be here in ten minutes, so you better go shower and shave."

"I don't have to shave," I said, my voice low.

"Have you seen those legs?"

"Yeah, it's not that bad." I lifted my leg and looked at my calf. Then, well, I flinched. "Okay, you're right. I'll shave." I looked at my phone and opened Hernandez's text. *Address?* I gave it to him before I tossed the phone aside. "'K, off I go."

"Is Sourpuss coming?" Marie asked, applying her eyeshadow.

She acted as if she hated him all the time, but every time we got together with him, Marie came to life. I'd bet my bottom dollar that she got off on their arguing. "Yep. Wear red. He likes it."

She rolled her eyes. "Now *you're* the crazy one."

I laughed and headed for the showers, feeling a little bit lighter for the first time since I'd gotten my heart broken by the guy who'd sworn he would always love me. I tried not to think about it much, but it was hard. Especially when my new guard was his freaking BFF. At first, I'd tried to avoid Hernandez out of principle. Dad kept sending him after me, though, and I'd realized I wasn't punishing Dad or Finn by avoiding the tail. I was punishing Hernandez, because he was getting in trouble for losing me.

So now I played along. I hated it.

I turned on the water, stripped, and stepped under the stream. The hot water woke me up even more, and I shaved and cleaned up as fast as I could manage with the jungle I'd been growing on my legs. As I dried off, I looked down at my tattoo. I wish I could say I regretted it, but I didn't. It represented a short period in my life where I'd been happy—really, truly happy—and even if he didn't love me anymore, he had.

And I'd loved him, too. So freaking much.

My heart wrenched, and I wrapped the towel around myself before making my way back to my room. I passed a few people on the way, but for the most part the halls were empty. When I opened the door, I called out, "You win. I'm no longer a hairy Amazon beast."

A man cleared his throat. "Uh, that's good."

"Riley?" I scanned the room and found him sitting on the edge of Marie's bed, his cheeks red. "You're early."

"You're naked." He raised a brow, looking me up and down casually. "Call it even?"

I clutched the towel tighter to my boobs, swallowing hard. It was longer than most dresses, yet I felt horribly exposed. "Uh, where's Marie?"

"Someone knocked on the door, and she left." His gaze dipped low again before slamming back up to my face. His gaze heated significantly, making me shift on my feet. "I guess I should do the same so you can get dressed. Or are we wearing towels to this party? I could totally rock that."

I laughed. "Yeah, you probably could. But I kinda need to get dressed, so…"

"I don't suppose I could sweet-talk you into letting me stay?" He stood up and crossed his arms. "I make excellent company."

"Bad boy," I said, laughing and pointing at the door. "Out."

He laughed and held his arms up in surrender. "Yes, ma'am."

"I'll call out to you when I'm decent," I said, grinning.

"You already look decent to me."

I cocked my head. "Are you flirting with me?"

"And if I am?" He brushed past me on his way to the hallway, his arm rubbing against my bare one. "Would that be so bad?"

I rolled my eyes and closed the door in his face. I couldn't answer that. Any girl would be lucky to have a guy like Riley flirting with her, but I wasn't *any* girl. I might not be with Finn anymore, but I knew I wasn't ready to fall for someone else.

I wasn't even sure if I could.

I slipped into my panties, bra, and then slid the dress over my head. It was soft, short, and sexy. For a second, I debated taking it off and changing into my usual jeans and loose T-shirt, but then I shook off the urge. I refused to be that girl anymore. Marie was right—enough was enough. It was time to move on…

Even if I still felt like I was dead inside.

"You can come in now," I called out, walking up to the mirror where all our makeup was. "I'm dressed."

As I applied light gray eyeshadow, Riley came back inside and sat down on my bed this time. He whistled through his teeth. "Damn, girl. You look good."

"Yeah, yeah." I leaned closer to apply my eyeliner. His gaze dipped down. *Oh my God, he's totally checking out my ass.* "Hey. Eyes at face level."

He met my eyes in the mirror. "They are at my face level. That just happens to be at your ass. It's a nice one, you know."

"Sorry to bail, I had to lend my curling iron to—" Marie stopped in the doorway, a smirk on her face as she took in me at the mirror and Riley on my bed. "Oh. Am I interrupting something?"

"No," I said.

"Yes," Riley said at the same time. Then he grinned. "I was staring at her...dress."

Marie snorted. "Yeah. Sure you were."

"He's being a typical dude. Staring at anything in a dress." I looked at Marie as I slammed the lid back on my eyeliner. She had on a short red dress that barely skimmed mid-thigh. "Speaking of which..."

She flushed. "Oh, shut up. It's the only one I had."

"Mmhm." I applied mascara, grinning the whole time. She had it bad, she just didn't want to admit it. As if on cue, my phone buzzed. I glanced at it and put the finishing touches on my lashes. My hair was still wet, so I grabbed a hair elastic off the shelf. "He's outside waiting for us."

"How much longer are you going to be?" Marie asked.

"Three minutes tops."

She backed toward the door. "I'll go let him know."

And then she was gone. I rolled my eyes. "She's half in love with him, you know."

"Who?"

"My new bodyguard, Hernandez." I checked out my hair. For once, my updo managed to look decent. I'd done a half-up, half-down twist. "He replaced...Finn."

I flinched. Even saying his name hurt.

"How are you doing with that?" He came up behind me but didn't touch. "Have you heard from him at all?"

"Nope, when we broke up, we broke up. I woke up the next morning, and he was gone. Haven't heard from him since. It's over." *Yeah. Even though I still slept with his shirt, I was so over him.* I smoothed my hair for lack of something better to do. I didn't like talking about it. It hurt too much. "How have you been?"

"Good." He studied me. "But you didn't tell me how you've been."

"I'm fine," I said softly. "Really. I don't like talking about it, or him. That's all. It hurts too much, you know?"

"I know. Hey, I like the darker red." He gave a small nod toward my hair. I'd dyed it a little darker after the breakup, and I had side bangs now. I was still adjusting to the darker red. "It's nice."

"Thanks."

"You're welcome. I like the bangs, too." He stepped closer. "Ready to go?"

I smiled at him gratefully. One of the best things about him was that he knew when not to push. "Yeah, just let me get some shoes."

Once I had a pair of heels on, I walked out into the hallway with Riley. Cory was walking down it at the same time as we left. He looked at Riley, and then stared at me. "Oh. Hey."

I gave him a little smile. We might not be friends anymore, but he *did* know my secret. I hadn't forgotten about that. "Hey, how's it going?"

"Good." Cory held his hand out. "I'm Cory."

"Riley Stapleton." He shook Cory's hand. "Nice to meet you."

Cory nodded and looked back at me. "Where's Finn?"

"We broke up." I swallowed. "We're on our way to a party, so I'll catch you later?"

"I'm going, too." Cory grinned. "So, yeah, you will."

Great. I nodded. "Bye." I headed down the stairs, grimacing. "Remember the guy I told you about who Finn hated?"

"That's him?" Riley asked dryly. "I can see why. I don't like the way he looks at you."

"Now you sound like *him.*"

Riley shrugged and opened the door at the bottom of the steps for me. "Sorry, but it's true. He's sleazy."

I rolled my eyes. "He's harmless as a—"

"Oh, don't be such an ass," Marie snapped. "God, why did I come out here at all?"

"I'm simply pointing out that if you wanted to wear a short dress, you should have put on—" Hernandez cut off, his eyes narrowing on me. "Oh. Hey, Carrie. What's he doing here?"

"Put on a what?" I asked, my eyes wide.

"Nothing," Marie snapped.

"Pair of underwear," Hernandez said at the same time. "That doesn't leave ass cheeks hanging out."

"I…I see." I looked at Marie, whose face was bright red, and she looked as if she wanted to punch Hernandez. I forced myself not to ask how he knew what she had on under her dress. Forcing my attention back to Hernandez, I smiled. "And *he's* here to go to the party with us."

Hernandez frowned. "You come down here an awful lot, considering your school is so far away."

"Yeah. I came down for the weekend to see Carrie." Riley eyed him, his blond hair reflecting the full moon. "Is that a problem?"

"No, of course not. It's just a long way to travel for a little party when you're going to school for law. How long did it take? Five hours?"

Riley laughed uneasily and rubbed his jaw. "Yeah, something like that."

I frowned at the way Hernandez was watching Riley. To quote Marie, he was looking at him with *judgey eyes*. "How do you know where he goes to school, and what his major is? From my dad?"

"No, from—" Hernandez hesitated. "I mean, yeah. Sure. Your dad."

My heart stopped before painfully speeding up. If he hadn't heard about Riley from my dad, that meant he'd spoken to Finn. Was he here, in Cali? I looked over my shoulder, half expecting to see him behind me. He wasn't. "You talked to him."

It wasn't a question.

Hernandez flexed his jaw. "Let's not do this. You ready to go?"

"Y-Yeah, of course." I took a steadying breath. "You're right."

"Carrie?" Riley placed his hand on my lower back. "You still want to go?"

No. "Of course. Let's go have some fun."

Hernandez looked at Riley's hand, stiffening. "After you guys."

I walked by him, Marie on my other side, trying to resist the urge to shrug Riley's hand off. It was an innocent enough touch, and despite what everyone seemed to think…

He wasn't in love with me.

CHAPTER SEVENTEEN

Carrie

The music was so loud I couldn't hear myself think, let alone carry on a freaking conversation. But I guess that was the point of a party like this. You were supposed to let loose, stop thinking, and just drink. Dance. Have fun. Be young and free.

I was trying so hard to do all of those things.

I lifted my cup to my mouth, draining the last of the wine. It tasted okay, but I missed my pink wine coolers that Finn had always kept stocked for me. I paused, the cup still pressed to my lips. That's the first time I'd thought about Finn without wanting to cry in…well, since the breakup.

Maybe that meant something.

"Want to dance?" Riley asked me, leaning down to shout in my ear. "With me, that is?"

My head spun a little bit from the amount of booze I had already. The last thing I should do is dance, yet that's exactly why I would. I'd been living my life doing all the things that I *should* be doing, instead of being crazy every once in a while.

Maybe it was time for a change of pace.

"Sure, let's go. But first…" I took his drink and finished it. When he looked at me with wide eyes, I laughed, tossing my head back and everything. "What?"

"Nothing at all. I like seeing you happy, is all."

He grabbed my hand and led me to the dancing area—which, in all reality, was nothing more than a cleared out living room. Couples danced all around us, half of them caught in the moves, and half of them caught up in each other. Some had stopped with the pretense of dancing, and were just plain old getting it on without caring who saw.

It made my cheeks go all hot, and it made me miss how Finn had made me feel when he touched me like the dude in the corner was touching his girl.

"Who says I haven't been happy?" I called out to Riley. "I'm good. Excellent. Wonderful."

And a horrible liar.

He pulled me in his arms and moved to the music without hesitation. Turned out, he was a pretty amazing dancer. Was there anything this guy *wasn't* good at? His hips swung to the music, mimicking sex, almost, and it was hot. Damn, the boy moved like Bruno Mars. The urge to fan my cheeks hit me strongly. "Since when do you dance like that?"

"Since forever. You just didn't notice before because you weren't looking." I stared at him in surprise, and he grabbed me and pulled me closer. "You going to dance, or stand there moping about Finn?"

I gave him my back, moving my body to the music. He brushed up against me, all hard muscle and hot skin. "Stop talking about him," I called over my shoulder. The tempo picked up, and we matched it effortlessly. Grinning, I moved closer, feeling so freaking alive. "He's not here, but you are."

"About time you noticed."

I looked back at him, ready to make some sarcastic remark, but he was watching me with a weird look in his eye. As soon as he saw me looking, though, it faded away and he grinned. I swallowed hard, realizing he'd been looking at me as if he *wanted* me. How often had he done that, and I missed it? Was I really that blind?

The song ended, and a slow one took its place. We both stood there awkwardly, staring at each other. I might be able to break it down with him, sexy style, but I couldn't be that close to him. I fanned my face with my hand. "I'm going to head outside for some fresh air. Want to get some more drinks and meet me out there?"

He nodded. "Don't wander off far."

"I won't. Besides, Hernandez is out there." I shrugged. "I'll be fine."

I walked away without waiting for an answer, needing to get away from him and all the possibilities that look he'd given me represented. It made me nervous and anxious at the same time. My stomach fisted into a knot, making me wonder if I was about to puke up all the wine I'd just drank. That would be a fitting end to this night, wouldn't it?

I stumbled out into the cool night, taking a big gulp of air. I could still hear the music, so I moved away from the doorway, wanting some peace and quiet. Someone stepped out of the shadows and I jumped, my hand to my chest. For a second, a split second, I thought it was going to be Finn.

It's how we met, after all. Outside a party.

But I was wrong. It was Cory. "Where are you going?"

"Nowhere. I needed some fresh air." I dropped my hand back to my side. "You scared me."

He laughed. "Sorry. Where's Riley?"

"Getting us some more drinks." I wrapped my arms around myself, eyeing him. I could tell with only one glance that he was drunk. Last time he'd gotten drunk at a party with me, it hadn't been pretty. "He'll be out any second."

"I'll only take a second." He walked right up to me, his jaw hard. "You're single again, and you're with a guy who looks like me. He's basically me, but not. Is he a senator's kid, too?"

I laughed, unable to stop myself. I'd been caught off guard by the cocky statement. "Um, I'm not with him. And he doesn't look like you at all."

"Yeah, he does. He comes from money, like us." He stumbled a little bit. "Answer my question, Carrie."

I backed up a step, stalling for time. Riley would come out soon, I was sure. "Which one?"

"Is he a senator's kid, too?"

I blinked. Why did he care? "Uh, yeah. He is."

"Of course." He smirked. "You had enough of playing on the wrong side of the tracks, huh? I don't blame you. Finn was a huge mistake."

I frowned at him and backed up. "Someone should really lock up the alcohol so you can't get a hold of it. When you drink, you don't play nice."

"I'm not drunk." He stumbled again, totally ruining the denial. "I'm just telling the truth. Finn was horrible for you. Stay on this side of the tracks," he slurred.

"Finn wasn't from the wrong side of the tracks. He was a good guy." I curled my hands into fists, taking another step back from him. He was pissing me off now, talking badly about Finn. He had no right. No right at all. It was deja vu. "Better than you've ever been."

Cory laughed and followed me, backing me up to the beach. "Doubtful. He's gutter trash."

My heart sped up, and I finally saw what Riley and Finn saw. For the first time ever, Cory creeped me out. "You're scaring me. Stop following me like that."

"Why? Because your big bad ex isn't here to beat me up? You don't have him here guarding you anymore. I could kidnap you now," he whispered, grinning evilly. "You're used to that, I bet. Being stolen away by ruffians. I bet you like it, too. You like it rough, don't you?"

"God. You're such an idiot," I snapped. "Leave me alone."

He grabbed my hand and jerked me closer. His breath reeked of cheap beer and even cheaper vodka. "You know, you *should* be nicer to me. I know things about you that no one else knows. And I've kept all your secrets…for now."

I tried to pull free, but he tightened his grip. "Let *go* of me."

"Fine." He released me and ran his hands down his face. "You treat me like I'm the enemy."

"You were mean to Finn," I said, rubbing my wrist. "And you're being mean right now, too." Where the hell was Hernandez, anyway? Shouldn't he have come out, even though I'd warned him only to show himself if it was life or death?

I scanned the shadows. Nothing.

"Well, he's not here anymore, is he?" He shrugged. "So why hold it against me? I was obviously right about him, or you'd still be with him."

"Just because he's gone doesn't make it okay to talk crap about him," I said, frowning at him. "You really don't get it, do you?"

He stepped closer and ran a finger over my jaw. "I never got what you saw in him, no. You should be with someone like me."

Over my dead body. "Stop it."

"You deserve so much better. Someone like me."

He lowered his face and kissed me before I could even remotely guess what he was going to do. His tongue probed my lips, making me gag. I gasped and shoved him back, swiping my hand over my mouth while trembling. "Don't do that again. We're not together, and we will *never* be together."

"That's why I did it. I had to do it just one more time." He balled his hands at his hips. "Before you're with that Riley guy next."

A scuffling sound came from the shadows. Hushed voices, too. Footsteps approached rapidly before slowing down. "Everything's fine, Hernan—" I broke off. It wasn't Hernandez; it was Riley. "Oh, hey."

"Hey." Riley held two bottles of water in either hand. "Everything okay?"

"Yeah, I was just leaving," Cory muttered. He gave me one last look before walking away. "See ya," he called out over his shoulder.

I let out a sigh of relief and looked at Riley. He was watching me closely. "Did he kiss you? I thought I saw…"

"He did. I told him not to do it again." I sat down on a big boulder and looked up at him. "He's always liked me, I guess. Which is why Finn hated him."

Finn.

"You still love him, don't you?" He perched next to me on the rock. "You're not over him even in the slightest."

I swallowed hard. "I don't know if I'll ever be *over* him, really. What I felt for him isn't something that just goes away with time. It'll always be there."

"Yeah. I get that."

I looked over at him. He looked pensive. "Are you still in love with your ex, too?"

"No." He laughed. "God, no. I don't think I really ever loved her. She was a girlfriend, but that's it. Nothing more."

"Have you ever been in love?"

"Well…" He looked over at me, and his eyes latched on to mine. "I think I could be, easily, but it's not the right time."

I sucked in a shaky breath, my heart wrenching. Darn it, I'd been a blind fool. Everyone was right. He wanted more from me, and I couldn't give it to him. "Riley, I can't—"

He leaned in and placed his fingers over my lips. "Don't. There's nothing to say. I know already."

"But—" I pulled his hand away from my lips, but didn't let go of his fingers. "There is. You're such a good guy. The perfect guy, really. I wish that things could be different. That I could be different. I'm just not ready to try again."

"I know." His fingers flexed on mine. "Do you think, once you are, that maybe we could, I don't know, get a coffee? Go to dinner?"

"You have to understand, the love I had for Finn?" I shook my head, not dropping his gaze. His eyes looked even greener in the moonlight. I didn't even realize that was possible. "I'm not sure it will ever fully go away. That's not fair to you. You deserve more than half a heart from a girl."

He reached out and cupped my cheek. It felt good. "Let me decide what I deserve, okay?"

I'd said something similar to Finn once. He'd pissed me off by deciding what was best for me without asking. Is that how Riley felt now? Frustrated and angry at me for trying to decide what's best for him? I didn't want to do that to him.

"Okay." I forced a smile, still holding his hand. "You really are a great guy, you know. If I'd met you first…"

His gaze dipped to my lips. "But you didn't."

"I didn't."

He set the water down, and framed my face with his other hand. "May I kiss you? Just a little kiss to see if we're compatible, before I try to win your heart?"

"I don't know." Speaking of hearts…mine picked up speed at the thought of kissing Riley. I'd only ever kissed Finn and Cory. There was no comparison there. Maybe with Riley it would be different. "I guess we could try if you want."

He grinned. "You make it sound like a prison sentence."

"Sorry." I laughed, reaching out to grasp his wrists lightly. "It's just—"

He leaned down and kissed me, cutting me off mid-sentence. His soft lips touched mine, applying the perfect amount of pressure. Perfect setting. Perfect weather. Perfect touch. Perfect guy. The gentle way he held me. The way he tilted his head just right to get access to my mouth. Everything about the kiss was *perfect*.

But he wasn't Finn. There were no explosions or fireworks.

It just felt nice.

He pulled back, resting his forehead on mine. "That wasn't so bad, was it?"

"N-No." I tightened my grip on his wrists. I wished I were different. Wished I were healed already so I could try this again with an open mind. "It was great."

"Good." He grinned down at me, looking way too happy. It made me feel guilty. "I can wait for you to be ready now."

"What if I'm never ready?"

He shrugged. "Then you'll never get to kiss me again."

"Ouch." I laughed. "That's harsh."

"I'm just kidding. You can kiss me anytime." He let me go. "You wanna kiss me again now, don't you? Admit it."

I smiled at him. He was so freaking charming that it was hard not to. "Actually, I think I'm going to go back to my room now. I'm tired."

"I'll go with you," he said quickly.

"*No.*" I winced at how harsh that sounded. I just needed to be alone right now. Kissing Riley and kind of liking it was like putting the nail in the proverbial coffin that held my relationship with Finn. I needed time to recover. "You stay and have fun since you drove this whole way down. Don't leave for me."

He studied me. "I want to, but I can tell you want to be alone, so I'll stay. Maybe we can have breakfast in the morning before I head back?"

"Sure, where are you staying?"

"With a buddy here." He quirked a brow. "Why? You offering to let me stay with you? 'Cause I could ditch him and crash with you instead."

"Ha! You could totally—" Something scratched on the concrete behind us, and a crashing sound broke the relative quietness of the night. I whirled around to look. "Hernandez, is that you? Are you okay?"

A shuffling sound, and then Hernandez came stumbling out of the shadows, tripping over his own feet. "Sorry, I, uh, I kicked a potted plant by accident."

I squinted at him. "You kicked a…plant?"

"Yep. That's me." He glowered over his shoulder. "Always being a clumsy asshole."

"Oookay." I stood up and picked up the bottle of water Riley got me. "Well, you're just in time. I'm ready to go back to my room, so you can walk me, and then go home."

He eyed Riley. "Alone, I assume?"

"Yes, of course." My cheeks heated. "If I wasn't going to be alone, I wouldn't ask you to walk with me."

He looked over his shoulder again. "I'm ready when you are."

I smiled at Riley. "Anyway…"

Riley came up to me and kissed my lips gently. "See you in the morning?"

"Sure. Nine?"

"It's a date," he said, grinning. He backed off, not dropping my gaze. "It's supposed to be sunny tomorrow, so maybe we can go to the beach, too."

The sun is finally shining, Ginger. Finn's voice echoed in my head, loud and clear. It was almost as if he'd actually said the words, and it hurt. Would he ever stop haunting me? My smile slipped. "Great. See you then."

I watched him head back into the party, tossing his water bottle from hand to hand. A super-hot girl walked up to him and started flirting, but he looked back at me. Well, crap. He really did like me. I wasn't sure what to do about that. I waved one last time before walking toward my dorm.

Hernandez fell into step beside me. "So…moving on, huh?"

"I don't know." I lifted a shoulder. It felt weird talking to him about this, when he may or may not be in contact with Finn. "Maybe."

"He seems…nice."

As if stuck in a time warp, Finn's words from all those months ago rang in my head: *Nice. That's the word for a puppy, not a man. Nice won't make you scream out in bed.* I straightened my spine and glanced around, half expecting to see him standing somewhere in the shadows, smirking at me. God, I was losing it. "Uh, yeah. He's very nice. There's nothing wrong with being nice."

"I never said there was." He shoved his hands in his pockets and looked over his shoulder again. "Where are you two meeting tomorrow for breakfast?"

"I don't know. He'll probably come up to my room first, and then we'll decide." I looked at him. "Why do you ask?"

"So I can follow you there." He raised a brow at me. "It's kind of my job," he lowered his head and mumbled, "no matter how much I might wish it wasn't."

"Why don't you quit if you hate it?"

"I can't." He looked at me, then glanced away. "I need to watch over you for him. He'd want me to."

"He doesn't love me anymore," I said, my voice soft. "You're off the hook."

He laughed. "No. I'm not."

We walked the rest of the way home in silence. I hesitated at the entrance to my dorm. Hernandez hovered, all of his weight on his left foot, as if perched to leave.

Still, I didn't move. My hand gripped the door tight. "Is he…is he okay?"

"Finn?" Hernandez looked away. "What makes you think I've talked to him recently?"

I tucked my hair behind my ear, my heart racing at the mere thought of hearing how Finn was doing. I was like a starved dog, desperate for any scrap of information I could get about him. "Please. Tell me if he's okay. That's all I want to know. I don't need to know anything else."

Hernandez looked out toward the shadows and shoved his hands in his pockets.

"I get wanting to move on, but don't do it if you're not ready. That's not fair to anyone involved."

"Has Finn moved on?" I asked. Immediately, I regretted the question. I didn't want to know. I held up a hand and scrunched my eyes tight. "You know what? Forget I asked that. Forget it all. Just go home."

I opened the door and walked inside, trying not to look back at him. Trying not to go back and beg him to answer my question. I *needed* to know.

I couldn't know.

CHAPTER EIGHTEEN

Finn

I rocked back on my heels and cursed under my breath, an empty hollowness residing where my heart used to beat. It had felt that way ever since I walked away from Carrie, and I didn't think it would ever go away, not without her in my life. She owned my heart, carrying it with her wherever she went, and she wasn't with me anymore. I missed her more than I missed having a heart. I'd finally learned how to *live* when I'd been with her, and now I wasn't living.

I was just surviving. Barely.

Dr. Montgomery opened the door and smiled at me. She wore her usual business suit, and her brown hair was pulled back in a bun. She was a creature of habit, if nothing else. "Griffin, you can come in now."

"All right."

I walked into the office and sat down on the couch. I drew the line at lying down on it, though. It was hard enough to walk in those doors. But after hitting rock bottom, I realized I needed help. And it *was* helping. I was still here, after all.

I almost hadn't been.

Dr. Montgomery settled in her chair. "So, how was your Friday night? What did you do? When you called for an emergency meeting, I figured something had to be up."

"It was...hard. Bad." I ran a hand over my hair. It was growing out a little bit now. It was as short as it would have been if I had been going to drill weekend. "I almost did something I would have regretted, but I held myself back."

"Did you try to hurt yourself again?" she asked, her forehead creased. "I thought we'd gotten past that point."

"No, that's not it."

"Were you upset over your honorable discharge from the Marines again?" she asked.

"No." I dragged my hand down my face. "And before you ask, no, Captain Richards didn't try to contact me about that job again."

Dr. Montgomery nodded. "Ah. Then it was Carrie. Did you try to go see her?"

"I *saw* her," I admitted, touching the scar on my forehead. "But I made sure I stayed hidden from her. She dyed her hair a different color—it's a darker red now. And she has bangs. She wears more lipstick, too. It's like she's trying to change herself now that I'm not there. She was with a guy we both know, and she looked happy. So fucking happy." I cut off. "Sorry."

"You can curse—God knows I do when I'm not working. This is a safe environment for you." She leaned forward. "So. How did seeing her look so happy and different make *you* feel?"

"Empty. So fucking empty." Rubbing my jaw, I laughed uneasily. "Lonely. Sad. Full of regret and wishes and useless hopes. What else would it make me feel? I love her so much it *hurts*, and she's not mine anymore. She never will be. I broke her heart."

She nodded. "But you let her go. Set her free. Do you now think that was the wrong decision?"

"Fuck if I know. I was so messed up, I wasn't even *me*." I tugged on my hair. "I wasn't good for her. She needed someone stronger than I was. A man who could protect her, be her partner. Not a burden."

Dr. Montgomery steepled her fingers. "But you think you could be that man now? Is that what you're saying?"

"I…I don't know. She looks pretty happy without me."

"Looks can often be deceiving." She leaned back and studied me. I hated when she looked at me like that. She saw way too much. "So can words. After all, you told her you didn't love her, but that was a lie."

"Yeah, well," I swallowed hard. "She didn't seem to be broken up or anything. She looked like she's moved on, and I'm happy for her. I am."

"But…?"

"But I miss her so damn much." I stood up and paced, my heart beating faster even though I swore it wasn't there. "I want to go up to her and beg her to forgive me, but then my head gets in the way. What if she's better off without me in her life? What if Riley makes her happier than I ever did or could? What right do I have to jump back into her life and fuck it all up again?"

She inclined her head, still watching me. "Is she with this Riley guy?"

"Not yet." I looked out the window. "My buddy is her guard. He says this is the first time this happened."

"The first time what happened?"

"They kissed." I looked at her. "I saw it."

She sat forward. "Did it trigger anything?"

"I had another nightmare last night." I looked out the window. "I'm not sure if it's because of that. They never really left. They just got less frequent."

"All right." She studied me, her eyes locked in on something I couldn't see. "What else did it trigger?"

"Nothing, besides the need to get her back." I sighed and headed back toward her. "And they're meeting up for breakfast."

"Ah, so there's something *starting*."

"I guess so." I turned around at the wall and headed back toward the window, my steps agitated. "But if there's nothing there yet, I'm not messing anything up, right? It's not like they're in love or anything."

"The real question is: Are you ready for all that talking to Carrie would entail? The possibilities? The pain?"

I looked at her. "Isn't that where you come in? Tell me. Am I ready?"

"You've been doing well. For all intents and purposes, you're more yourself then you were when you showed up here the first time." She crossed her arms. "Tell me again about that night. The night you turned it all around."

I sat down on the couch and rubbed my temples. "Why?"

"Just trust me this time, Griffin."

I rested my elbows on my knees. I hated when people used my full name. It reminded me of the senator. "I was drunk off my ass and went to Carrie's dorm. It was the lowest point in my life." I looked up at her.

"I was ready to end it all; the pain was just too much. I couldn't take it anymore. Couldn't stand that I was the only one alive, and I was alone. And I missed her so damn much."

She nodded. "And then…?"

"I went to the store to get rope to hang myself," I whispered. "I deserved a rough death. Slow, painful, horrible. The whole way to the store, I was so fucking calm. No panic, no doubts. It's what I wanted to do. But when I held the rope in my hand, deciding the best type…something stopped me. I thought about her, and I couldn't do it. I couldn't do that to her. It would devastate her knowing I'd died alone and miserable."

"Good." She cocked her head. "And then…?"

"I took a deep breath, put down the rope, and walked to my buddy's house, which used to be mine. Pounded on the door till he answered, and I told him I needed help before I hurt myself." I sighed. "You already know this shit. Why are we going over it again?"

"I have a point." She pursed her lips. "And he said…?"

"'No shit, dude. You look like a fucking zombie.'" My lips twitched into a reluctant smile. "Then he hugged me, made me shower, and I slept for a day and a half. I made an appointment to see you, and I've been getting better every day. Really getting better, not just trying to."

"And you haven't thought about ending it all again?"

"No, not even once." I dragged a hand down my face. "Does that mean I'm ready? Is that your point?"

"I don't know. When you saw her with Riley, did you want to hurt yourself?"

"What? No." I shook my head. "I was upset, but I'm done with that portion of my recovery, if you could call it that. I don't even think about it anymore. It won't make the pain go away. Nothing will. I miss my dad. Miss my friends. And I miss her the most, because she's still here, but not with me."

"What do you do instead of thinking about hurting yourself?"

"I accept the pain. Deal with it. Move the fuck on." I tugged on my hair. "Life is full of shit. There's not much to be done for it, and I've accepted it. My PTSD isn't gone, but I'm coping."

"What are your plans for the future?"

I laughed. "I have no idea. I'm out of the Marines, thanks to my injuries, and I'm not in private security anymore."

"Do you want to be in either one?"

"I got offered a job with a private security firm." I shrugged. "I said no."

She nodded. "Why did you do that?"

"It was in Chicago." I paused, knowing what she wanted to hear from me. "She's here, in California. Why would I move there?"

"Ah, so you don't want to leave her, but you don't want to be with her?"

"I never said that," I snapped. "I said I wasn't sure if I would be best for her. That's why I'm here, asking you if I'm ready. If I can try to get her to forgive me yet or not."

She pushed her glasses up on her nose, her green eyes on me. "If she rejected you, would the pain send you spiraling again? Would you want to hurt yourself? Drink a few bottles of beer? Pop a few pills? Buy a rope?"

"No. I don't know. I don't think so." I scrubbed my face with my hands. "I love her. That's all I fucking know. Every day I spend away from her is a day I'm in hell."

"Sometimes loving someone is letting them go," she said softly, her eyes still on me. "I can't tell you whether you're better for her than this Riley guy is. No one can, except for her. Maybe you *should* talk to her. Test it out. Let her decide this time, since you decided for her last time."

My heart twisted at the thought of going up to her. Actually saying hello. Seeing if she hated me. Oh, fuck. What if she looked at me with hatred shining in those pretty blue eyes I loved so much? What then? "She could despise me," I rasped. "What if she can't even look at me without wanting to punch me?"

"Then that's a cross you'll have to bear," she said, taking her glasses off. "The question is, do you want to know for sure, or do you want to spend your whole life wondering what would have happened if only you'd said hello?"

I swallowed. "I don't know. Can't you just tell me what's better? Fix it?"

"I'm sorry, but I can't do that," she said, smiling a sad smile at me. "This one's up to you."

I stood and dragged a hand through my hair. "Fine. I'll think about it."

"I look forward to hearing which option you chose on Tuesday." She also stood up, smoothing her black skirt. "But Griffin?"

"Yeah?"

"Don't jump blindly into either choice. If you do see her, make sure you take things slow. You have to remember: She thinks you don't love her. You broke her heart into pieces, no matter how honorable your intentions might have been. These things take time to heal. Even if she rejects your offer of friendship at first, try to be patient. She might come around." She pointed her pen at me. "And that's all you should offer in the beginning. Friendship. Another chance to get things right. No rushing into anything in a single day."

I nodded. "Thanks, Doc."

"Good luck."

I left the office, paid my copay, and stepped out into the sunlight. Squinting into the brightness, I headed for my bike. It had taken a while for my arm to heal, but now I could act like myself again. I rode my bike. I hung with Hernandez. But...

I didn't have a job. Didn't have a plan. Didn't have Carrie.

I scanned the crowd on Ocean Drive, looking for a redhead out of habit more than anything. I knew she was around her somewhere, eating breakfast with Riley. The desire to find out where she was hit me pretty strong, but I shook it off. If and when I saw her again, it wouldn't be with Riley watching. We would be alone.

Maybe I'd buy her some flowers.

I revved the engine, looking over my shoulder at the spot where Carrie used to sit. There hadn't been another woman in my life since her. Even at rock bottom, I couldn't let myself fall even lower. Carrie owned my heart, and no other woman would do.

It had to be *her*, damn it.

"Hey, how did it go?" Hernandez shouted in my ear from behind me.

Jumping, I looked over my shoulder, shut off the engine, and frowned at him. "Aren't you supposed to be guarding Carrie?"

"I am. She's in that restaurant." He pointed over his shoulder at a restaurant that was about three hundred feet away. "With Riley the Perfect."

I picked up my helmet. "Shit, man. I gotta go before she sees me."

"So you're not allowed to approach her yet?"

140

"It's not that." I gripped my helmet tight. "I don't know what I'm doing yet, but I'm not making rash decisions this time."

Hernandez grinned. "That sounds like a therapist talking."

"It was her advice." I lifted a shoulder. "It seemed like it made sense, so I'm gonna take it. And while I might say hi to her at some point, it won't be while she's on a date with another guy."

Hernandez nodded. "She almost saw you last night, when she kissed Riley and you knocked over that damn pot with your elbow."

I flinched. "Yeah. I wasn't watching where I was going."

I'd been too busy watching her *kiss* Riley.

"I noticed," Hernandez said dryly.

The restaurant door opened, making a bell jingle. Both Hernandez and I turned slowly. I knew it was going to be her. Just knew it. She walked out, holding Riley's hand and laughing, and a fist punched in my chest. Riley's eyes latched with mine, but Carrie didn't look this way.

I knew the second he realized it was me. He paled and went all tense.

I slammed my helmet over my head and started my engine, watching as Hernandez headed her way without another word to me. She still didn't see me, so I revved the bike and took off. As I passed her, I saw her turn my way with wide eyes, her mouth parted. She spun as I passed, following me with her eyes. I drove faster.

If I didn't get away now, I'd go back.

And I'd beg her to love me again, Riley be damned.

CHAPTER NINETEEN

Carrie

I walked Riley to his car with my mind a million miles away on the motorcyclist that I was ninety-nine percent sure had been Finn. I hadn't seen his face or anything, but there was no doubt in my mind that I'd seen Finn today.

Same type of bike. Same type of build. Same helmet.

"You're thinking about that guy on the bike, aren't you?" Riley asked, his voice level. "I saw him, you know. Before he put the helmet on."

I stopped walking. "Wait. What?"

"I know you're not mentioning it because you don't want to hurt my feelings, but you're dying to know if it was Finn." He met my eyes. He looked so handsome in the sunlight. So tall and perfect. It almost made me sick to my stomach just looking up at him. "I can tell you, if you want."

I sucked in a shaky breath. "I'm sorry. I know you want—"

"Sh." He hugged me close, resting his cheek on the top of my head. It was intimate and yet withdrawn at the same time. "We both know what I want, but it doesn't mean you have to give it to me. If you still have feelings for him…"

"Sometimes, I wish you were Finn. That you'd been sent here to protect me, not him." I rested my hands on his arms. "It would be so much easier."

"Me too." He tilted my face up to his. "Maybe you could move on from the past at some point, though? From his hold over you?"

I swallowed past my aching throat. I wasn't sure how to answer that. "I don't know. He still owns the majority of my feelings; I know that. I don't know what I feel for him anymore, but he fills my head all the time."

"Fair enough." He stared at my mouth, his eyes darkening. "How about one more kiss before I go?"

Before I could answer, his lips were on mine again. He kissed me, and it felt good. I even felt a little bit of desire stirring within me. But it just wasn't Finn.

It wasn't fair.

He deepened the kiss, his tongue touching mine. Even though I wanted to pull away, to end it, I kissed him back. Heck, I even pulled him closer. I owed it to both of us to at least try to feel something here. To try to get over Finn. Something within me came to life, a small flicker of something, but it almost wasn't strong enough to notice.

I curled my hands behind his neck, moaning into his mouth, and he crushed me against his chest. When he groaned and cupped my butt, hauling me closer against his erection, desire hit me pretty hard, but it didn't feel *right*. Panic crept up my throat, choking me. I gasped and lurched back, my hand covering my mouth. "I'm s-sorry. I can't. N-Not yet."

"I'm sorry. I got carried away." He gave me a small smile. "But that was perfect. Just perfect, Carrie."

Yeah. Perfect. "I know. It was…nice." *Nice won't make you scream out in bed, Ginger.* "Unexpected, even."

He grinned. "I'll take it."

"Riley…" My heart wrenched. "Was it him?"

The grin slipped away. I felt like crap for asking, but I had to know. He slid his shades in place. "Yeah. It was Finn. He looked better than the last time we saw him. More whole." He looked away. "Are you going to get back together with him now?"

"No." I shook my head for emphasis. "Absolutely not. He's over me."

Riley hesitated. "I'm killing my own case here, but I have to be honest or I'll never be able to live with myself. The way he looked at you today? He didn't look *over* you. He looked like he wanted you back, Carrie."

A small thrill shot through me, but I stifled it. He'd hurt me. Broke my heart. Even if he was regretting it now, it didn't mean I would fall into his arms and hug him.

My heart was still broken.

"Well, it's a little too late for that now." I crossed my arms and forced a smile. If I were smart, I'd fall for Riley. I'd forget all about the boy who'd broken my heart. If only my darn heart would get the memo. "Thanks for visiting me this weekend. I had fun."

"Should we do it again soon?"

I hesitated. My heart said *no*, but my mind screamed *yes*. "You know I'm still not over him, right? I can't commit to you fully yet."

"But you could in the future? I could definitely work with those odds. I'm a gambling man when the occasion calls for it."

I bit down on my lip. "I want to, but I can't promise anything."

"Especially since he's back."

"That's not why—"

"Carrie. I get it. You loved him, and still do—maybe, kind of, sort of." He cupped my cheek, his thumb resting on my chin. It made me think of how Finn used to do something similar, but he'd run his thumb over my lower lip instead. My stomach clenched tight at the memory. "Those feelings might come back to the front if he comes to see you. And if that does happen, that's okay. I know what I'm up against, but unless you get back together with him? I'm not going anywhere. I'm determined to throw my hat in the ring, or whatever people say nowadays."

Tears filled my eyes, but I laughed. "You're too good for me."

Funny. Finn used to say that to me all the time. I finally understood what he meant now. Hindsight was twenty-twenty, after all.

"Nah. I'm just patient and understanding and...okay, maybe I'm a little too good." He kissed me, smiling against my lips when I laughed again. "I'll call you later this week to see if you want to get together. No pressure or anything, but I'll be expecting a yes. Don't break my heart, Carrie."

I shook my head at his teasing. "Okay."

After watching him drive away, I headed back toward my dorm. Hernandez stepped out from the shadows once I got close to him, a disinterested look in his eyes. "Here."

"Um...thanks." I took what he handed to me. It was a small rose. "You're giving me a rose?"

He rolled his eyes. "No. Read the little paper."

I opened the tiny scrap of paper that someone had wrapped around it. *Keep smiling.* I looked up at Hernandez, feeling more confused than anything. "Who gave you this?"

"No one. I found it on your car, so I took it off to make sure it wasn't a death threat or something."

I blinked down at it. It was yellow. Yellow roses were my favorite. "Maybe it was from Riley?"

He looked away. "Maybe," he mumbled. "So. What's next for today?"

I sniffed the rose and walked toward my car. "I don't know." I stole a glance at him. "Have you seen Marie this morning? Is she back at the dorm?"

"I don't know. Last I saw, she was out with some guy getting coffee." Hernandez tightened his fists. "She was wearing the same clothes she had on last night."

"Oh. That must have been Sean. He seems like a nice enough guy." When Hernandez clenched his jaw, I looked over at him. "You know, if you want her, you should just ask her out before she gets serious with some other guy—maybe even Sean. Right now, they're having fun. There aren't feelings involved or anything."

He gave me an incredulous look. "Why in the hell would I want to do that?"

"Because you seem to like her. And believe it or not? I think she likes you, too." I stopped at my door. "You should ask her out already. We'd planned on doing a double date when Finn came home, if you recall. We can't double-date anymore, but you could take her out without me."

He frowned at me. "Yeah, I don't think so. We would be horrible together."

"If you say so."

"I do." He leaned on the passenger side. "So, you staying in, or going out?"

"Um..." I looked up at the sky. It was a pretty warm day, and there was a good breeze for an early spring morning. I hadn't been surfing since...well, since Finn. Suddenly, it seemed like the best idea ever to get out there again. To do something that I hadn't done in months. To get back to living. "Actually, I'm going to go surfing."

His brows slammed down. "You can't. Finn said you're not allowed to go out without him."

"He did, yes, back when he was my bodyguard and my boyfriend. He isn't either of those things anymore." I raised my brows. "So why should it matter? It's irrelevant."

"Carrie…" He frowned. "You can't go out there alone. Finn had his reasons for not wanting you out there alone, no matter where he is or what he's doing now."

Or who he's doing it with, I added in my head.

"Yeah, well, I don't care what his reasons are. I'm an adult, and he isn't my boss, boyfriend, or father." I crossed my arms, the rose still in my hand. "Last time I checked, he didn't have any say on what I did with myself. Not since he walked away. If I want to surf, I'll freaking surf. You can't stop me."

He dropped his head back and glared up at the sky. "Days like this? I hate my fucking job even more."

"Sorry." I opened the door. "But I'm going anyway."

I climbed up the stairs, feeling free. Feeling light. And for the first time in a while, I was excited about something. I pushed open my door and headed for my bikini and wetsuit. Marie sat on the bed, reading a biology book. "Hey. Whatcha doing?"

"I'm going surfing." I grinned over my shoulder at her and tossed the yellow rose on my pillow. "What are you up to besides doing the walk of shame at a coffee shop?"

She flushed. "Nothing like that happened. I just fell asleep at Sean's place." Then she paused. "Wait. How did you know I got coffee this morning?"

"Besides the cup in your hand? Hernandez saw you." I yanked my shirt over my head. "You might want to look away. I'm about to be naked."

She huffed and turned away. "Why the hell is he watching *me* now? Who does he think he is? He doesn't work for *my* dad."

"I don't think he was watching you." I took my bra off and slipped the bikini in its place. "He just happened to come across you."

"Well, he can just happen to kiss my ass, too." Marie set her coffee down hard. "Is he out there?"

"Yep. He's pissed because I'm surfing."

She stood up. She had on a pair of short shorts and combat boots, paired with a flowing purple tank top. She looked beautiful in her anger. It brought a color to her cheeks that had been missing before. "He's about to be even more pissed after I'm done with him."

She stormed out without another word. I blinked after her.

"Okay, then," I muttered. After I finished changing, I grabbed my board and headed downstairs. I passed Cory, but ignored him. We were *so* done, no matter how much he knew about me. My bullshit meter had filled up and overflowed. I came through the doors just in time to see Marie stomping away from Hernandez. He watched her with a confused look on his face, shaking his head. I almost felt sorry for him.

I walked right by him. "I'm going now."

"I don't like this." He walked beside me, glaring the whole time. "You shouldn't be out there alone."

"I'll be fine. Turns out, I kinda like being alone. There's no one to boss me around, and no one to let down. " I flipped my hair over my shoulder and unlocked the car. "You can watch from the beach if you'd like. Want a ride?"

He sighed. "Sure. Why not?"

The whole time we drove to the beach, my heart raced. I was actually going to do this. Go out there without Finn. It was exhilarating. Scary. Fun. And more importantly, it would prove I didn't need him anymore. I didn't need him to have fun. If I could do this, well, I could move on. I could be free of him.

Maybe, with time, I could even be happy again.

I pulled into my normal spot. There weren't a lot of people out there in the water. It was too late for optimal waves, but I didn't care. I was going to have fun anyway. I hopped out of my car and grabbed my board, closing my eyes and inhaling the fresh beach smell. On the West Coast, it smelled so clean. Crisp, even. The waves crashed on the sand, creating a soothing sound that never ceased to calm my nerves. Today was no exception. I kicked off my flip-flops, eager to get my bare toes in the sand again.

Hernandez shoved his phone in his pocket and scanned the beach. "Where do you surf?"

"Out there." I pointed to my normal spot. It's where Finn had always taken me, and I couldn't imagine going anywhere else. Maybe it was habit; maybe it was sentiment. Maybe I was a glutton for punishment. All I knew was I liked the memories, as painful as they might be at times. "See? There's even a bench over there where you can sit and watch."

He nodded. "Don't kill yourself, or *he'll* kill *me*."

"Don't worry, my dad will never know you let me surf," I called over my shoulder, tossing my flip-flops at him. "Hold these, will ya?"

"Yes, ma'am," he called out sarcastically. "Want me to braid your hair and tell you all my secrets, too?"

I ignored him, grinning as I headed for the surf. As soon as my feet touched the water, I laughed out loud. This was it. This was what I'd needed today. I swam out to the optimal surfing point and climbed on my board. Wringing my hair out, I tilted my face up to the sun, letting it all soak in. Letting the freedom hit me.

I could do this. I could move on. Get over him.

Try again.

"Hey, Ginger." A shadow fell over me, and for a second I thought I was imagining things again. Hearing things. "You know you're not supposed to be out here alone."

I opened my eyes slowly, as if I might find out I'd imagined the whole thing if I dared to peek. It was him. *Finn.* My heart lurched, painfully accelerating so hard it seemed as if it was trying to jump out of my chest and back into his hands where it used to be.

I scanned him, looking for any signs of the haunted man he'd used to be. He still had the scars. Still looked tired as hell. His brown hair had grown in a bit; looking about the same length as it had been last time he'd gone to drill. And his arm was out of the cast. He wasn't wearing dog tags. In fact, he wore nothing but his black wetsuit and a cautious look in his eyes. He looked good. Healthy. Happy.

Holy. Freaking. Crap.

CHAPTER TWENTY

Finn

I watched her, my heart pounding in my ears full speed ahead. I hadn't been planning on saying hello to her. I'd been planning on watching her from far, far away. Hernandez had texted me to let me know she was going out in the water, and I'd rushed so I could get there before her. Waiting. Watching. Guarding.

The usual.

But then I'd seen her, sitting in the sun, looking pretty as hell with her wild red hair blowing in the breeze, and something inside me had broken. Maybe it was something that had been holding me back, restraint even. But now that she was out here, in my territory, there was no holding back.

Her hair was longer, reaching all the way down to the small of her back while wet, and it looked even darker than before since it was damp. Her blue eyes looked bluer than I remembered, too. Fucking gorgeous. That's what she was. She was perfection, while I was not. I was finally starting to be okay with that fact, though. That I wasn't perfect and never would be.

She was just staring at me.

Finally, she seemed to snap out of it. She licked her gorgeous lips, her gaze skimming over me all over again. Did she like what she saw? I'd grown my hair longer for her. It helped camouflage my scar a little. That had to help my appearance somewhat.

She shook her head slightly. When she spoke, her voice came out hoarse. "You…You're *here.*"

"I am." I tugged on my hair, watching her. "I've been here for a while, actually. A little over a month now, I guess. Maybe two."

It had been two months, one day, three hours, and twelve minutes, to be exact. She didn't say anything. Just stared at me, not moving besides the lull of the waves that made her board sway. I cleared my throat. "Did you get my flower?"

She blinked at that. "That was from you?"

"Yeah." I rubbed my head. "I left it on your car earlier."

"W-Why?"

I shrugged. "Because I wanted to."

"I…see. Why come back out here?" She met my eyes again. "Instead of staying in D.C.?"

"There's nothing for me in D.C. anymore."

She cocked her head. "And there's something for you here?"

"Yes." *You. I love you. Take me back. Forgive me. Make me whole again.* "The weather's nicer. And there's surfing. Hernandez. My bike…" *You.*

"I see." She stared at me, not moving. "You—" She cleared her throat. "You look good. Better. Are you?"

I couldn't believe she was being so damn polite. "Thanks. Yeah, I am." My heart twisted and turned. "You look beautiful, as always. So fucking beautiful."

"Th-Thank you." She took a deep breath, color slowly coming back to her cheeks. "I don't know what to say to you right now. This feels weird."

I tried to smile at her. It probably came across as a grimace mixed with a grin. It hurt to feel so damn awkward around her. We'd never been like this. "A little bit, yeah. But we've never had to deal with the aftermath of…after saying all that we said."

"And you never snuck away in the middle of the night on me, either," she said slowly, her bright eyes still on me.

"About that?" I looked down at my hands. Should I tell her it was all a lie? That I'd been trying to save her from me? Would she even fucking care? Time to find out. "I fucked up. I never meant—"

"Don't." She glared at me. Now she was pissed. *This* is what I'd expected to see. "Don't go apologizing or backpedaling. And don't you dare try to take it back. You said how you felt, and you left. I shouldn't have even brought it up. You caught me off guard, is all." She let her hand fall back to the board. "I wasn't expecting to see you out here. Actually, I wasn't expecting to see you at all. I told you not to check on me, remember? Said I didn't want to see you again."

Yeah. I remembered. But I couldn't stay away. "I'm sorry. I really am." I twisted my lips. "It's not safe for you to be surfing alone. You know that, Ginger."

She lifted her chin, her blue eyes flaring with anger and maybe a hint of something else. Sadness, maybe. "I'm fine on my own, thank you very much. I've been just fine without you here watching over me, and I'll continue to be fine. I don't need you watching me to make sure I don't drown. I have Hernandez."

I gripped the surfboard. I'd been right. She was fine without me. Didn't need me like I needed her. "Hernandez can't fucking surf."

"Yeah, but he can swim. And even if he couldn't? Even if I drowned out here? That's my problem, not yours." She looked away. "You're not my guard or my boyfriend anymore, so stop acting like you're either one."

I flinched. "I know you're not mine anymore. That's not why I'm here. I was planning on surfing already. You're not the only one who surfs on weekends, if you recall. I'm the one who brought you here in the first place."

She bit down hard on her lip, looking flustered and upset with my reappearance in her life. I shouldn't have said hi, damn it. She fingered her necklace, and I stared at in in disbelief. It was the one I'd given her. She still wore it. "You weren't supposed to come find me. I told you—"

"You're wearing our necklace," I said, my voice sounding way too fucking weak. "You didn't throw it away after I left?"

She dropped it immediately. "No. I didn't throw it away." Her cheeks red, she looked away from me. "I-I forgot all about it, honestly."

Something told me that wasn't true. She was lying to me. She knew she was wearing it, and she wore it because it reminded her of me. I knew it. Happiness rushed through my veins. For the first time in months, I let myself believe I stood a chance with her. Let myself believe I might be able to make her love me again.

God knows I needed her to feel alive.

"Ginger. Fuck, I miss you so—"

"*Don't.*" She shook her head, her eyes spitting sharp blades of fire my way. "You don't get to say that to me. Just leave me alone. I'm out here for some peace and quiet, not for a trip down memory lane. We've 'caught up,'" she used her fingers to make quotations marks, "enough. Now go back to leaving me alone, like we agreed upon."

I gripped my board tighter. "I can't leave you."

"You didn't have that issue in D.C." She glowered at me, her eyes still spitting fire. "I haven't forgotten what you said, and I'm sure you haven't forgotten what I said. Goodbye, Finn."

She closed her eyes, obviously intending to ignore me until I left. I sat there quietly, not so much as making a splash, letting my heart break some more. Hell, I was used to it now. After a while, she cracked her eye open and looked at me. I inclined my head and looked her over, trying to act as if there was nothing strange about us being out here alone again. "Yeah, I'm still here."

"I see that," she said, frustration clear in her voice. "What are you trying to do, Finn? What do you want from me? Is there a point to this visit?"

"I wanted to see you again," I said, my voice light. Just being near her, talking to her, felt like fucking heaven. I missed her so damn much. I tugged on my hair. "It's the first time I felt strong enough to come up to you. I didn't want to come back till I was better."

Her gaze flew to mine. "And you're better now?"

"I think so." I swallowed hard. "How have you been, though?"

She turned her head away, hiding her pretty face from mine. "Ask Hernandez how I'm doing if you want to know." She glowered toward where he sat on a bench by the beach. He looked like he was texting someone, or surfing the web instead of the ocean. "I'm sure he could tell you everything you want to know about me."

"I'm not asking him anything. I'm asking you." I hesitated. "I know I'm not supposed to say it, but I've missed you, Ginger. So damn much."

"You really shouldn't call me that anymore," she said, her voice breaking. "It's not right. We're not together, and that was what you called me when—" She broke off, rubbing her hand on her forehead. "It's not right."

"I'm sorry. So fucking sorry." I swallowed hard, my throat aching with the pain I'd caused her. I wanted to wrap her up in my arms and never let go again. To love her like I should have all those months ago. "I never wanted to do this to you. To us."

She looked at me again. The pain in those baby blues hurt. "But you did it anyway."

"I did." I nodded once. "I wish I could take it all away, Carrie. I really do."

"Well, you can't. It's over. When you told me—" She broke off, shaking her head. "You know what? I'm not saying it. Not fighting with you. Our days of fighting are over. We're over. You saw to that."

I gritted my teeth so hard it hurt. "I know. I'll never stop regretting it, and I will never get over it. Over you."

She made a small sound. "Don't go there."

"Why not?" I paddled closer to her. "Are you and Riley an item now?"

She stiffened and held her hand out, wanting me to stay away, I could only assume. "That's not any of your business. *You're* the one who broke up with *me*. That means you don't get to ask about my personal life anymore."

I narrowed my gaze on her. "I might not be your boyfriend anymore, but it doesn't mean I'm fucking blind, deaf, or dumb." I paddled closer, despite her upheld hand. "I saw you kissing him. You looked like you liked it."

She turned to me, her eyes wide. "You were there?"

"Have you ever known Hernandez to knock over a fucking pot?" I asked, raising a brow. I stopped when I was three feet away from her. Close enough to touch, but not so close that I would. "I knocked it over when I backed away, not wanting to watch you 'moving on.' Not wanting to accept that you could be happy with someone besides me when I'm so fucking miserable without you."

"Then you shouldn't have looked," she snapped, her cheeks flushed. "You don't get to come here and swoop in, trying to make me fall into your arms again. It's not going to happen."

I gripped the surfboard. "Tell me about it."

"And how dare you ask me about my love life? Because I'm *so* sure you've been perfectly celibate since you left me," she said, her grip tight on the board. She might be acting as if she was making a point, but I could tell she was dying to know. "You haven't touched a single girl since you left me, right?"

"I haven't wanted another woman at all," I said, dropping my voice low. "I haven't been with anyone else since the first moment you kissed me on my curb. I swear it on my father's grave."

She stared at me, her eyes wide and her lips parted. For a second, just a second, her eyes softened. She didn't look angry. But then she shook her head and glanced away. "It doesn't matter."

Pain sliced through me. It didn't matter to her that I'd been faithful to her? She didn't care anymore. "No, I guess not."

Her back remained ramrod straight. "How long have you been watching me?"

"For a little while. I've been trying to stay away, though. Trying to let you move on." I cleared my throat. "I saw you at the window, when you thought you saw me. It was the night I decided to fix myself."

I didn't mention the wanting-to-kill-myself part. It wasn't necessary.

She frowned at me. "Did you drive away like you did this morning?"

"Ah." I leaned back on my board, relaxing my stance. "You saw me, huh?"

"Of course I saw you," she said, her eyes glaring at me. God, I loved it when she looked at me like that. All fiery and passionate and *hot*. "You were on your bike and you drove right past me. It was kind of hard to miss."

"Riley saw me." I cocked my head. "Did he tell you that he saw me, or did he hide that fact from you?"

She pressed her lips together. "Yeah, he told me it was you. He would never lie to me, unlike you."

Of course he'd told her I was back. Riley was that kind of guy. It made me fucking sick. "He's a good guy. Far better than me. I've never denied that."

"I know he is." She lifted her chin. "I'm *trying* to like him. To care for him as more than friends. You showing up isn't making it any easier on me."

Delight hit me, hard and swift. So she didn't have feelings for him yet. That meant I wasn't too late. I laughed. "If you have to try, it isn't fucking working. There's this thing called *chemistry* between a man and a woman. It's either there, or it isn't. I don't remember us having to *try* to like each other."

"Yeah, and that worked out so well for us, didn't it?" She glowered my way. "Life is just a bucket of sunshine and rainbows now."

"Love isn't always easy," I said, silently begging her to realize that we weren't done yet. I hadn't been thinking clearly. I'd messed up, and I knew it. If she gave me another chance, I'd never let her go again. "I made a mistake back in D.C. One I've regretted since the moment I sobered up enough to realize what I'd done. I shouldn't have left you. *Ever.*"

She closed her eyes. "But you did."

"I know. Believe me, I fucking know it." I reached out and tried to grab her hands, but she lurched back. I let mine fall back to my lap, empty.

Tears slipped down her cheeks. "*You broke my heart.*"

"I broke mine, too." I dragged my hands down my face, releasing a ragged breath. "I was fucked up. More so than I ever let you see. You have no idea how dark I was."

"Which was the problem. You didn't let me in." She swiped her hand across her cheeks with jerky motions. "You didn't trust me, or trust in our love. You just lied and left."

"I know. But if you give—"

She shook her head, her whole body tense. "Don't. Don't ask me that."

"*Please.*"

She covered her face, shaking her head. "I can't do this right now. I was getting better. I was finally feeling alive again. And now you're here, telling me you're sorry? What am I supposed to do with that?"

"Forgive me," I said, my voice raw. "Give me another chance."

"To what? Leave me again? Lie some more?" She looked at me, her eyes shining with tears. "You have no idea what that did to me, because you just *walked away.*"

"I know." I held my hands out. "I'm sorry. I can't say I'm sorry enough times, I know, but I am."

"That doesn't mean you get me back." She lifted her chin. "Riley wouldn't hurt me. He wouldn't leave me broken hearted."

"Only because you don't love him," I said, frustration coursing through me. "He can't hurt you if he doesn't have that power over you."

"Which is why he's the better choice," she cried out. "I don't want to be in love anymore. Love isn't worth the pain. Not if it hurts like this. It isn't safe. It's not real. It leaves all too fast, as soon as one person decides they're done." She pressed her hand to her chest, tears streaming down her face. "I can't do this anymore. I don't want to be in pain. I don't want to be in love."

"You don't have to be in pain anymore," I whispered, reaching out for her hand. "I can make it better, and you can make me better, too. I was *always* better with you."

She shook her head and yanked her fingers out of reach at the last second. "No, you weren't. You were miserable. Always trying to change yourself for me and my dad." She looked over her shoulder. I knew what she was doing. She was going to escape. "You think you want me, but you don't. Not really."

"*No.*" I grabbed her knee, my fingers firm on her. "I'm better with you. Don't fucking leave me."

She shoved my hand off with her elbow. "No, you're not. Look what happened to you when you were with me. You were broken and beaten and at the lowest point in your life. I brought you nothing but pain, and you did the same to me."

"My pain wasn't because of you," I argued. "You made me so fucking happy."

"It was because of *me!*" She shouted, tears still running down her cheeks. "You tried to change for me. It's my fault you got injured. It's all my fault, Finn! You left me, and then you got better. Don't you see? We're no good for each other. It's *over.*"

I wanted to push her further. To see if she still had feelings for me, but then she looked at me with tears in her bright eyes. "You're wrong. Don't do this."

She laid down on the board and started forward. "You left me, and you're better off for it. Look in the mirror if you don't believe me."

"I'm only better because of you." I curled my hands into fists, yanking on my hair. "You saved me, even without you at my side, it was you who saved me that night."

She paddled faster and called over her shoulder, "I'm no good for you. Go be happy with someone else. You won't find your happily ever after with me anymore."

She rode the wave away. I could have followed her. Could have forced her to continue this conversation, but I sensed it wouldn't go the way I wanted it to. I'd have to bide my time and wait till she was ready to see me again.

But I wasn't giving up on us. Not again.

I wouldn't make that mistake twice.

CHAPTER TWENTY-ONE

Carrie

A few days later, on Friday afternoon, I came out of my last class of the day and found Marie standing outside the exit. She fidgeted while nibbling on her lower lip. As I approached, I noticed she looked upset. I hurried to her side, not sure what was going on. "Hey, what's up?"

She grabbed my hands. "He's there. At our room. Waiting for you again. Just like he has been every single day since he came back. With a pink rose this time."

Finn. Every single day, he'd shown up at my door and asked me to go out to eat with him. Or surfing. Or to the soup kitchen. And he always had a flower with a cute little message on it. *Keep smiling. Don't give up. You make me happy. Forgive me.*

He wasn't giving up. And I was scared one of these times I'd give in.

I smoothed my hair and blotted my recently glossed lips. Pink today. "Seriously?"

"Seriously." Marie eyed me. "But I have a feeling you knew that. Is that a new shirt you're wearing?"

I tugged at it. "No. Yes. Maybe."

"Don't do it. Don't give in," she warned. "He'll hurt you."

The night he came back, I'd told her how Finn had showed back up in my life, after radio silence for months. Once her surprise wore off, she'd

161

been angry at him for bombarding me like that. I'd listened to her rant and rave and call him names, but the whole time, I'd been thinking about him—and I hadn't been calling him names.

I'd been too busy thinking about how he looked better. How he'd filled out a little bit more again, since he'd been so skinny when he came home. I'd been thinking about how his hair was short, but long enough for me to run my fingers through it as he kissed me. But mostly, I'd been thinking about how wonderful he'd looked sitting on that surfboard.

Too bad he'd only gotten better after he left me.

"What should we do?" Marie asked, wringing her hands. "I told him to leave, like usual, but he just stared me down…like usual."

I sighed. "Right now? I'm going to go eat. If he's still there when I get back, I'll deal with him just like all the other times." I paused. "Pink, huh?"

"Yep. Pink." Finn came around the corner, holding out a pink rose. "Oh, and *he's* not there anymore. He's here, and he's starving, too. Let's go eat."

I narrowed my eyes on him, not taking the rose. "You're not coming."

He wiggled the rose. It had a note attached, like usual. I still didn't take it. "Come on, Ginger. You know you want it."

He wore a light blue T-shirt with a motorcycle on it and a pair of ripped jeans. He had on black shades, and he looked freaking hot. Way too hot for me to keep pushing him away. Damn him. His ink swirled up his biceps, and I knew exactly how they intertwined on his chest, right near the tattoo he'd gotten for me.

He'd never seen the one I'd gotten for him.

"No, I don't," I responded, gripping my bag. "I thought I was perfectly clear yesterday, and the day before that, and the day before that, and all the other days that you've showed up at my place with a present, that I'm *not* interested in restarting our relationship."

"Liar."

He stepped into my space, and his cologne washed over me. I closed my eyes, savoring the familiar scent. Smelling him like this made me want to throw myself into his arms and beg him to never leave me again. It made me want to forget.

"I'm the liar?" I snapped, whirling on my heel and ignoring him. I felt so freaking alive right now, with him next to me provoking me all

162

over again.

Marie walked with me, shooting Finn an anxious look. "Hey, thanks for stopping by, but we're going to go eat now."

He grinned at Marie. "Good. I'm starving. Take the flower."

"Dude," Marie looked at him, her eyes wide. "We didn't invite you, and she doesn't want the flower."

"Sure she does," he said, frowning at Marie. "She loves flowers. They make her happy. So do inspirational messages. She used to get one sent to her phone every day."

"I still do," I said, my heart picking up speed. "That's why you give me little notes?"

"Yeah." He held his hand out. "Please take it."

I reached out and took his flower, my hand so tight on the stem that a thorn dug into my palm. "Th-Thanks."

"Don't mention it." He shoved his hands in his pockets, still walking beside me. "I know pink isn't your favorite color to wear, but it reminded me of the hangers I got you. Remember those?"

Of course I remembered them. He'd gotten them for me so I could keep clothes at his place. Ignoring his question, I opened the little note he'd attached to the stem. *I'm sorry.* Swallowing hard, I looked back up at him. "Finn..."

He locked gazes with me. "Wanna go to Islands with me? I have my Harley here. We can take the back roads, like we used to. Enjoy the fresh spring air that God gave us today. It would be a shame to miss out on it."

I stopped walking and curled my fist even tighter on the pink rose. God, yes, I wanted to get on his bike with him. Of course I did. But that's why I couldn't. "No, thank you."

He *tsk*ed me. "Carrie Wallington, I'm ashamed of you. You've lost your fun streak since I left. Your desire for adventure is dead." He took his sunglasses off and walked backward, his gaze locked with mine. "The Carrie I knew wouldn't turn down a ride from me, even if she was pissed. Get on the bike. You know you want to."

I shook my head, but he was right. I really freaking wanted to. "That was before we broke up. I'm not her anymore."

"You'd have gotten on the damn bike before. You changed."

"Says the man who broke up with me because I *hadn't* changed while he had," I said, crossing my arms over my chest. "Be careful what you wish for."

He held his hands out at his sides, pouting at me. Actually. Pouting. He used to give it to me back when we were dating and he wanted to get his way on something. I couldn't resist that look, darn it. Not now. Not then. Not ever. "Ginger, get on the bike. Let's go for a ride for old time's sake."

I wavered. I knew he sensed it, too, because his eyes lit up. "*No.*"

Marie watched us both, looking about as happy as a kid stuck between two quarrelling parents. "This isn't awkward for me at all," she drawled, studying her nails. "Want me to leave?"

"Yes," Finn said.

"No," I said at the same time. "Stay right there."

She craned her neck. "Oh, look. It's Hernandez. I'm going to go fight with him for a little bit."

She took off like her butt was on fire. "*Marie,*" I called out. But it was useless. She wasn't coming back. I turned on Finn, my hands clenched at my sides. "You need to stop doing this."

"I can't." He leaned against the side of the building. "I miss you."

I closed my eyes. "You need to stop saying that."

"Fine. Then make me *not* miss you." I sensed him moving closer, so I snapped my eyes open. He froze. "Go on a ride with me."

"I *can't.*"

"Just one little ride." He reached out and pushed a tendril of hair behind my ear. "I promise to behave myself. Come on. You miss it, don't you?"

"It doesn't matter if I do," I said. "I'm not going anywhere with you."

"If you go with me and hate it," he said, clenching his jaw. "I'll stop coming by your dorm. I'll stop giving you messages and flowers. I'll leave you alone."

I swallowed hard. He'd leave me alone? No more flowers and inspirational notes? The idea was as tempting as it was painful. I was such a mess of emotions right now that I didn't know which way was up and which way was down anymore. "I don't know. There's too much…" *Love. Pain. Desire.*

When I didn't finish my sentence, he offered me a small smile. "Well, let's find out. If you still hate me when we're done, and don't want to see me again, I'll back off. Give you some time and space. Stop showing up every day." He held his hand out. "Let's go for a ride and for some lunch. You're done with classes for the day."

I frowned at him, not bothering to admit I didn't hate him. I could never truly hate him. "Someone has an inside source."

"Maybe." He shrugged. "What can I say? You're my favorite subject."

"Then you shouldn't have dropped out." I walked past him. "I'll go with you, but then you'll be leaving me alone. Be prepared. And friends don't hold hands, Coram."

He laughed and followed me, sounding way too happy for someone who was about to be told to hit the road. "Fair enough."

I looked at him again, unable to believe this was the same Finn who had broken up with me. "Why are you acting so normal now?"

He stole a glance at me. His blue eyes shined even brighter in the sunlight, making them seem unrealistically blue. "I told you, I'm better. I go to a therapist now, just like you suggested I should," he said softly. "She's helping me a lot."

I nodded. "I'm glad." I stole another glance at him. "And your arm?"

"Better." He looked down at it, wiggling his fingers. "I only get aches here and there. The headaches are a bitch, though."

I frowned. "You still get them?"

"I'm told I'll always get them." He shrugged. "But I'm not on meds any longer. I just lie down if it gets too rough. And I don't drink."

I stopped by his bike. He had my helmet sitting on it, and I felt a sharp pang of loneliness at the sight. God, I'd missed him. It was true. I watched him closely. He looked so different, and yet exactly the same. "This is weird, isn't it? I should go…"

"No. It's not weird at all. It's just the new normal." He grinned at me and grabbed my helmet off the bike, looking eternally optimistic. "Put this on, get on the bike, and it'll all feel right again."

I took my bag off and handed it to him, just like I used to do. Looking down at the rose in my hand, I tucked it into the bag as an afterthought. He slid it over his shoulder and sat down, lowering his own helmet over his head. I looked back at Marie, who shot me a *Really?!* look. I shrugged and slid the helmet on before settling onto the back of the bike. But once I was there, I didn't know what to do. Should I hold him like I used to, or was it not necessary to get quite so close?

He looked over his shoulder. "What?"

"Nothing," I said quickly. I gripped the side of his shirt loosely, leaving plenty of room between us. His skin burned through the fabric, and his hard muscles taunted me, and I hadn't even touched him. God, he felt so freaking good. And even scarier was the fact that it felt so *right*. As if I'd finally found the missing piece of me I'd lost. "I'm r-ready."

"Only if you're hoping to fall off the back and skin your pretty little ass," he called out. "Hold on tighter, or you'll throw off our balance."

I scooted up more, still not touching my front to his back. To do so would be dangerous to my mental well-being. "Better?"

He shook his head and twirled his finger in a circle. "Scoot closer. I told you I would behave, and I will. Hold me like you used to. Friends do that on bikes, I assure you."

"*Fine.*" Rolling my eyes, I glared at his back and slammed my body fully against his. I held back a groan, just barely, but he didn't even bother to try. Hearing him groan made me want to do something else to make him do it again. It reminded me of the sound he always made when I used to…uh, never mind what it reminded me of. "Better?"

"Fuck yeah."

He revved the engine and pulled away from the curb. As soon as the wind hit my face, I grinned bigger than I had in a long time. Being back on his bike, holding on to him, it felt *right*. He swerved in and out of traffic, taking the slow roads to our old restaurant. I hadn't been there since he left for…wherever it was that he went. I still didn't know.

I wonder if he could tell me now?

Man, I had so many questions. Questions I had every intention of asking him once we were at Islands. There was so much I wanted to know. He revved the engine harder, zipping between two cars. I laughed, and if I wasn't mistaken?

So did he. I'd missed that, too. So freaking much.

By the time we pulled into the parking lot, I couldn't hold back my excitement at being back on his bike. Of being with him, if I was being honest. I wasn't. I hopped off the bike and tore my helmet off, laughing. "That was freaking *awesome*."

He laughed, watching me with a warmth in his eyes I hadn't seen in way too freaking long. It stole my breath away. "Yeah, it was."

I smoothed my hair with a shaking hand. "When did you start riding again?"

"Two weeks ago," he said, running his hands over his head. He didn't need to worry about his hair being messy. He looked perfect, as always. "I wasn't ready until then. But my therapist told me I should try again, so I did."

"What does she say about me?"

"She said I should reach out to you, if I was ready." He met my eyes. "So I did."

"And you listened to her." I set my helmet down and twisted my hair into a ponytail. Finn liked it down better, but since we weren't dating anymore? Ponytail it was. I hated wearing my hair down. "That shows a lot about where you are."

"I won't pretend I'm a hundred percent better," he said, motioning me forward. He fell into step beside me as I walked toward the mall where Islands was. "But I'm not a hot mess anymore, either."

He placed his hand at my lower back, just like Riley had last week. But instead of feeling a little awkward, Finn's hand made me all itchy and wound up inside. "Well, there's that. But friends don't hold on to each other. Hands to yourself."

He dropped his hand back to his side. "Damn, you're right…again." He looked at me, giving me a grin. "So what's up with you? Still studying and being a good girl?"

I shivered, a burst of desire sweeping through my veins. Last time he asked me if I'd been a good girl, I'd gone down on my knees in front of him. What a freaking time I'd had. Of course, that had been *after* he told me he might be leaving, and then he had.

I stared at him for so long that he blinked at me.

"Carrie?" he said, looking at me with narrowed eyes. "You okay?"

Quickly, I looked away from him, shaking off the memories. "Y-Yes, of course. My grades are as good as ever. I've had more time to study ever since—"

"Since I was an ass and left?"

"If the shoe fits." I tucked my side bangs behind my ear. "In this case, you might as well be Cinderella."

"I like the new cut and color, by the way."

"You noticed?" I touched my hair self-consciously. "It's not a big change or anything. Just a shade darker."

"I noticed the second I saw you. Favorite subject, remember?"

I shook my head. "Yeah. Sure."

He twisted his lips and opened the door for me. His gaze fell on the spot where he'd bruised me inadvertently. It had faded a long time ago. I wish I could say the same about the rest of the pain he'd inflicted upon me.

I watched him as he walked up to the receptionist, giving her his megawatt smile. She practically melted into a puddle right then and there, and I wanted to gouge her eyes out for it. I guess friends weren't supposed to feel that way. I had a lot to learn about being friends with Finn…if we could even make it work.

I didn't want to hurt him anymore.

CHAPTER TWENTY-TWO
Finn

I watched Carrie close her small hands around the gigantic burger on her plate, her eyes shining with excitement. I knew, right then, that this was the best fucking move I could have ever made. Start out as friends, just like we did before, and eventually? Maybe she would love me again. Fuck, I hoped she loved me again.

Knowing she didn't love me anymore was killing me.

I fingered the envelope in my pocket; uncertain whether or not I should give it to her. Hell, I was uncertain of everything. Twelve times now, I'd reached for her hand, and covered it up by grabbing my drink instead. I was on my fifth fucking lemonade. I didn't even really like lemonade. I'd just ordered it because I'd been too distracted by her to pay attention to the menu. Ten times, I'd gone to entwine my ankle with hers under the table, just like we used to, but quickly jerked my foot back to my side. And six times, I'd almost went in for a kiss, but hidden it by grabbing the dessert card off the table.

Being her friend again was *hard*.

She moaned and closed her eyes, slowly chewing. My cock came to life at the sound, since it's the same one she made whenever I made love to her. Her face was lost in rapturous delight, and, oh my fucking God, I wanted her so badly. Needed her. I cleared my throat and picked up my own burger, unable to look away even though it physically hurt to watch her.

I sank my teeth into the burger, hoping it distracted me from the need that currently attempted to kill me. It did. I chewed, letting out my own groan. Her eyes flew open and she watched me with heated eyes. Oh, fuck. She liked that sound, too.

I didn't know whether that was a good or bad sign right now.

I swallowed past the suffocating need choking me. Trying to play it cool, I lifted the burger. "It's so fucking good."

She nodded slowly, her gaze on my mouth. "Yeah. Yeah, it is."

Need punched me with iron knuckles in the gut.

Before I begged her to forgive me and take me back—and before I could ruin the tenuous peace we had going between us—I shoved the burger in my mouth and took another bite. This time, I groaned even longer, and I even rolled my eyes back in my head a little bit, because why the fuck not? She kept staring at me as if she wanted to close her mouth around *me* instead, and if she was tempted?

I was going to push my luck.

She made a small sound and picked up her lemonade, downing almost the whole glass in one gulp. "It's so freaking hot in here, isn't it?"

"Yeah." I lifted my shirt a little bit, fanning my abs and showing her the goods. It worked. After her gaze dropped, it flew back up to mine. "They need to turn the air on or something."

She frowned at me. "Totally."

I took another bite, once again groaning deep and low. She bit down on her lower lip, watching me with hunger in her eyes. When I chuckled, the hunger faded away, only to be replaced my calculation. She grinned, too. The kind of grin that told me she was up to no good.

Thank God.

Her gaze latched with mine, she took a bite of her burger, letting out the longest, most drawn out moan she'd ever voiced. It was fucking *hot*. "Oh. My. God. Yes." She breathed in tiny little spurts, as if I was going down on her right here and there. "That's *so* good."

Some twenty-year-old brat kid looked over at her, his mouth ajar. It took all my control not to punch the fucker in the face. Those noises were for me. Or, at least, they had been, once upon a time. Another dude looked over, and he looked vaguely familiar to me. He'd been at the beach the other day, when Carrie and I had been surfing.

Coincidence…or not?

I looked back at Carrie, forcing myself to pretend I didn't notice him. "You're playing a dangerous game, Ginger."

She patted at her lips with a napkin, never looking away from me. "I have no idea what you mean. I'm just eating." She leaned in. "Unless you have something to admit to, Coram?"

"Not at all," I said, smiling. I reached out and ran a thumb over her lower lip. "Sorry. You had a little something on your lip."

Her eyes were blazing at me now. "Oh, really?"

"Really," I said as innocently as I could manage. I sucked on my thumb, licking away all traces of her. "Mm. Tastes good. Almost as good as you do."

She gasped, looking over her shoulder as if scared someone might have heard. "You're…you're so…"

"Perfect? Funny? Adorable?"

"*Annoying*," she offered. But the sparkling in her eyes ruined the anger effect she was trying to give off. "Incorrigible. Ridiculous."

I lifted a shoulder, my heart soaring. *Fuck me.* Did I really just think that my heart soared? What the hell was wrong with me? "I can live with those titles, Ginger."

She rolled her eyes. "Of course you can."

"I'm also stubborn. I don't give up easily. Remember that one, too."

She froze with the burger in her mouth. As she took a bite, chewing slowly, I let her absorb that information. I bit down on my burger, studying her as I did so. She looked at me like someone who wanted to be more than friends would, but I didn't point that out. "You know we can't be more than buddies."

I swallowed. "Funny, I heard you said the same thing to Riley the other day when he left."

She stomped her foot. "Oooh, I'm going to *kill* Hernandez."

I laughed. "It's not his fault. I'm irresistible to him, too." I pointed my burger at her. "You should add that to your list of my faults."

She snorted. "Yeah. I'll get right on that. *Not.*"

We ate our burgers in silence, no more competitive sexual groaning going on, but I sensed her watching me the whole time. Every time I looked at her, she quickly turned away. As if she didn't want me to know she watched me. She shouldn't have bothered with the attempted subterfuge. I could feel her eyes burning into me.

After we were finished, I picked up my lemonade. "This was nice."

"Yeah." She leaned back in the booth. "What are you doing with your life? Are you still in the Marines?"

I shook my head, my heart twisting. I still couldn't believe I was out. Honorable discharge and all that, but still. It was so fucking weird. "No. I got honorably discharged, so there wasn't any shame or anything."

She blinked at me. "Oh. So you're actually out?"

"I'm out."

"Are you still in security?" she asked, pursing her lips. Her eyes were narrowed, as if she was figuring something out. "Or do you want to be?"

"No, I'm not still in security. I'm currently jobless." I looked where the guy who'd set my teeth on edge earlier had been. He was gone. I relaxed slightly. "I got offered a job, but I turned it down."

She picked up her lemonade and finished it. "Why?"

"It was in Chicago."

"Ah." She *clunked* the cup down. "No surfing."

I hesitated. Should I be honest? I had nothing to lose anymore. Nothing at all. "No, there's no you."

She froze. "What do you mean?"

"I didn't want to go there because you weren't there." I grabbed her hand, squeezing it between both of mine. I still had scars on my knuckles from the night I'd gone insane in her parents' house. Did they stand out to her as much as they stood out to me? "I wanted to be here with you. I *need* to be near you to live."

She pulled free. "I know what this is all about. Dad hired you again, didn't he? You're guarding me again and don't want to tell me."

I choked on a laugh. "What? Are you fucking crazy? *No.* He didn't contact me, and I haven't talked to him since I left. Why would he? He fired me."

"I don't believe you. You told me you didn't love me anymore. You looked me in the eye and said it." She pressed her lips together. "Now you want to live near me? It makes no sense."

My stomach hollowed out. "I didn't mean it. I was trying to save you. I never stopped loving you, and none of the things that happened to me were your fault."

"Yes, they were."

"No. They. Weren't." I locked gazes with her. "I only said that because I knew you'd believe it. I knew you felt bad, so I used that against you. I'm sorry for that, too, but I never stopped loving you. I lied about that."

"Stop." She reared back, her face pale. "Just stop."

"*I can't.*" I pressed a hand to my heart. "No one will love you like I do, Ginger. I always have. I always will. Even if you hate me for the rest of your long, healthy life, I'll still love you forever. I don't know how to stop. I can't." I reached into my pocket and pulled out a note I'd written her. "Read this later. Please?"

She made a broken sound and slid out of the booth without taking the note. "I can't do this—can't love you like you want me to. I told you, I'm done with love. It *hurts* too much. I made up my mind. You need to stop coming to my dorm. Stop begging me to forgive you. Stop trying to be my friend. Just stop everything."

She bolted for the door. I tossed some cash down on the table and followed her, grabbing the note on my way out, my heart shattering into a thousand pieces even as it sped up. I had a bad feeling that something was about to happen. And when I got that feeling, I was usually right. I followed her out into the dull afternoon sun, scanning the crowd for any signs that something might be amiss.

Nothing stood out to me, except I didn't see Hernandez. That might be nothing, since he knew she was with me, but it might *be* something, too. I shot him a quick text, keeping my phone in my hand as I followed Carrie.

When she saw me behind her, she glowered at me and hurried her steps. She rifled in her purse, pulled her phone out, and put it to her ear. When she stopped walking and stood there, talking rapidly while scanning the crowd, I stopped, too. Talking into her phone, she nodded before heading for the exit. I trailed her, keeping a good distance behind her. Hernandez was missing, so like it or not, I was kind of her guard right now.

She must have spotted me following her, because she whirled on her heel. "Finn. Go. Away. You promised you would after this."

"I will, but not until you're home."

"I will be soon." She gripped her bag tight, not meeting my eyes. "Marie is coming for me."

I crossed my arms and searched the crowd. No sign of the dude who had caught my attention, but another man I didn't know stood to the side, watching Carrie way too fucking closely for my liking. "Fine. But I'm not leaving until she does. I think someone's wa—"

"I thought you weren't my freaking guard anymore," she snapped, eyes flashing. Her red hair blew in the breeze, and she looked picture perfect. I wanted to kiss that frown right off her face, in front of everyone in this outdoor mall. "Yet here you are, guarding me yet again."

I twisted my lips. "Hernandez didn't come, so I have to watch over you. And I saw someone—"

"Actually, you don't." She tossed her hair over her shoulder. "I'm fine alone."

"Jesus, woman, will you let me fucking talk?" Which reminded me why I'd written the note in the first place. So I could get all my words out like Dr. Montgomery suggested. I stepped closer, towering over her short frame. I shook the note in front of her face. "Take this."

"No." She shook her head. "I don't want it. It won't change anything."

I opened it. "Dear Ginger," I started. "I know I was wrong when I left you. I know I broke your heart, but the thing is? I broke mine more. I can't live without you. When I wake up, you're there—but you're not there. When I laugh at something on TV, I look to your spot on my couch to see if you laughed too—but you're not there. When I roll over in bed, I stretch my hand out, looking for your smooth skin—but you're not there."

"Oh my God, stop." She covered her ears, tears streaming down her flushed face. "*Please.*"

Pain sliced through me, but there was no way in hell I would stop now. "Even when I was out of my fucking mind with grief and rage, even when I wanted to fucking die and almost did, you saved me. I was going to end it all the night you saw me outside you room, but when I stood in the store picking out a rope—you were there. You *saved* me. You didn't ruin me. You are all I need in my life to live, and without you, I'm not living. Without you—"

"Wait. Y-You wanted to *die*?" She took a step toward me but stopped herself short. "You almost killed yourself?"

She was close enough for me to touch her now.

I didn't.

"I'm not done yet." I dragged my hands down my face. "Without you, I will never be whole, because half of me will always be gone. You complete me, and without that, I'll—"

She pushed my shoulders hard. "Damn you. You can't *die*."

I lowered my arm, giving up on reading the letter right now. "I know. And I'm not." I fisted my hands. "I'm here, watching you hate me, and I'm not going anywhere. It's my turn to have the broken heart. I can handle that. But it won't make me stop fucking caring, damn it." I lifted my arm. "Without that, I'll keep living, but I'll die alone, because no one else will ever replace you. I. Am. Not. *Leaving*. Not this time." I looked up at her again. "Please forgive me. Please love me again, because I can't stop loving you. I won't. I don't want to be your friend. I want to be your forever. The sun is always shining when I'm with you. Love always, Finn."

She pushed my shoulders ever harder this time, her wet cheeks shining in the dull sunlight. "Fuck you!"

I stood my ground, even though it hurt to see her look at me as if I was the enemy again. I'd done this to myself. I deserved every second of her anger, and more. It was better than her being upset, if nothing else. I crumpled up the paper in my fist. "That's what the letter said."

She growled and smacked my arm. "God, I *hate* you sometimes."

"I love you all the time," I said.

"Stop saying that."

"Or what?" I cocked a brow. "You'll kiss me into submission, like the good old days?"

Her eyes flared, and she stared at my mouth. I could tell she was contemplating it, so I acted without thinking. I hauled her close, spun her against the wall, and kissed her. Our lips met explosively, fireworks going off and all that sappy, sentimental garbage most women said happened when people kissed.

Thing is? Most of them are lying.

But this was real.

Her hands closed on my shoulders, and for a second I thought she was going to push me away. But then she dug her nails into my skin and hauled me closer, whimpering and parting her lips. I slipped my tongue in with a growl, deepening the kiss until I felt her melt against me. When she was all liquid desire, I cupped her ass and lifted her slightly, needing to feel her against me.

Needing her.

She gasped and broke off the kiss, her cheeks bright red. "Oh my God."

"Please." I kissed her again, soft. My heart thundered in my chest, drowning out the sounds of the people all around us. "Don't push me away. I *need* you. Love me again, Ginger."

"Finn…" Her hands hesitated, and she looked up, her blue eyes shining up at me. I held my breath, waiting for her to say *yes*. Hoping she wouldn't send me away, because it just might rip me in half. "I—"

"Carrie?" Riley said, his voice hard. "Are you okay? Marie sent me here to get you."

She bit down on her lip hard, still staring at me. But I could see the difference. The moment had passed, and she was going to reject me. She wasn't looking up at me with warmth. She was scared. Angry. Hurt. But not in love.

It was over.

CHAPTER TWENTY-THREE

Carrie

Oh my God. This was so unfair. I'd been fighting and fighting to move on from Finn when all along…he'd been hiding within me. I thought I could get over him? Well, he'd never left. How could I move on when I was still hopelessly in love with him? The second his lips touched mine, it was like I'd finally come home.

The weight that had been sitting on my shoulders lifted, and I could finally breathe again. It was like I'd been stuck in some deep, endless slumber—and nothing could wake me up but his kiss. Like Snow White or something. That might sound stupid, but it was true. It had always been, and would always be, Finn. There was no escaping it, and if I kept trying, I might drive myself insane in the process.

I could probably love Riley. I could probably be happy.

But he wouldn't make me feel like *this*.

I looked past Finn to Riley, and I could tell he was upset. He deserved better than this. He deserved to feel this way with a girl who felt this way about him. I let go of Finn, and he stepped back, his head lowered. "I need to…I need…Riley. I have to go to him."

Finn nodded, his mouth pressed tight and his eyes achingly hollow. "I know. Go ahead. A deal is a deal."

I didn't know what he meant by that, but I tried to push it aside so I could focus on what needed to be done. As I walked over to Riley, I bent down and picked up the note Finn had written for me as I walked. I could feel Finn's eyes on me. "Riley, I'm—"

"I know. I can see it. There's nothing to say. No explanations or apologies needed. I knew I was the underdog in this match." He shrugged. "I guess I just hoped you had a thing for the underdog. Or that I'd have a sweeping win, Rocky style."

I held his hands, squeezing them. "I'm so sorry. I think I could love you eventually. It would be so much easier. So much…just more everything."

He offered me a small smile. "A wise man once said that the heart wants what the heart wants."

"That wise man was you."

"Was it?" He cocked his head. "I should write that down. It's good advice."

I laughed a little bit. "It is."

"I guess I'm taking my hat back, huh? It's a good thing I look so hot in a hat."

"Yes," I whispered. "I believe love like this, as disastrous as it can be, only happens to a person once in a lifetime. You deserve to find someone who feels that way about you."

Riley cupped my cheek. "If you were mine, I'd never let you go. You deserve a guy who will stand by you, no matter what."

"Thank you." I smiled and dropped back down to my normal height. "Your girl is out there. You'll find her soon. I know it."

He smiled sadly. "We'll see about that."

"Want to say hi to Finn?" I looked over my shoulder. "He really does…like…you." I spun in a circle, searching the crowd. "Wait. Where did he go?"

Riley frowned. "He was just there, watching us."

"Finn?" I called out, rising on tiptoe. I spun in a circle. "Something's wrong. I know it."

Riley scratched his head. "What could possibly be wrong? We're in a crowded mall."

"You don't understand." I grabbed his hand. "I know him, and he wouldn't leave me alone. He'd never leave me unguarded like this."

"Calm down. You're with me. Maybe that's why he left." Riley started leading me to the exit. "Let's get to my car and we'll call him. Maybe he's already on his bike, waiting to follow us back to the college. Okay?"

I looked over my shoulder. "No. I *know* something's wrong."

"Then we'll find him." He squeezed my hand. "Try calling him."

We started for the exit, me fumbling for my phone in my pocket, but someone stepped in our path. He wore a hoodie that covered his face, and he reeked of smoke. I couldn't see his face, but his dirty hand held what looked like an equally filthy blade. "We have your boyfriend, and he's unconscious. You want him to live? You'll both come with us, Ms. Wallington."

My heart stopped. "What did you do with him?"

"It doesn't matter if you don't get walking," the guy said, showing the blade in his hand even more fully to us, "'cause he'll be dead."

Riley stiffened. "We're in a crowded mall. You can't abduct us here."

Another guy came behind us, pressing a knife against my lower back. "Do what he says, princess."

I tried to look over my shoulder. The guy in front of us snarled. "Don't turn around. Don't fight. Just *walk*."

"No," I said, surprised at how steady my voice sounded.

"Carrie," Riley said, his voice cracking. "Do what they say. He has a knife to your back."

The guy in front of us slashed out at Riley. Riley hissed and jerked back, his hand to his arm. Blood soaked the white shirt, and he glared at the criminal with fury in his eyes. "You *asshole*. I'll kill—"

"Okay, we're going!" I said, my heart racing. "Riley. Look at me."

Riley whirled my way, still looking as if he was ready to fight both these men all on his own. He'd lose. Two to one. "We can take them."

"We have her boyfriend," the guy behind me hissed. "How will you save him, too?"

The guy in front of us smirked. "You'll never find him."

"We're coming." I swallowed hard. "Who put you up to this?"

"A friend of a friend. We were only supposed to scare you, and make this one look like a fool," he said, tipping his head to Riley. "But then we realized you're both worth more money than the other kid offered us. Now, out to the parking lot, real easy like, and no one gets hurt."

Riley's hand tightened on mine. The blood had spread over his forearm, soaking the whole lower half of his sleeve. "Let's go. Do what they say."

I walked with him, my eyes straight ahead the whole time. "Are you okay?"

"I'm fine." Riley's hand tightened on mine. The guy behind me pressed the knife deeper against my back. "Pissed, but fine."

I nodded. I was terrified, so much so that my legs shook. But we'd be okay. These guys would ransom us off, and this nightmare would be over. Finn would be okay, too. Things could go back to normal. Oh, who was I kidding? This was my freaking life. Two kidnapping attempts in one lifetime meant my life would never be normal.

We reached a shady van with dark windows. Of course. This kidnapper didn't have an original bone in his body. For some reason, I wanted to laugh at this whole scenario. Maybe it was paranoia, maybe it was me going crazy.

All I knew was that this seemed extremely funny.

The guy in front of us opened the back door of the blue van and said, "Get in. Quickly."

Before Riley could move, the guy behind us hit the ground twitching. I whirled, my eyes wide as the dude struggled to breathe, his face turning blue. Riley leapt on him, twisting his arms behind his back, forcing the guy onto his knees. Finn leapt around us, attacking the other kidnapper before he could even react. He hit the ground, too, and Finn knelt behind him, choking the dude out and breathing heavily, his eyes narrowed as he searched the rest of the parking lot.

His hard muscles flexed as he gripped the guy tight. I watched as the kidnapper lost all color to his face and finally passed out. Finn hadn't even broken a freaking sweat. "I already took out the driver. Were they with anyone else?"

"I-I don't know," I said quickly, looking around. "I thought they h-had you."

"No, they had Hernandez. I already saved him, though. I saw him get taken. I almost missed it, but when I looked away from you two…I saw Hernandez." He let go of the guy, and his lifeless body slumped to the ground. "Then he was gone, so I followed him."

I let out a sigh of relief. Finn was okay. So were we. It was over. But this whole thing felt fake, as if it were a dream.

Finn stood up and came around us, punching the other guy in the face. He slumped over, too, knocked out cold, and Riley let go of his arms, his face pinched tight in anger. "Thanks, man."

"It's nothing," Finn said, reaching into the van and pulling out some rope. I'd known he was lethal, but seeing him in action again was both frightening and yet...somewhat *hot*. Knowing he could save me from anyone or anything made me all warm and gooey inside. "I was here. Carrie? Are you okay?"

I nodded. "Y-Yes."

He'd never let me down again, and I knew it.

His gaze scanned over me. He opened the van and pulled out rope, tying the kidnappers' feet and hands together effortlessly. It wasn't until he opened the van that I saw another guy in there, also hogtied. He was awake now. "Did they hurt you?"

"N-No. They cut Riley, though." I looked at Riley. I was still holding his hand, but he seemed to need it, so I didn't let go. He looked shaken up. "We're okay. I thought they had *you*."

He snorted. "But they didn't. They'd never have gotten me. I'm surprised they got Hernandez. He must have been distracted by something."

Marie came running up, out of breath. "Is everything okay? I was on the phone with Hernandez, fighting with him over whether he was able to find you, and then he was gone. It sounded like..." Her eyes went wide. "Why are there two unconscious dudes on the ground?"

"We were almost kidnapped, and they knocked out Hernandez." When Marie paled, I quickly added, "We're all fine, though. It was over before it started because of Finn."

Marie looked horrified. "Oh my God. Are you okay?"

"Yes. I am, I swear."

Looking in the van, she nodded distractedly. "Where is he? Where's Hernandez?"

"I left him in Islands after I found him unconscious. He's probably awake by now." Finn looked up from his position on the ground. "You can go check on him, if you'd like."

Marie took off without a backward glance.

"Thank you, Finn," Riley said again, stepping forward. He still didn't drop my hand. "You saved us."

Finn finished tying up the first suspect, stood up, and went to the second. "It's nothing, man." He looked at me before quickly glancing away. "Absolutely nothing."

I let go of Riley when my phone rang. "It's my dad. How does he know already?"

"Hernandez called him, I bet." Finn looked at me and nodded. "Answer it. Tell him what happened. I'm going to stand guard till the cops get here in case there are more of these assholes out here."

I picked up the phone, and instantly my dad started. "Who is this? Give me back my baby girl or I'll—"

"It's me. I'm okay. I'm safe. We're all safe," I said, not bothering with small talk. The world started spinning, as if I'd forgotten to breathe or something. "Finn was here with Riley and me, and he saved us."

Dad was silent for a second. "Who did this to you?"

"I have no idea, but Finn tied up the suspects, so I'm assuming the cops can find out." I took a shaky breath, trying not to break down now that it was all said and done. Funny, I didn't feel scared before, but now? I was literally falling apart. As a matter of fact, I just might faint. Funny. I'd never done that before. "Finn was here, so he took care of it. And we're okay. We're all okay. O-Okay."

Finn tied the man's arms together, his gaze locked on me the whole time. "Riley, hug her or *I* will. She's going in to shock and needs comfort. Comfort her."

Riley hesitated. "Dude, we're not—"

"I don't give a shit," Finn growled. "Just fucking do it already, man."

"Okay," Riley said, pulling me into his arms and kissing my temple. "It's okay. We're here. We're fine."

I just stared straight ahead, not sure what to say or do. It was like I was broken. I held the phone to my ear still, and Dad kept talking, asking a million questions, but I couldn't make a sound.

Finn reached out for my cheek, but then pulled back. After a low curse, he said, "It's okay. You'll be all right." Finn took the phone from my hand. "Sir, she's in shock right now and can't talk, but she's okay. There were three suspects that I took care of. I'm keeping an eye out for others, but there's no sign of any." Sirens sounded in the distance. "The cops are almost here. I called them after I got the first guy, as I searched for Carrie." He was quiet. "Yes, sir. He was with her." Another pause. "No, sir. He's fine. So is she." He blinked. "I'm fine too, sir. So is Hernandez." He nodded. "I'll let her know to expect you." He hung up and put my phone in his pocket. "Your dad is on his way."

I nodded. Or at least I think I did. I tried to say something, anything, but nothing came out. My mouth just opened and closed. Finn stepped forward, his eyes on me, but then he stopped. His fist unfurled, curled again, and he turned away. "She's still freaking out. You need to calm her the fuck down, Riley. Come *on*."

"Shh, you're okay." Riley hugged me closer. Police cars rolled into the parking lot, screeching to a halt by us. I barely noticed them. "What happens now?"

"Police will want statements and all that, but once they're done, you go home and let them do their jobs." Finn tugged on his hair, still watching me. "She's not fucking okay, damn it. Fix it!"

Riley let go of me, making an angry sound. "Maybe *you* should try to fix her. You're the one she loves! She probably just needs you."

"She doesn't—" Finn shook his head and growled. "Fuck it. Come here, Ginger."

He yanked me into his arms. He hugged me so tight I could barely breathe...and yet suddenly, I *could*. I clung to him, releasing a sob. "I-I was...so scared, Finn."

"Shh." He kissed my head, his arms going even tighter around me. "I'm here. I won't let anything happen to you. *Ever*."

I nodded, burying my face in his chest. "Don't leave me again. Swear it."

"I swear. I'll never leave you again," he whispered brokenly. His heart thundered against my cheek, and I hugged him as hard as I could. He didn't seem to mind. If anything, it made him kiss me even harder the next time. "Even when you're with someone else, I'll take care of you. I love you so damn much."

I shook my head. Didn't he realize what I was saying? I was his, and always would be. "There's no—"

A cop cleared his throat. "We need to speak with her, please?"

Finn tightened his arms around me. "If she's ready."

"I'm r-ready." I let go of Finn reluctantly, but entwined his fingers with mine. "Stay with me?"

He gave me a sad smile. "Always. But what about Riley?"

I looked at Riley. He was talking to an officer and walking toward a paramedic. "He looks okay, right? They'll fix his arm in the ambulance."

Finn nodded, looking confused. "Yeah, but…"

"He'll be brought to the station, too," the officer said, motioning toward his own car. "Let's get her somewhere safe and then they can reunite in the station."

I nodded and took a deep breath. "All right. Let's go."

"Just you, ma'am," the officer said, eyeing Finn. "He can follow in another car."

"He stays with me, or I don't go." I hugged his arm close to mine, gripping his biceps with my free hand. "He's with me."

Finn flexed his jaw. "I go with her if she wants me to."

The officer sighed. "Who are you?"

"Her bodyguard," Finn said, before I could open my mouth to answer. He cocked his head toward the van. "I'm the one who tied them up."

"Oh. Good." He opened the back door. "We need to talk to you, too."

Finn slid into the backseat, not letting go of me. "I'm all yours," he said softly.

I swallowed hard, clinging to him.

Had he been talking to me or the officer?

CHAPTER TWENTY-FOUR

Finn

Hours later, and a million questions later, I finally got released from the interrogation room. I don't know if that's what it actually was, but man, it had felt like it. They'd asked me so many questions, over and over again, that my fucking head hurt more than ever. I rubbed my temples, wanting nothing more than to lie down in a dark room for a whole day.

"Griffin." A door opened beside me and Senator Wallington stepped out, looking as impeccable as always in his gray three-piece suit. "A word?"

Shit. "Yes, of course."

I followed him into the empty room…well, almost empty. Mrs. Wallington stood in the corner, watching me cautiously. "Griffin."

"Mrs. Wallington." I nodded at her and turned back to Senator Wallington. "You two got here way too fast. Or was I really in there that long?"

"We were actually in Arizona for a meeting. We arrived a little more than an hour ago."

"Oh." I dragged my hands down my face. "You're here to ask me to leave Carrie alone, I assume?"

Mrs. Wallington stepped forward. "Griffin—"

"Wait, let me talk first." I lifted my chin. "I was a mess before, and I know it. I wasn't worthy of Carrie like that, but I got better. I've been going to therapy, and I don't take pills or drink."

Senator Wallington shook his head. "But you left her. Walked away and didn't even care."

"I *cared*." I fisted my hands. "I cared way too much."

Mrs. Wallington nodded. "You did. I know that. But what makes you think you're better for her now?"

"Because I'm me again, and I love her more than anything. I love her enough to walk away when I needed to. I'm not walking away again, not if she wants me." I met Senator Wallington's eyes. "She doesn't forgive me yet, but if she ever does, you can be damn sure I will never break her heart again. I'll cherish her till I die. She's…she's my life."

Mrs. Wallington's eyes filled with tears. "I believe you."

"Margie," Senator Wallington hissed. He gave her a long look before turning to me with hard eyes. "Why were you there today?"

"I know I shouldn't have been there, since I don't work for you anymore, but I was—and that's a good thing. I was able to help Hernandez."

"I heard." He crossed his arms and studied me. "You look better. Less…"

"Messed up?"

He nodded. "Yes. That."

Mrs. Wallington gasped. "Don't be rude, Hugh."

"He's right, though," I said, smiling at her. "I am less messed up now."

"Good." He stepped closer, his gaze dipping over me. "I won't pretend you're my choice for her, but if you make her happy, and keep yourself in check, I'm willing to give you a second chance. I might even approve of you, over time."

"Me too," Mrs. Wallington said, resting her hand on my arm. "I know how much you love her, Griffin." She cocked her head. "Finn, I mean."

I blinked, my hands hovering at my sides. What. The. Fuck? "Ma'am…?"

"It's what she calls you, right?" She smiled at me, her eyes tearing up. "If you're going to be with her, we should call you that, too."

Senator Wallington cleared his throat. "I saw what happened to her when you left. I don't want to ever see that again." He held his hand out for mine, waiting. "I'm willing to accept you not because I have to, but because I think in the end…you just might be the best partner for her. You'll die for her. Live for her. Do anything to keep her safe."

I swallowed hard. "Always. But sir, she's with Riley now."

"No, she's not. We tried to urge that along, but it's not going to happen." He frowned at me. "You better love her the right way this time, because I'm determined to see her happy again. No drinking. No drugs. No punching walls."

"I'm better now. Still not the same guy I used to be, and I don't think I ever will be, but I love her with all my heart." I tugged on my hair, eyeing Mrs. Wallington. "I only left her because I wasn't good for her. I—"

He waved his hand. "We all know you were in a dark place, yes, but you seem better now. I hear you go to therapy twice a week, and the nightmares have mostly stopped?"

I stared him down. "Sir, have you been reading my medical records?"

"No." He laughed. "Your roommate, otherwise known as Hernandez, is keeping me informed. He told me when you came back, and I've been watching you ever since. Watching you heal."

"But why?" I asked, more confused than ever. "I don't understand."

"Because I want Carrie to be happy, and you're the one who makes her happy." He laid a hand on my shoulder and squeezed. "Speaking of which, do you want your old job back, Griffin…er, Finn? With our permission to date and love our daughter for the rest of your life, as long as you treat her like you should?"

I swallowed hard. "I have to talk to her first. See if that's what she wants. But I…I want to go to college. I think Richards is still going to pay for me to go, even though I'm not a Marine anymore. He told me he was."

"Then go to the same college as Carrie," Mrs. Wallington said. "That would be perfect."

Senator Wallington motioned in the general direction of the campus. "I'll even pay for your education myself as part of your salary if that's what it takes for you to come back. But if you ever hurt her again, I'll—"

Mrs. Wallington stepped forward. "What he *means*, Finn, is we forgive you. We're willing to move on instead of dwelling on the past." Mrs. Wallington held on to her husband's arm. "Isn't that right, Hugh?"

He flinched. "Yes. That's right."

"Thank you. I…I don't know what to say," I said, my throat feeling way too damn tight.

"She's waiting for you out there," Mrs. Wallington said. "You ready to go back to her?"

I looked at the door. "What about Riley?"

"He's there, too," Senator Wallington said, opening the door. "But I told you, she doesn't love him. I'd *prefer* her to love him, to be honest, but she just doesn't."

"I'll guard her, even if she's with him." I gritted my teeth. "I'll do it anyway, so I might as well get paid for it. I can't trust anyone else. What about Hernandez?"

"He quit already. Said being a Marine was enough danger for any one man," the senator said, straightening his tie. "I never saw him as long-term. I was just waiting."

I cocked a brow. "For?"

"You. I knew you'd be back."

"So did I," Mrs. Wallington said.

I shook my head. This was the weirdest fucking conversation ever. "If she does take me back, I'm not changing for you." I stared him down, running my fingers over my scar. "She likes me the way I am. Or, she did, anyway."

He inclined his head. "Fair enough. As long as you treat her right this time, I can work with that. But if you—"

"*Hugh.*"

Senator Wallington cut off, shooting me one last look before heading for the door. I didn't say anything else. I followed them out into the main area, my heart thundering in my ears. Were they right? Did Carrie want me, even though Riley had come back into the picture at the worst moment? We entered the room, and I saw her immediately. Her hair was down now, and she sat next to Riley.

She looked fucking exhausted.

We walked over to them, me a few steps behind the Wallingtons. Carrie looked up, cried out, and flung herself into my arms. "Are you okay? They had you in there forever."

I hesitated only a second before I closed my arms around her tight. Riley locked gazes with me, nodding once. Saying he was okay with this type of contact with his girlfriend, I suppose. "I'm okay. I just have a headache."

She let go of me, framed my face with her hands, and nodded. "Let's get you home."

188

"You mean to Hernandez's place?"

"He's not there. He said he was leaving the job and the apartment—since the apartment belongs to Carrie's guard," Senator Wallington said, heading for the door. "We'll take you there."

I had no idea what was going on, but I didn't want to ask Carrie in front of them.

My questions would have to wait.

We all piled in to the limo, mostly silent. Finally, Carrie spoke. "Apparently, they came after us because of Cory."

"Cory?" I snapped, my head lifting instantly. "What did he do?'

"He hired them to scare us, and make Riley look like a fool since he couldn't protect me." She shrugged. "Cory thought that would make me break up with Riley, I guess. Or maybe he thought it would scare Riley off. I don't know."

I curled my hands into fists. I'd kill the fucker. "They did more than scare you both."

"Yeah, they broke the plan. They decided to ransom us off for money and leave us somewhere to be found afterward," Riley said, looking down at his bandaged arm. "They were looking for money for their next fix, and thought they found it in us."

"*Cory*," I snarled, rage choking me. "I always knew that guy was trouble."

She nodded. "You were right. I should have believed you. He'll be facing charges now."

I snorted. "He should face me. I'll make him sorry he ever thought of endangering you."

"Agreed," Senator Wallington said. "For once."

We all fell silent until the limo stopped in front of my old place. I nodded my head at Riley and the Wallingtons. Finally, I locked eyes with Carrie. "Thanks for the ride."

"You bet," Carrie said, her hands clutched in her lap.

I nodded and got out of the car, heading up the walkway. Swallowing hard, I dug my key out of my pocket. It had been way too fucking hard to walk away from Carrie again. You'd think I would be used to it by now.

"Hey, wait up!" Carrie called out.

I stopped, my heart lurching. Slowly, I turned. The limo left, but Carrie stayed. I didn't know what to think of that. "Yeah?"

"Did you mean it?"

I gripped my keys tight. "Did I mean what?"

"That you still loved me, and never stopped?"

"Of course," I said. "I love you, and nothing will ever—"

She flung herself in my arms, kissing me into silence. I dropped the keys to the ground, picking her up and hugging her against my chest. By the time the kiss ended, we were both out of breath. She pulled back, her cheeks flushed and her blue eyes shining. "Can I come up with you?"

"Yes." I nodded, feeling completely flustered. "Of course."

She bent down, picked up the keys, and headed for the door without breaking stride. "Did you know Hernandez never slept in your bed?"

I rubbed my jaw and followed her, using all my strength and resolve to not grab her and pick up where that kiss had ended. What did it mean? Did it mean she loved me, too? That she forgave me? Fuck, I hoped so. "I did. He was on the couch when I came back. He said it didn't feel right taking over my place when he had his own a few miles away. So I've been sleeping in my bed, and he's been on the couch."

"He never got rid of his place?"

"Nah. He owns it." I glanced her way. "He's had it ever since his grandfather died. He just stayed here for the job."

She shook her head. "He never wanted this job."

"No." I took the keys out of her hand and unlocked the door. "He did it for me."

"I know." She walked inside. She took it all in, her face a mixture of hope and nostalgia. "Now we talk."

I closed the door and tossed the keys on the table. "Okay."

"Do…" She sat down on the bed, bouncing to test it out. She looked back toward the pillow, frowning when she saw the purple rose on the pillow. Reaching out, she picked it up and looked at me. "What's this?"

"I was going to give it to you, but then decided the note was too much." I shifted on my feet. "Too soon, because you hadn't forgiven me yet."

She looked down at it, her fingers lightly caressing the petals. "Can I read it?"

"Yeah, I guess so." I crossed the room and grabbed six more. I'd struggled to pick the right message today. "Here's the rest."

She looked up at me, her eyes filling with tears. "Were these all too personal, too?"

I nodded. "Yes."

She took a deep breath and unrolled the paper. "*Love me.*"

"Yeah." I tossed the red one on the bed. I hadn't even realized that people dyed roses all these crazy colors until recently. I thought they only came in red or pink. "This one says: *The sun is shining. Love me.*" The pale green one. "*I can't live without you. Love me.*" Pink next. "*You look beautiful. Love me.*" Another pink one. "*I'll never make you cry again. Love me.*" Last, the yellow one. I tossed that in her lap. "*I want to marry you. Love me.*"

She looked up at me, tears falling down her cheeks, and picked up the yellow one, holding it to her chest. "God, Finn."

"I'm going to be honest with you here." I paced her way, nibbling on my thumbnail. "I'll never be the same guy you fell in love with. I still get headaches, I have scars, and I occasionally have those nightmares, too. I don't drink to hide the pain anymore, and I don't abuse pain pills anymore, either. I was in a dark, dark hole the last time we were together, but I'm better now."

She stood up, still holding the yellow rose. "Finn—"

"Wait. Before you say anything, I know you could do better. I know Riley is better. But damn it, you love me. You even said it. It might be scary and hard, but I want to spend the rest of my life with you. Making you laugh. Making you cry. Making love to you. I want to be yours…and I need you to be mine. Please. I'm begging you—and I don't fucking beg. You know that."

Tears shined in her eyes. "Are you done yet?"

"I…no." I tugged on my hair, looking at the half-dozen roses scattered across my bed. "I love you, and no one will ever love you like I do. I know I fucked up, and I'll spend my whole life making it up to you, if you'll let me. Please, just let me love you. *Love me.*"

"Yes. Yes, yes, and yes." She launched herself into my arms, hugging me tight and crying. "I love you, too. I do. I love you so much."

"Y-You do?" I looked down at her, my mind spinning and my heart racing. "You still love me?"

"Yes, I love you, you idiot." She cupped my cheeks. "I've laughed with you. I've been blissfully happy with you. I've cried with you. I've cried for you. I've been scared for you. I've hurt for you and from you. I've even been broken hearted over you." She looked up at me, tears rolling down her cheeks. "But I never want to be *without* you again."

"Then you won't be. I swear it."

She lifted her face. "Good. Now kiss me before I die."

CHAPTER TWENTY-FIVE

Carrie

The second his mouth closed over mine, I lost myself. I gave myself over to him willingly, knowing this was the right choice. No second-guessing or wondering. This was Finn, and I was me. We belonged together like this. It was the way we were supposed to be. His tongue touched mine, and he growled, pressing me back on the bed. I wrapped my arms around his neck, holding him close. There was no way I'd ever let go of him again. Not even if he pushed me away. Not even if he tried to make me not love him anymore.

Love like this wasn't meant to die.

He pressed his hard length against me, and I spread my legs so he could rest within them. We both moaned when he fell into place, but we didn't stop kissing. I don't think I could have even if someone forced me to. He slid his hand under my butt, lifting me against his erection. I rolled my hips, desire twisting and turning in my belly.

He broke off the kiss with a gasp, dropping his forehead on mine. "I can't believe we're back here again. I didn't think you'd ever forgive me."

"I love you." I sat up and watched him as he pulled his shirt over his head. "Love is forgiveness, compromise, and dedication. I think we have that all covered. Now get *naked*."

"Fuck yeah." He tossed his shirt over his shoulder, his steamy blue eyes latching on to mine. "Your turn."

I shook my head. "You need to be naked first, because once I get my hands on you? I'm not stopping."

He undid his fly and dropped his shorts, kicking out of them easily. After he shimmied out of his boxer briefs, he stood there naked for the first time since his accident. Staring at me, waiting, letting *me* look my fill. He had scars all over his arm, and the scar on his head was still there, obviously. His muscles were as toned as ever, and he looked tanner than he used to be. He looked nervous, as if I might not like what I saw.

He didn't need to worry. He was *Finn*.

"You're perfect," I said, slowly standing. I trailed my fingers over the red, jagged scars on his arm and shoulder. "Every mark on your body, whether it's ink or a scar, tells a story. I want to know it all. I want to be there for it all from now on."

He relaxed, his eyes lighting up again. "You will be. I swear it."

"I know. I do too. Without you, I go out of my mind."

He laughed. "Yeah. Me too."

"I have a surprise for you." I undid my shorts, letting them fall to the floor. I stared at his tattoo. The one he'd gotten for me. *The sun is finally shining.* On his other shoulder, he'd gotten a new tattoo. It said *Ginger.* Even when we were apart, he'd gotten my name on his shoulder. I blinked back tears. God, I loved him. "I hope you like it, because I have a feeling it doesn't mean the same thing to you as it once did. But it means a lot to me."

He cocked his head. "I'm trying to concentrate, but you're getting naked. I'm finding it increasingly hard to listen."

"It's part of the surprise." I kicked out of my underwear and then grabbed my shirt hem. "I got something for you for Christmas, but I didn't have a chance to show you."

He nodded, his gaze on my stomach area…or maybe lower. "Show me," he rasped. "Hurry, please."

I took a breath and lifted my shirt over my head, letting it hit the floor behind me. The bra came off next, but Finn wasn't watching my movements anymore. He'd spotted my gift since I was officially wearing nothing but his necklace and his tattoo. As he stood there, staring at me, I waited. Letting *him* look *his* fill this time. "D-Do you like it?"

He closed the distance between us. Reaching out, he traced his fingers over the ink with a featherlight touch. "You got our tattoo? When?"

"When you were overseas." I rested my hands on his arms. "I know you don't like saying it anymore, probably because it reminds you of what you went through over there, but I—"

"I fucking love it." He pushed me back on the bed, lowering himself down my body to kiss the ink. "And I fucking love you, too. So damn much."

His hand skimmed lower and dipped down between my legs. I almost fell apart right then and there, because it had been so freaking long since I'd been touched like that. I let my legs fall open and moaned. "Oh my God."

"Jesus, I missed this. Missed you." And then he thrust a finger inside me. I cried out, arching my hips, my eyes rolling back in my head. It felt that good. "You're so hot when you're flushed with need, Ginger."

"P-Please," I begged, moving my hips higher. "More."

He chuckled, the sound low and so sexy it drove me even more insane. My pulse raced, and I moved my hips again, groaning when he thrust inside at the same time. "I am so incredibly moved and touched that you did that for me," he said, withdrawing and then thrusting two fingers inside. "But before I get all sappy and sentimental and shit, I'm going to make you scream my name so fucking loud it hurts."

"God, yes," I breathed. "*Finn.*"

He slid down my body till he knelt on the floor next to the bed. Without a second's warning, he closed his hands on the sides of my hips and his mouth was on my clit. As his tongue moved over me in slow, sensuous circles, I slowly drifted away to a place where nothing mattered but us. Nothing but this.

He cupped my butt, lifting me higher against his hot mouth, and increased the pressure. His fingers dug into my skin, making me cry out from the mixture of pleasure and pressure, and he scraped his teeth against me. It had been so long since I'd had him, so long since I'd felt anything even remotely close to this, that it didn't take much to send me soaring over the edge.

And, man, did I freaking fly. "Finn," I cried out, my entire body bursting with pleasure. "Oh my God. Oh my God."

He let me hit the mattress again, growling as he climbed on top of me and claimed my mouth with a tortured kiss. After he rolled a condom on, he lifted my hips and thrust into me in one hard drive, not stopping once he was all the way inside of me. He pulled out and slammed into me again, making my entire body convulse from pleasure. I screamed into his mouth, unable to hold back the frantic noises escaping me, and closed my legs around his waist.

Freaking *heaven*.

He broke off the kiss and rested his forehead on mine, breathing heavily. His muscled arms flexed on either side of my head, and he rolled his hips gently. "Shit, Ginger. Are you okay? Was I too rough on—?"

"No." I dug my heels into his butt, smacking his arm in frustration. "Don't stop. Keep going. *Harder*."

He growled and moved within me. Slow at first, but quickly picking up speed and friction. I dragged my nails down his back, moaning and whimpering and God only knows what else I did. My body was focused on him and what he was doing to me. Nothing else registered at all. I was so lost in him that I didn't even know or care what I said or shouted or even cried.

As long as he kept pumping his hips like that and kissing me, that's all that mattered. He bit down on my neck, letting out a grueling moan. "I'm so fucking close. I need you to come again, Ginger."

He reached between us, squeezed my nipple between his finger and thumb with the perfect amount of force, and thrust harder. "Yes," I cried out. "Oh my God, yes."

He thrust into me so hard the bed moved across the floor with a loud screech. His hard biceps were so strained his veins were pronounced, and he closed his eyes, his face lost in pleasure. It was so freaking hot, watching him like this. Knowing I was the only one who got to see him like this. I clung to him even tighter. "Fuck, Carrie."

"Let go. I have you," I said, kissing him. "I'm all yours, love."

He let out a broken sound and moved inside of me without abandon. I dug my nails into his shoulders as the bed moved across the floor, the tightness in my stomach coiling so hard that I knew I was close to exploding again. He pinched my nipple, rough and hard, his tongue moving against mine, and I came.

"*Carrie*." He growled and pumped into me once more, harder than ever before, and his body went rock hard as he orgasmed. He collapsed on top of me, his breathing harsh. "Holy shit."

"Yeah." I grinned. "It's been way too long."

He lifted up onto his elbows and smiled down at me, sweeping the hair off my face with his hand. "I feel a hell of a lot less tense now, that's for fucking sure."

"You and me both." I flexed my legs around him, not wanting to let go…like…ever. "You know I wasn't with anyone else while you were gone, right?"

He kissed my nose. "I'd hoped so, but if you moved on when I was gone, it would be fine. I don't have a right to—"

"I didn't." My cheeks heated. "You're the only one who makes me feel this way, and you're the only one who ever will."

He kissed me tenderly before pushing off me. "We need a shower. I want to wash the filth of those assholes Cody hired off us."

I laughed. "You mean Cory?"

"Nope. Cody." He lifted me into his arms. "He doesn't deserve a real name."

I rested my head on his shoulder as he walked into the bathroom. I flicked the light with my toes. He set me down on my feet, kissed the tip of my nose, and turned on the water. "Still like it scalding hot?"

"Yep." I pulled out two towels and rummaged under the sink for supplies. Two bottles caught my attention. "You still have my shampoo?"

He dropped something into the trash and turned a little bit red. "Yeah. I liked to sniff it when I missed you, which was every night before bedtime. Sometimes in the morning, too." He rolled his eyes. "And there goes my man card yet again."

"You never lost it, and never will. Not with me." I hugged the bottles close to my naked body. "Besides, I slept with your shirt, so I'm not one to talk."

"You did?"

"I did," I admitted. "Do. Whatever."

He laughed and swept me into his arms. He carried me into the shower, depositing me directly into the stream of water. "Are you okay? I mean, after the scare and all…"

"I'm fine." I reached up and cupped his face. "I'm not here because I'm in shock or anything."

"I know." He kissed me. "And I'm not here because your father asked me to be your guard again."

"I know. You're—wait. What?" I peeked up at him as he massaged my scalp under the water. "Did he ask you?"

"Yeah, he did. I want to make sure it's okay with you." His fingers stilled. "He's also giving me a second chance to prove myself. Your mother is, too. I'm not sure what to think about that."

"I'm not too surprised. They want me to be happy, and you make me happy." I rose on tiptoe and kissed him. "Do you want to accept the job?"

"I think I will. Since I'll be guarding you for the rest of my life, I might as well get paid for it and keep some annoying dude from following us around all the time." He poured out the shampoo and rubbed it into my hair. "He offered to pay for my college, but Captain Richards has already informed me that he'll still pay even though I'm a civilian now. I don't know if I can accept that, though."

"Accept it." I frowned at him. "Are you insane? Of course you accept it. He's offering to help you, and you earned it."

"But why? Because I lived and no one else did?"

"Because you were injured, and that was part of the deal—you going to college on his dime. Trust me, he can afford it." I rested my hands over his heart. "And if you won't accept help from Captain Richards, then accept it from my father. He owes it to you after all the crap he's given you."

He stepped back and tugged on his hair. "I don't know. I'll think about it."

I gazed at him, admiring the view. His ink was stark against his flawless skin. His broad shoulders tapered down over his hard pecs, and then narrowed to his impossibly taut abs. His cock—yes, I still blushed at that word—jutted out from his light brown curls, and he looked beautiful.

Delicious, even.

I'd never seen a more welcome sight than him, standing naked and wet in the shower with me. And I never would again. After he finished rinsing my hair, I grabbed his hand before he could snatch up the conditioner. "So...ready for round two?"

His eyes darkened. "Are *you*?"

"Heck yeah." I nodded for good measure, running my fingers down his chest, over his abs, and closing my hand over his cock. "And three..."

"And four..." He dropped his head back against the white tile. I skimmed my fingers over the head of his erection before jerking him in my fist. "Fuck, that feels good, Ginger."

I sank to my knees. "I know what will feel even better."

"Yes." He threaded his fingers in my hair, his Adam's apple bobbing as he swallowed hard. "Do it. *Now*."

I sucked him into my mouth hard, rolling my tongue over him just like he liked. He tightened his fists in my hair, urging me closer. His body flexed and moved, and he gently pumped his hips into my mouth as I sucked on him. I tasted his semen before he tried to pull away, but I dug my hands into his butt and refused to let go.

I wanted to do this. To taste him.

"Ginger, I'm going to come," he growled, pulling my hair. "Let me make you come, too."

I shook my head and sucked harder, moaning. He growled and moved his hips, seeming to give in. He rested his shoulders against the wall and pulled me closer, instead of pushing me away. When I scraped my teeth over the tip of him, he cried out and came. It was such a heady feeling, knowing I'd done this to him. Made him feel this good.

I swallowed, finally letting go of him after one last kiss to the tip of his cock. He collapsed against the wall, breathing unevenly, his hand still fisted in my hair. "You've been a bad girl," he said, his tone broken.

He tugged me up by my hair, and I stood. Once I was on my feet, he spun me around and entered me from behind. I slammed my hands against the wall, and my forehead smacked against it, too. "*Finn*."

He reached around the front of me, pressing his fingers against my clit. "My turn to make you scream, Ginger."

As he moved inside of me harder and faster, his hands seemed to be everywhere. He skimmed over my breasts, pinching my nipples, and then dipped down. As soon as he touched me there again, I tensed. He thrust hard. I threw my head back and screamed, my nails scratching uselessly over the tiled wall as I came. "*Yes*. Oh my God."

He moved inside me once, twice, three times, his grip on my hips so tight it almost hurt—but in a good way. He dropped his forehead against the shower wall, cradling me in his arms from behind. "Holy shit, you're going to kill me."

"Never." I slid off him and spun around, wrapping my arms around his neck. "I love you too much."

Grinning, he trailed his fingers over my tattoo. "I love you, too. The sun is always shining around you, Ginger."

My heart warmed. "Indeed it is."

And I had a feeling it would never stop.

CHAPTER TWENTY-SIX

Finn

Four months later

I climbed off my bike and hung my helmet on the bars, taking a calming breath and smoothing my hair as I did so. The crisp early September morning air smelled fresh, sending awareness through my veins. Waking me up. It felt renewing, almost. Since this was the start of a new chapter of my life, it felt fitting. These past few months with Carrie had been pure heaven. We fought. We kissed. We made up. We loved.

I never thought I could be so damn happy.

My phone buzzed, and I pulled it out of my pocket. Senator Wallington. *Good luck, Finn. Let me know how it goes. Give Carrie my love, too. We miss you two already.*

I smiled. We'd spent the summer with them, getting to know each other better. I could almost say that they actually liked me now. They got to see the "me" I was without the pain and grief. It had been good for us. *Thank you, sir.*

I still couldn't believe how much he'd changed. But then again, we'd all changed. I sure as hell had, and so had Carrie. It stood to reason that he would have, too.

My phone buzzed again. *Talk to you later.*

"Who was that?" Carrie asked, smoothing her hair and coming up beside me.

"Your dad." I slipped my phone into my pocket and offered her my arm. "He was wishing me luck."

"Oh, that's nice. I bet he—" She checked her phone and frowned. "Hey. I got nothing."

I shrugged. "What can I say? I'm the favorite child now."

"Only because you can talk with him in his study for hours about politics without getting bored." She pouted, stealing a peek at me. "I had to escape. He can't blame me. Even Riley left after an hour."

I laughed. "That's 'cause he's not as cool as me."

"I know it." She wrapped her hand around my bicep. "But after we spent all summer living with them, I think my father really does love you more than me in some ways—and I love that fact, just for the record."

"That's not true." I grinned. "Okay. Maybe it's a little bit true."

She smacked my abs with her free hand. "*Ha-ha*, really funny, fresh meat."

"Hey, you promised not to call me that."

She laughed. "No, I promised not to call you that in bed. I didn't say anything about not doing it here. And I never promised not to laugh at you if you get lost on campus."

"Brat," I said, kissing her temple. I slid my bag higher on my shoulder and handed her hers. "Somehow I think I'll be fine, though, with or without your help."

"You think?" She smiled at me. "Are you ready for this?"

"Of course I am." I rolled my eyes. "I've been on this campus since last year. What difference is taking a few classes going to make?"

"Tell me that when you're buried in homework later this week."

I readjusted so I could put my arm over her shoulder. "As long as you help me study? I won't give a damn."

"You know I will." She wrapped her arm around my waist and hesitated. "You know...I was thinking."

"Sounds dangerous," I quipped.

She smacked my arm. "Stop it."

"Fine. I'll behave." I grinned and yanked my bag up higher on my shoulder. "What's up?"

"We're going to be studying so much, and at the same school, so I thought," she peeked up at me, "maybe I could move in with you? I mean, I practically live there now, but we could make it official."

I stopped walking, my heart thundering in my ears. "R-Really? You want to?"

"I do." She smiled up at me. "If you do."

"Fuck yes." I picked her up and swung her in a circle. "Yes! Are you sure?"

"I'm as positive as a proton," she said, grinning.

"Me too."

She laughed, and the melody washed over me, washing away any nerves I had—that I'd deny I had if anyone asked. I had her with me. What could ever possibly go wrong? She loved me, and I loved her.

Life was fucking good.

I kissed her, my mouth melding to hers perfectly. Which made sense, since she was made for me. I pulled back and grinned so big my cheeks fucking hurt. "If we weren't on our way to class, I'd celebrate this with you my favorite way—naked and wet."

Desire flared in her eyes. "Meet you out here at twelve for a nooner at home?"

"Yes." I kissed her one last time. "I love you."

"I love you, too."

I looked to the left and sighed. "I have to go this way to my economics class."

"And I go this way to trigonometry." She backed away from me, our fingers still entwined. "Then tonight, we'll tell my dad together? About us living together?"

I groaned, not letting go. "Do we have to? He liked me, but will he like this?"

"I don't know." She grinned. "But we'll find out the best way possible."

"Together."

"Always," she said, looking at me with so much love it almost hurt. "Now get your butt to class, freshman."

"Yes, ma'am." I let go of her reluctantly. "Look in your bag first, though."

She reached in and pulled out a yellow rose. Grinning, she read the message. "*I'll miss you. Love me.*" I'd ended the note the same way as I had the day we'd gotten back together. It was easily one of the best days of my life. She looked up at me, her blue eyes shining in the sun. "I'll miss you, too. And I do."

I blew her a kiss. "Stay in class and don't wander off, since I won't be watching you."

She laughed and called out over her shoulder, "You worry about me too much. Good luck!"

"I'll never worry enough when it comes to you," I said under my breath, watching her walk away. She took my heart with her, but I knew it would be safe in her hands.

Always.

EPILOGUE

Finn

Seven years later

I watched Carrie from across the room, my arms tightening on the precious bundle in my arms as I juggled the phone with my free hand. She stretched her arms up, trying to get the last ornament on the perfect branch toward the top of the tree, her lips pursed in determination. The pink rose I'd given her earlier lay on the table behind her, the message still attached to the stem.

"Are you still there?"

"Yeah, sorry." I forced myself to focus on the conversation I was having with Carrie's father. "We'll be there first thing in the morning for Christmas breakfast."

"Coffee starts at eight," her dad said. I heard paper crinkling, which probably meant he was wrapping his presents at the last minute like usual. "Did Carrie tell you to make the fruit salad? She told me she would remember."

I laughed. "Yeah. It's all ready to go. We'll see you tomorrow, sir. Tell Margie I said merry Christmas."

My father-in-law sighed. "If I ever finish wrapping these godforsaken presents, I will. I should really just hire someone to do it."

But he wouldn't, because he liked doing it. "Well, good luck. I have to hang up now, because your daughter needs help with the tree."

"Don't let her knock it over like she did last year," Senator Wallington said. "She might hurt—"

I rolled my eyes. "I won't, sir."

"All right. Merry Christmas Eve."

"Same to you." I hung up and tossed my phone on the sofa, turning back toward Carrie just in time to hear her curse under her breath. "I heard that, Mrs. Coram."

She shot me a frustrated look, her blue eyes blazing at me. "I'm going to get this last one on if it kills me, I swear it."

"I *can* help you, you know." I crossed the room slowly, trying not to upset my balance. "I am a bit taller than you."

"Nope. I get the red ones, not you." She looked at me, her gaze dropping low and then slipping back up. "It's our Christmas Eve tradition."

I grinned. "Yeah, it is. Then when we're done, we drink and have hot, sweaty—"

"Sh," she hissed, her cheeks going red. "She'll hear you."

"I think we're safe," I whispered, stopping directly in front of her. The colored lights on our tree twinkled merrily, and all that was left was the ornament in Carrie's hand and the angel—which came last, of course. "She doesn't really speak English."

"Still. It's the principle." She peeked at me, a sly grin on her face. "We don't want to have to foot that therapy bill, trust me. We cost way too much."

I rolled my eyes. "Believe me, I know that."

Carrie had changed her major the second year of college. After seeing how much Dr. Montgomery had helped me, she decided she wanted to do that for other people like me. Wanted to help soldiers and others who suffered from PTSD. She worked on base now, and she always looked so damn happy.

I liked to think I had something to do with that.

And I liked that we worked in the same building, so we got to have lunch together every single fucking day. It was heaven, and I never failed to thank God for giving me my Ginger. She was my life. My partner. My world. My everything.

Sometimes it all seemed too good to be true.

She was a therapist, and I was a computer engineer, just like we'd both wanted. We still lived in Cali, thank fucking God. D.C. was way too cold, even if her parents still lived there half the year. They spent a lot of time out here, too.

Everything in our life was perfect. Scarily, unrealistically *perfect*.

Carrie waved her hand in front of my face, laughing when I jumped slightly. "Hello? Earth to Finn?"

I caught her hand and kissed it, right above her wedding ring. I must've zoned out. I still did that sometimes. Got lost in thought. "Sorry, Ginger. I was lost in time."

"What were you thinking about?" she asked, a soft smile on those perfect lips of hers.

"You." I leaned forward and kissed her, loving the way she tasted, even after all these years. "Always you."

She closed her hands on my shoulders before pulling back and looking down for a quick second. "You two ready for the angel?"

I looked down at the baby in my arms, smiling with so much fucking happiness I swear my heart would burst. Our red-haired daughter, Susan Marie Coram, fluttered her lashes open and looked up at me with the same blue eyes as her mother. She was only three months old, but already I knew she would own my heart as fully as her mother did.

"We've been ready for years," I said, making my voice higher as I held Susan's hand. She cooed and closed her tiny little fingers around mine. "She's so f-f—" I cut myself off. I was trying to cut back on the cursing. "—uh, fetchingly perfect."

Carrie laughed, picked up the angel, and came over to us, her eyes on me the whole time. "How could she not be? She came from us." She trailed her fingers over the scar on my forehead, smiling. Then she laid the angel on Susan's belly. "You're up, princess."

I walked up to the tree, lifting Susan above my head. With my help— *aka* I did it myself—we put the angel on top of the tree. Backing up far enough to really see it, I eyed the tree skeptically. We'd gotten better over the years, because it actually looked evenly spread out. Perry Como crowed in the background, and lasagna cooked in the oven.

It was tradition.

No sooner did I nod in satisfaction than the timer dinged. I looked down at Susan. She was fast asleep. Good, it was time for me to have some one-on-one time with her mama. I smiled at Carrie, my heart so full it had to be close to bursting. "You get the lasagna out, and I'll lay down Susan."

"Okay." She walked by me, heading toward the kitchen, her hips swinging with each step she took. She wore a red dress and a pair of red heels. Fucking hot. "Hurry up."

"Oh, I will."

After watching her go, I climbed the stairs to Susan's nursery. I laid her down to rest and snuck into the master bedroom to grab my present for Carrie out of my underwear drawer. I'd gotten her another sun pendant, but this one was white gold with a diamond in the middle of the pendant. She'd love it.

I stopped two steps into the room. Lying in the middle of the bed was my wife, and she didn't have anything on except a pair of red heels and a seductive smile. "Merry Christmas to me," I said, shutting the door behind me.

She opened her arms. "Come here, love."

I crossed the room, climbed onto the king bed, and lowered myself on top of her. She moaned and closed her arms around my neck, arching her back seductively. Trailing my fingers down her side, toward her hip, I kissed her. Her tongue tangled with mine, fighting for control before she gave it to me.

I moaned and deepened the kiss, wedging myself between her legs. Breaking the kiss off, I whispered, "I love you, Ginger."

She smiled up at me, tracing her fingers over my faded scar. "I love you, too."

Unable to resist her when she looked so fucking hot, I kissed her again. I never could resist her, and never would be able to for as long as I lived...because she loved me—and *needed* me—just as much as I needed her.

Imagine that.

BONUS SCENE

Finn

This scene takes place a few weeks after the end of OUT OF TIME, but a couple of weeks before the beginning of OUT OF MIND.

I woke up slowly, blinking away the sunlight streaming through the hospital windows. I must have dozed off for a little while. By some miracle of miracles, I hadn't had a nightmare. I usually did. Sighing, I reached out and pushed the morphine button on the machine next to me. My head and arm hurt like a fucking bitch.

The door opened, and I tensed. My last visitor had been Senator Wallington. He'd reminded me exactly how beneath his daughter I was, then left. Ya know, the usual. But this time? It was a most welcome visitor. Carrie's red head peeked inside the hospital room.

"I'm awake," I said, smiling and adjusting myself against the pillows. "Come in."

She grinned at me and slipped through the crack of the door. "I came by earlier, but you were sleeping, so I went to the gift shop. Here. It's for you."

"Thank you." I took the yellow rose she held out for me, not quite sure what I was supposed to do with a flower. I was a dude. We were supposed to be the one's giving out the flowers—not the other way around. "I didn't realize they made yellow roses."

"They make them in every color imaginable," she said, sitting down on the side of the bed gently. "You're probably wondering why I got you a flower, right?"

I chuckled and stared down at the gentle bud. "Uh, yeah, kind of."

"From what I've seen, roses are the toughest flowers out there. One year, my mother's gardener planted the garden way too early. A frost came through, and it killed all the flowers outside." She leaned in and touched the soft petal. "All of them except the roses. They were the only flowers that thrived, despite the cold and the frost. They had the biggest batch ever that year. And they were gorgeous."

I swallowed hard. "Oh yeah?"

"Yeah." She cupped my cheek. Her soft touch was so soothing and perfect that I closed my eyes and savored it. "And those roses remind me of you—of us. You are so strong, and I know it'll be tough, but you'll get through this, and you'll be stronger because of it. I know it."

My heart clenched. "We'll get through this." I squeezed her hand with my one good one. "Together, we can do anything."

"Together," she echoed, her eyes filled with tears that didn't spill out. "I love you."

"I love you, too, Ginger."

I kissed her, my lips fleeting over hers. My grip tightened on her hand, and she strained to get closer. I drew in a ragged breath, my body responding to her closeness. Her tongue flicked over mine, making my stomach get tight and other things go hard. What I wouldn't give to be out of this hospital room, and back in California with her in my apartment so I could take care of this need for her that was trying to kill me.

But we wouldn't have privacy until I got out of this one in D.C., though, so we had a while to go. With that knowledge ringing in my head, I pulled away. "I can't wait to go home."

She sighed. "Me too. It'll be here soon. We just have to get back to my parents house, then get through Christmas. Then things will go back to normal."

Normal? Nothing about me was normal anymore. I was a fucking mess. But I smiled for her even though I knew it was a crock of shit. "Yeah. Normal."

Her smile faltered, as if she saw through my façade, but she didn't say anything. Her phone dinged. She didn't pick it up. "We're going to be okay," she said again.

"Yeah, we will." I hoped to hell we would, anyway. "Are you going to see who messaged you?"

"It's just my daily inspirational message of the day." She lifted a shoulder. "You know how I love those little messages."

I ran my thumb over her lip. "I love that you love those little messages. It's a-dork-able."

She flushed. "Shut up."

"Gladly." I leaned in, the morphine making me feel high and kinda out of it. "Or you could shut me up."

"Gladly," she echoed, completely oblivious to the fact that I was a fucking wreck.

She kissed me, and I tried to stop thinking. Stop feeling.

To just stop it all.

NOTE FROM THE AUTHOR

Dear Reader,

Some of you might have recognized this already, but the epilogue in this book is almost exactly pulled out of Finn's thoughts in *Out of Time*. When he and Carrie are decorating their first Christmas tree, he thinks to himself:

If Captain Richards asked me where I wanted to be in ten years, I'd have an answer for him. I'd want to be right here, decorating a sloppy tree with Carrie. Maybe with a baby in my arms. That's where I wanted to be. And I would be, damn it.

Well, Finn got what he wanted, and I hope you all did, as well. I've had tons of fun writing Carrie and Finn's story, and I hope to see you again soon. Even though Finn and Carrie got their happily ever after... Marie, Hernandez, and Riley didn't.

At least...not yet.

If someone asked me where I saw myself in the next ten years, I'd have an answer too—just like Finn. I'll be right here, writing stories for you. Thank you for letting me do that for you. I feel so very blessed.

Till next time? The sun is finally shining.

Love,

Me